TJ HAWK

Papua

Generative AI was not used in the drafting, editing, design, or production of this book. 100% author-created content.

Author: TJ Hawk
Date Published: September 2024
Publisher: Terry Mallon
Cover design: Cover layout and graphics by Terry Mallon.
Cover photo: Mongabay.com

Books by TJ Hawk

Gar Randolph Series

The Ghost of Siam

Sungtan's Gold

Salvaged

Papua

Kolovalu's Revenge

Historical Fiction

Brothers of Fortune, A Story of the Philippines

Autobiography

Walk Run Fly

Cast of Characters

Bembol Chief Engineer on Gar's 220-foot support vessel, Tanigue

Chambo A 6'4" pilot and Operations Center Director for Grey Hawk. He flies the Cessna Sky Courrier and manages all maintenance on the quadcopter.

Devon V-22 Osprey pilot on loan from the USAF to help test Gar's quadcopter, called Icarus

Gar Works as a contractor for the Department of Defense and is on loan to the Department of Homeland Security. He owns Grey Hawk International, which operates two experimental Raptor aircraft, a Cessna Sky Courrier, a prototype helicopter called Galileo, and an experimental quadcopter.

Mac Team leader of a 6-member team sent by a Washington D.C. Agency

Marlo Personable Captain of Gar's 220-foot support vessel, Tanigue

Momma Grace Native lady on Wakde Island who runs a rustic coffee shop near the pier

Ming Fu One of Gar's Raptor pilots. Worked at Grey Hawk International for two years before returning to Washington D.C. to work for Gen Smithberger.

Quinn V-22 Osprey pilot on loan from the USAF to help test Gar's quadcopter, called Icarus

Rava Research botanist working with her brother, Rip, in Papua

Rip Neurologist studying neural pathway creation using plant extracts obtained by his sister Rava from Papuan natives

Saturday Native from Wakde Island, who committed himself to protecting Rip and Rava after they saved his son's life with one of their plant potions

Smithberger, General Tommy "Grits" MGen (Ret) Deputy Director of the Department of Homeland Security, and Gar's boss.

Wu, Xi-han Wu's harsh upbringing and bullied past hardened him into an evil-minded virologist. He manages three teams who experiment with viral effects along the Taritatu River.

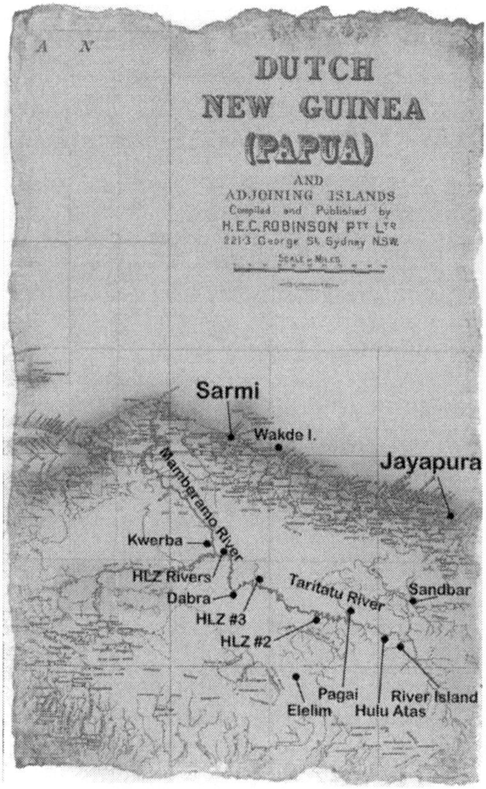
DUTCH
NEW GUINEA
(PAPUA)
AND
ADJOINING ISLANDS
Compiled and Published by
H. E. C. ROBINSON PTY LTD
221-3 George St. Sydney N.S.W.
Sarmi
Wakde I.
Jayapura
Mamberamo River
Kwerba
HLZ Rivers
Dabra
HLZ #3
HLZ #2
Taritatu River
Sandbar
Pagai
Elelim
Hulu Atas
River Island

ONE

BEAMS OF LIGHT JUMPED FROM DESKTOP TO desktop.

"Here, this is Siraj's desk," Wu hissed.

An eerie quiet blanketed Jayapura's downtown district. 2 a.m. A solitary car passed outside, only the muted whine of its engine and the squeak of its tires rolling across empty pavement resonated inside the darkened laboratory.

They snapped pics of research papers and prepared to force open the top desk drawer. Something rustled outside.

A lone security guard crumpled his candy bar wrapper before tossing it toward the hallway trash receptacle. It ricocheted off the top and fell to the side.

"Damn," he mumbled to himself. "I live without luck."

"Quick, grab those papers, and let's go," Wu ordered.

They slipped out the window an instant before the lab door opened.

As the guard casually entered and walked around the lab, thoughts of the upcoming weekend filled his mind. The solitude of night duty suited him. He noticed scattered papers on Siraj's desk and thought it odd. Siraj normally impressed him as being overly fastidious with his work.

A muted commotion at street level caught his attention and he walked to the window. Someone left it ajar, open. He saw two men hurry across the street to their car.

The thought of them having just been here, in the lab, flashed through his mind. But rather than make a formal entry in his log, he'd leave a note for Siraj. That way, he wouldn't get involved in an investigation if anything turned up amiss.

"Good afternoon, Grey Hawk International," Chambo announced in a relaxed, professional tone.

Static hissed through the phone, then a troubled voice.

"Hello. My name is Dr. Ripon Siraj. I need to talk with Gar."

"Sorry, he's not available for the next two hours. Can I help with anything?"

"I need help, rather quickly, I'm afraid. Please inform Gar that Rava and I are proceeding to Point Echo. I'll message him with all the details. He'll know what to do."

Click. The line went dead.

Chambo sensed trouble. Siraj's desperation had bled through the phone. Chambo had a feeling things would spin up soon.

Rip turned to Rava with his usual adventurous look. "I've got just about everything set for tonight. Have you gathered your things?"

"Yes, brother. For the past week, I've stuffed extra clothes into my bag and hid them in my lab locker."

Rip had done the same. He gathered research documents and carefully sealed them in storage baggies before locking them in his well-worn briefcase. He'd left unassociated technical papers in their place that suggested his research focused on developing new experimental pain-relief medicines from the plants Rava bought from the natives.

The Laboratorium Kesehatan Jayapura where Rip and Rava leased lab time remained busy throughout the day until roughly 3 p.m. when most technicians took time off for dinner. A handful of lab techs returned to work from 6 p.m. until 10 p.m. on Monday through Thursday. Fridays ended early.

Long shadows from nearby buildings stretched across the lab's few windows as Friday evening's neon lights came to life. Rip had created several meaningless lab tests to provide an excuse for working late. He'd conferred with the senior technician and agreed to lock the lab doors on the way out. After everyone left, he walked into the men's room and shaved his thick black beard. While at it, he also trimmed his already shaved head. He fitted a nicely trimmed hairpiece before sitting at his computer and preparing the message for Gar.

Rava entered the women's bathroom where she dyed her dark hair a shade of blond. Before leaving the building, she planned to twist and clip it into a bun.

Rip had purchased an all-expenses-paid weekend stay at a nearby beach resort earlier in the week and proposed an unusual vacation deal to one of the younger lab techs. Rip liked the kid and routinely teased him about his scraggly beard.

"I received this super promotional package for a weekend stay at a coastal resort about fifty miles east of here," Rip told him. "It includes room and meals, but I can't take advantage of it because I've already committed to a jungle excursion south of Jayapura."

Rip leaned his head close to the technician and whispered, "Take these rooms for you and your girlfriend. I can't use them, and they definitely shouldn't go to waste. The only catch is that you'll need to use my car as the rooms are somehow tied to its registration. If I can use your car to get around this weekend, you can have the rooms."

"Wow, thanks. My Toyota is old and has a couple of dents, but it runs fine."

A muscular Oriental peered over the magazine he pretended to read as Rip's car pulled from the parking ramp. The Asian started his car's engine and tailed who he thought to be Rip and Rava eastward as they headed for the resort.

A disguised Rip and Rava looked like a younger couple an hour later as they exited the stairwell into the underground car park area and walked toward the dusty old Toyota hatchback. They eased left onto Raya Abepura Road without drawing attention. Their escape route led them west past the Sentani Airport before bending south around the west end of Lake Sentani. Rip had known that driving along jungle roads at night in Papua would be prohibitively dangerous, so he and Rava planned to stop for the night at the Luther Yawan Christian Church. Rip had met its pastor a year earlier when quite by chance, they struck up a conversation while dining at a small outdoor restaurant in Jayapura. The pastor had invited them to spend a night whenever they wanted and tonight seemed to be the perfect opportunity.

Gar landed the odd-looking quadcopter and switched off its electric motors. Chambo greeted him with a glass of iced tea.

"Got a rather unusual call while you amused yourself with this goofy aircraft. The caller identified himself as Dr. Ripon Siraj and said he needed your help. Do you even know this guy?"

Gar thought for a second.

"I suspected this call would eventually come. Rip is an old friend who's currently working for General Smithberger in Papua. Somewhere in our safe is a manila envelope with his name on the outside. I think it's time we take a closer look."

Garfield "Gar" Randolph owned an unusual company called Grey Hawk International. Its principal base of operations consisted of several hangars on the eastern tarmac of U-Tapao International Airport in Thailand. The company functioned as an agent of the U.S. government for resolving sensitive issues on foreign soil. Gar came under the direction of Major General, retired, Tommy "Grits" Smithberger, the deputy director of the Department of Homeland Security.

Over the past years, the public purpose of the company grew from a simple fly-for-hire outfit to a research and development node for advanced aviation technologies. Gar prided himself and his company on work in prop and engine noise reduction, visual stealth, aerodynamic efficiencies, and more recently, artificial intelligence and virtual reality integration. What started as a bold investment by a young college graduate slowly became an effective tool for the government. In addition to the more or less public purpose, a vastly more clandestine mission existed.

Grey Hawk performed a unique mission and did it with equally unique aircraft. Gar's austere hangar initially housed a Cessna 208B Grand Caravan. Smithberger called him one day with a proposition to replace his unpressurized single-engine Grand Caravan with a new, more capable Cessna SkyCourrier. The team immediately started modifying it for more stealthy operations.

The latest addition to the fleet arrived in crates several months ago, a revolutionary electric/combustion/nuclear-powered quadcopter. It occupied most of Grey Hawk's second hangar, where it remained out of sight to all but those assembling and testing its systems. Gar had been the only person to fly it, although he'd planned to recruit several more pilots in the not-too-distant future.

Chambo had joined Grey Hawk International several years earlier as part of a support package for two of Gar's more unique Raptor aircraft. He'd soon found his niche as the operations manager. His larger-than-life personality and organized approach to complex projects and missions brought a fun-loving professional approach to daily operations. In many ways, he'd become Gar's right-hand man.

Gar and Chambo entered Grey Hawk's air-conditioned operations room and looked for a couple of convenient over-stuffed chairs where they could discuss Rip's call.

"Let's project a map of New Guinea on the wall," Gar suggested. "I'll dig out that envelope from Rip."

Chambo started flipping switches before briefing what little he knew about Papua.

"Did you know that Papua is the second largest island in the world after Greenland? It's divided in half with Papua New Guinea to the east and simply Papua to the west. That western part originally existed as Dutch New Guinea but later became a part of Indonesia. Its Grasberg mine at one point produced more copper and gold than anywhere else in the world. But mostly, it's a vast jungle with few roads penetrating inland from the coastline. I think there are still cannibals running about."

Chambo rarely surprised Gar, but his knowledge of Papua did just that.

"Wow Chambo, you never cease to amaze me. Don't tell me you're planning a vacation there or have relatives from the mountains."

Gar chuckled to himself as he sat at the conference table across from him. Chambo smiled inwardly, knowing he'd caught his boss off-guard.

Gar carefully opened Rip's envelope. A USB drive slid out as he extracted the remaining single sheet of paper. He read it aloud.

> Dear Gar,
> The USB drive contains a unique encryption algorithm should I need to message you. Plug it into your computer before opening your email application. Since you're reading this, the time is probably now. In the meantime, here's a list of locations with random identifiers should I reference them.

Gar thought for a moment before responding. "There's not much we can do right now. The Point Echo Rip mentioned appears to be a coastal town called Sarmi. Let's find that on the map."

Chambo searched the internet for Sarmi.

"It has a small seaport and a nearby airport. Other than that, it looks pretty remote."

Gar studied the map.

"You know, Rip is an interesting and very smart guy.

"I first met him at Mammoth Mountain Ski Area, or more precisely, along a tiny creek near his Airbnb. Narrow pathways in that area had eight-foot-high snow walls. They made me feel like a mouse looking for cheese in a maze. He'd taken a wrong turn on the way to his apartment, which seemed an understandable mistake after having sloshed down more than a few shots of whisky. He fell into the creek, and I almost followed him into the same mess, but stopped in time to realize what had happened and ultimately pulled him out. Our friendship took root.

"Rip went on to become a medical research scientist, specializing in neurological disorders. He's quite meticulous yet comes across as the polar opposite of geeky. His younger sister, who I might add has beauty that matches her brain, specializes in medical botany. They shared laboratory findings in Los Angeles for a short while before shifting their work to Papua. General Smithberger has them working on one of his pet projects. Not long after I'd introduced Rip to the General, he and his sister packed up and moved."

"You seem to know everyone," Chambo interjected. "Dang."

"Get me if Rip calls again. He must have been desperate to have called in the first place."

Gar worried about Rip and his sister. If Rip called in need of help, he absolutely needed it.

TWO

RIP'S EMAIL APPEARED ON GAR'S SCREEN ALONG with its telltale notification beep. Gar reached for Rip's envelope, poured out his USB device, and plugged it into one of the computer ports. After a few screen flashes and scrolling text, the message appeared.

> Gar,
> As you know, I'm with my sister Rava in Jayapura. While I've been analyzing a variety of potions that affect neurons and neural pathways (which make up the essence of our nervous system), Rava has ventured into the jungles in search of medicinal plants. Until recently, various tribesmen provided promising specimens and everything seemed fine.
>
> But strange situations started popping up. Several of Rava's tribal contacts disappeared. We sensed strangers watching us, and our lab experienced a break-in. We've decided to quietly leave Jayapura and establish a much lower profile elsewhere. Shortly after I hit the send key,

we'll start driving northwest, roughly following the coastline to Point Echo.

Gen Smithberger supports our research, and I'm about to ask him to bless our plan of action. It'll include potential support from Grey Hawk, such as airlift into the more remote regions of the jungle where Rava convinced me the most important plants grow. We'll also need a few pieces of laboratory equipment to replace, in part, the lab we're about to abandon.

I wanted to give you a sliver of advanced notice before Grits surprises you.

Thank you and as always, we wish you well.
Rip

Gar read the message again and wondered who wanted his research, and why.

"Chambo, where are Marlo and his new ship? Let's get him headed to Rayong as soon as possible, like within the next few hours."

Gar had added an eighty-foot converted fishing trawler to all the stealthy aircraft he'd accumulated. Marlo sold it to him several years earlier and agreed to remain as its captain.

General Smithberger soon realized its utility and envisioned an even larger, more versatile ship that could support helicopter operations. He seized the opportunity to buy such a vessel when one became available.

Smithberger and the Secretary of the Navy shared thoughts on future projects over a Crown Royal at the Army-Navy Club on a cold, blustering December night. As the Secretary mentioned his vision for modifying an advanced fast support vessel built in the NetherlandsSmithberger envisioned several applications of his own, ones that wouldn't require major modifications. The Secretary had his ear.

Purchasing the 210-foot luxury vessel had been a mistake in the mind of the U.S. Navy and the Secretary wanted it gone before Congress caught wind of his spending fiasco. Smithberger quietly acquired it along with five key crew members who would sail it to Subic Bay in the Philippines.

A new off-black veneer featuring rust streaks and corrosion blotches applied after its arrival transformed it into what appeared to be a derelict vessel one step short of the ship cemetery. With such a degraded appearance, the vessel could ease in and out of most ports without attracting undue attention. Gar asked Marlo to temporarily mothball his trawler and take command of the yacht. A handful of Filipino engineers and bridge-mates accompanied him. Their technical expertise and indigenous appearance complimented the ship's well-worn veneer. Marlo often worked alone even with his expanded crew force. On more than one occasion during the ship's sea trials, he'd felt like the captain of a ghost ship.

Chambo returned from his desk in the hangar.

"I've talked to Marlo. He's at Subic Bay with full fuel and says he can easily average fifteen knots once underway. He'll be here in five days at that speed."

Smithberger had fallen asleep in his bedroom recliner. He'd settled into the overstuffed lounger an hour earlier to clear his mind while reading an autobiography he'd picked up at the Pentagon Book Store. The relatively quiet beep on his smartphone triggered his mind. He sat up, stretched, and looked to see who'd sent the message. It turned out to be two messages from Rip. The first one pushed the encryption interface to Smithberger's phone. The second message appeared and it warranted his attention.

General Smithberger,
Rava and I are on the verge of an exciting breakthrough, but we've got trouble on our doorstep. Explaining the breakthrough should add clarity to the trouble portion, so I'll start there.

A tribesman from deep in the coastal jungles gave Rava a plant his people use to prevent a wide range of diseases. I've run a variety of tests and am shocked to find that it generates near-universal antibodies. It looks genuinely promising.

More interesting, I've discovered additional properties that stretch its usefulness to much greater limits. It has the effect of stimulating damaged neurons to repair themselves. Neurons are our nerve cells. They translate raw input into an electrical impulse and transfer it cell-to-cell via a neural pathway that ultimately triggers our brain cells. For example, if a neuron experiences heat, it sends an impulse to the brain that interprets it as HOT!

I've found that the same plant extract seems to encourage the growth of new, or alternative, neural pathways. Hypothetically, if we could manipulate the creation of specific neural pathways, we could transmit camera-like inputs into the optic nerve and create vision for a blind person. Injections, or perhaps even skin applications, could accomplish this.

Here's another thought . . . say we take a highly sensitive chemical detector and convert its signals into a format that our nasal neural network can recognize. Humans might smell with the acuity of a rescue or drug-sniffing dog.

I see many positive applications for humanity–the blind could see, the paralyzed could walk, we could all perceive the world around us more clearly, smell better, and so much more.

It could, unfortunately, spur more nefarious activities like the theft of scientific development for short-term profit. Let's think about even darker applications like the creation of a super-healthy military force, or the reduction of our humanness into a more robotic existence. This plant's broad immunization properties could encourage bio-warfare where one side has universal immunity. I think those might well be the reasons for the trouble we're experiencing.

Rava's jungle contacts are slowly disappearing. It's as if someone else is grilling them for information and eliminating them so they can no longer support her efforts.

Unknown people secretly watched us. I noticed a young Asian following me several times during the past weeks. Three nights ago, someone broke into our lab and went through my technical papers. The incursion went mostly unnoticed and unreported. Thank goodness I tend to be cautious and keep my important research papers with me at night. In their place, I leave a separate set of more or less meaningless documents.

Rava and I are secretly moving out of Jayapura later tonight to Point Echo where we hope to continue our studies. I've mentioned the move to Gar and asked if he could provide a small level of airlift and laboratory support.

The good news is that I think we're onto something important, and I would like to continue researching it. Since this deviates from our initial contract, I'm asking for your permission to continue as planned. Here's what we'll need to do that . . .

Smithberger began pacing back and forth, thoughtful, worried. He had a lot at play here, not just Rip and Rava in Papua. His larger plan focused on the development of more effective aircraft operations in contested airspace. The technological leap he hoped to make had at its core the ability to take the pilot out of his traditional flying role and transform him into a mission manager. It included an ever-increasing use of man-machine interfaces where raw signal inputs would translate into neural pulses that would be transmitted from sensor to converter to a neural transfer point, and ultimately to the brain. The sensor element for the most part already existed.

The Defense Advanced Research Projects Agency had made great strides in the signal conversion process, and Rip appeared to be solving the neural transfer and neural pathway elements. Gar stood ready with his quadcopter to function as the testbed.

Smithberger's mind jumped from element to element of his master project. He eased back into the recliner, found a cigar, lit it, and let his mind slow down. He breathed a sigh of relief at having delivered the quadcopter none too soon. Once Gar learned to fly it and tested it for endurance, stealth, and general utility, advanced testing could begin. He wondered if it'd be ready for Papua and supporting Rip. If he could do that, it'd be a great trial run. He made a mental note to ask.

Chambo twitched when the phone rang.

"Grey Hawk International."

Smithberger's voice sounded at the other end. "Chambo, can you get Gar on the line, please?"

"Yes sir."

He swiveled his chair toward Gar "It's the General."

As Gar came on the line, Smithberger puffed cigar smoke from his mouth.

"Rip needs your help in Papua and I'm trying to determine how you can best provide what he wants. Is that quadcopter flying yet?"

Gar chuckled to himself for anticipating this very phone call.

"Sir, we're calling the quadcopter Icarus even though its rotors are neither feathers nor wax. I flew it earlier today and can confirm that its basic controllability works as advertised.

"I have to admit that I've had a couple of hours to think about a support package for Rip. Marlo will arrive with our yacht in a couple of days and I'd like to make several modifications to it before we set sail for Papua. The first task will be to reconfigure the sub-deck under the helipad into a laboratory. I don't know what equipment it'll need, nor do I know exactly how to source it. Nonetheless, I'll get a working lab set up before departing.

"I'd like to clear the rear deck so that we can take our helicopter or maybe even Icarus. We'll depart once I line up full-time pilots and complete the basic acceptance tests."

Smithberger relaxed slightly and drew gently on his cigar. He let the smoke in his mouth linger as he savored its rich flavor. Eventually, he subconsciously exhaled.

"I like the direction you're going.

"This may be preaching to the choir, but I feel compelled to warn you of the dangers you'll face.

"Papua presents a naturally hostile environment complete with impassable swamplands bordering most rivers, venomous slithering creatures, tribal conflicts where its few natives exist, and a vast army of annoying bugs who feast on humans using their miniature tiger teeth. There are few roads and those that do exist often start and end at alternative versions of nowhere. Rivers are the unifying conduit of travel and they similarly host a variety of nasty creatures, including crocodiles and flesh-eating fish.

"Did I mention cannibals? Well, you're lucky because most of them stick to the highlands. But if one of them invites you for dinner, stay away from any large pots near the fire. Most tribes speak a unique language. There are almost three hundred of them–they're different and unrelated to each other. As a result, it's nearly impossible to fully understand tribesmen without years of exposure, so good luck there.

"The reason I point all this out is that I want you to be prepared for the worst. There are several issues concerning, what is it . . . Icarus. I'd like to know if you can fly missions in super-stealth mode. I'm not ready to have anyone see such an aircraft yet. And, I'd like to know if Icarus can operate for extended periods without refueling. Helping Rip should provide the perfect opportunity for validating those concerns along with the aircraft's other physical upgrades.

"Rip is researching the technical end of how I envision aircraft to be operated in the future. Your crews will be the direct beneficiaries of his work. Keeping him alive and productive in Papua might speed up the process. Here's what you'll be up against politically.

"Foreign governments are keenly interested in the medicinal aspects of Rip's research. Their efforts range from stealing new drugs and reaping huge profits by being the first to market, to developing a friendly force immune to the bio-warfare agents they develop. I believe at least one Asian country is after Rip's research. They've already killed several of the tribesmen who provided plants to his sister, Rava. They've made one attempt to steal Rip's research, and it appears they're becoming even more aggressive.

"I'd like you to gather a team that can protect Rip and Rava while at the same time validating Icarus. Let me know what funding and additional support are required, and good luck."

Smithberger hung up. Gar had his marching orders. He needed a plan, and he needed to set it into action.

Rip,
I'm gathering the troops and getting ready to head your way. It'll take almost three weeks for our ship to arrive at Point Echo, so keep a low profile until then.

One of my areas of interest will be flying you into the jungle as close as possible to where the tribesman found

Rava's medicinal plants. We'll try to remain at nearby jungle openings, if there are any, and provide at least a modicum of security. It sounds as though alternate transportation such as motorcycles or even para-gliders may be impractical. Any thoughts on small boats or canoes?

Besides airlift and physical security, is there anything else I'm missing?
Regards,
Gar

He hit the send key, got up, and walked into the hangar.

"Chambo, I've got a list of taskers for you to work on. Regarding Icarus, let's make sure the noise-canceling rotor housings are intact and verify that the skin cameras and surface displays are working. We won't be flying it again until we fly it to the deck of Marlo's yacht. I'd like to have a team clear the aft deck once Marlo arrives so the pilots can park Icarus there. We'll need a protective cover to shield it from the salty ocean spray, and more importantly, from curious eyes.

"Let's hire locals to construct two ten-foot canoes out of Kevlar and fiberglass. Make them look like native canoes from Papua. You can probably find descriptive pictures on the internet. Build internal fuel tanks and buy a couple of small engines to power them. They should have hardware so that we can attach them directly to the bottom of Icarus."

Chambo scribbled the last of his notes.

"Are you going to be the only pilot for this mission?" he asked. "What about maintenance?"

Gar had given this some thought.

"I'm flying to Tokyo later tonight to get additional pilots. I should be able to do all the ground training on the way to Papua. For maintenance, you'd be the perfect solution. Do you get seasick?"

THREE

RIP'S LAB-TECH CO-WORKER AND HIS GIRLFRIEND approached the coastal resort's receptionist.

"May I have the keys to our cabaña? It should be reserved under the name Siraj."

She glanced at the reservation ledger and reached under the countertop for them.

"You'll be staying in one of our lovely beach units. It's down the road a bit, and there's space to park your car nearby."

The two lovers arranged their luggage and relaxed before heading to the beach. He'd entered the bathroom and looked into the mirror to examine his teeth, all the time envisioning his soon-to-begin carnal adventure. A sudden thud against the door . . . a muffled call. His girlfriend kicked and the commotion broke his train of thought. She'd wandered onto the lanai when a stranger grabbed her from behind and pressed his hand over her mouth. A gun barrel jabbed against her rib cage.

The stranger forcibly maneuvered her back into the room.

"I'll shoot the girl if you don't comply," he threatened. "I want all your research papers, and I want to hear the details of your experiments."

Anger filled the tech's veins.

"I don't have any. . ."

At that moment, the girl drove her elbow into the assailant. His fingers instinctively twitched. The gun fired and the girl slumped to the floor. A candle dislodged from its spot on a low table during her fall. Curtains caught fire, then the ceiling. The tech charged the intruder and grabbed his gun. It fired again, and the tech collapsed next to his girlfriend.

The intruder seethed inside as his simple plan unraveled. He frantically looked for the research papers, knowing they existed somewhere. Searing heat singed the hair on his arms and eyebrows and forced him to withdraw, empty-handed. He ran from the structure toward his car, got it started, and drove into the dark. The cabaña blazed beyond control.

Rip and Rava arrived at Luther Yawan Christian Church several hours after sunset. Rava breathed a sigh of relief as they pulled into its grassy yard.

"Thank goodness they paved the roads the whole way. I don't feel comfortable driving around here in the middle of the night."

"I agree," Rip concurred in a relieved tone. "We'll get an early start in the morning and hopefully find a new home before another sunset."

Rip leaned across the front seat of their car toward Rava as they prepared for the next leg of their journey. He held up a weather-beaten map and drew his finger along a road from the church to Sarmi.

"Aah, see here. It connects this series of villages located roughly along the coast. At least we shouldn't get lost. I think it's the only road, and I'd bet anything branching left or right transitions into a rutted pathway rather quickly. Let's get started."

Rava relaxed, the muscles in her neck loosened once she and Rip pulled onto the recently laid pavement. Jungle growth slowly closed in and brought with it a rich, fragrant aroma of dew rising off its floor. The soothing sensation would, unfortunately, lose its grip on her senses as the more oppressive heat took hold. Small home fires began warming water for morning coffee. The dried wood produced a wispy white smoke that rode air currents horizontally through the palm trees while highlighting beams of morning sunlight.

"Do you think we'll eventually explore far enough into the jungle to find our miracle plants?" Rava asked. "The last native gave me directions to a possible location this side of the high mountains."

"I don't know," responded Rip, "but Gar has always been incredibly reliable. If he says he's coming, I think we'll be okay and he'll get us to where we want to go."

"Tell me about Gar. The one time I met him, he seemed . . . polite. But is he interesting?"

"He's one of the more unusual fellows I've ever known. Our parents would approve. He places great value on the work he does, which, to my knowledge, is mostly secretive. Those who work with him carry a deep respect for their leader. I remember him telling me about his mother and father taking him to food shelters during Chicago's bitter winter months. He heated soup and mingled with those he fed. He appreciates the troubles of others and knows the struggles of the impoverished. It's a mystery why he never married. He'd be a prize for any woman, yet he deflects their advances and siren-like callings. He's a most interesting man."

Rava absorbed her brother's words as she watched the jungle blur along the roadway.

"That's perfect because I don't want a man in my life right now. How will he travel to Sarmi? Is he going to meet us there?"

"I don't know. It'll take time to organize everything, but once he figures all that out, I expect to hear something. We'll blend into the local area in the meantime and familiarize ourselves with the airport and seaport. The map shows a little island nearby. I'd like to rent a boat and explore it as well."

They rode in silence for the next twenty minutes. Rip recalled comments the pastor had shared.

"You know, I learned something last night that I hadn't thought about until the pastor mentioned it. He told me about private aircraft operators flying natives and missionaries to remote locations.

"I asked, 'What airplanes?' and he told me about the Missionary Airlift Fellowship that flies Cessna Grand Caravans. A few other outfits offer the same fly-for-hire option. They routinely charter flights to a number of the less austere landing strips. The 'barely useable' category of landing strips is occasionally requested, but not nearly as often.

"With luck, we'll have Gar to get us around. That'll keep our whereabouts much more private. But the thought occurred to me that maybe those scalawags chasing us might try to charter an aircraft. I asked the pastor about it, and he assured me that the missionaries would know, and if he asked, they'd pass that info to him. He gets wind of ninety-nine percent of their non-standard flights because he's always a potential passenger. I gave him my satellite phone number."

As midday approached, Rip stopped to refuel at a small Pemex gas station. Rava surveyed the area from the passenger seat.

"There's a little restaurant. Let's stop."

She managed a few local food phrases when the owner approached their table and pointed toward the seafood display. He seemed to know what she wanted, nodded his head, and disappeared into the back room. Rava turned to Rip.

"I think I ordered ikan bakar, sago seeds, and rice."

"What on earth are the first two?" Rip asked. "I understood the rice."

He chuckled to himself.

"The ikan bakar is also called kapeting raja, or more commonly, king crab legs. My fingers are crossed that I'm correct on this. Sago is more traditional here. It's made from a pith or palm tree heart. They mash it to a pulp and serve it in a variety of ways. It's supposed to lower blood pressure and contain a fair amount of potassium. The seeds help in a lot of ways, but mostly they lower the strain on your heart. The natives believe it prevents birth defects. Anyway, I didn't have many choices. Hope you like it."

By late afternoon they'd passed Sarmi's coastal airport and drove around a small cove leading to the center of town. A rather garish hotel called Jasmine caught Rava's eye and looked inviting. They stopped. Its spartan interior appeared bland and uninteresting but perfect for their temporary needs.

They showered in their room before descending an old staircase to the empty dining area. Iced fruit drinks relaxed the tension of the past few days. A television in the room's corner began blaring the daily news and they couldn't help but hear about a scientist and a research botanist who'd been murdered near Jayapura. The hair on their necks bristled. A cold shock took hold. Rip looked at Rava.

"That should have been us," he whispered.

Rava silently mouthed the words, "Oh my God."

They drove back along the coast to Sarmi's municipal airport the next day. Two small aircraft had been parked outside a correspondingly small hangar and next to it stood an office building.

"How often do commercial flights come and go?" Rava asked its sole attendant.

The young man looked up and mentally assessed the person asking the question. He didn't recognize Rava and assumed she wanted to book a flight rather than inspect his work.

"There's a flight every Thursday afternoon. It goes from here to Jayapura. If you need to get to Sorong or further west, you'll have to first fly east to Jayapura and then fly directly from there."

"Do you have aircraft fuel available here?"

"Yes, of course, he answered with a puzzled look on his face. "But it's often in limited supply. Why do you ask?"

"Oh, I'm just curious. My father once flew in Papua, and I always wondered about such things."

He perked up a bit. "Did you ever hear of General Mac Arthur's airstrip on Wakde? It's a small island group about twenty miles south of here. If you've got the time, it'd be a great day trip."

Rava listened intently, thinking they might be safer on a remote island than here in Sarmi.

"Tell me what you know about the island. We might rent a boat and go exploring."

He recalled what his parents had told him.

"I think the Americans fought the Japanese there during World War Two. The Japanese carved a coral runway out of the palm trees and built a small base. It must have been a fighter base because it didn't appear to be very large.

"A battle raged and the Japanese fought courageously from well-entrenched positions. But after several days and many banzai charges, the island fell into American hands. My parents lived nearby on the mainland and could hear the fighting.

"There are sunken remains of a battleship nearby. My friends and I camped there one weekend and looked for it but never did find anything. Wakde has nice beaches and the local village sells food. Other than a few surfers, the island remains pretty isolated."

"Wow, it sounds interesting," Rava responded. "You call it Wakde? Right."

Rip and Rava casually assessed Sarmi's little airfield as they left, looking for signs of equipment like forklifts or cargo pallets. They saw none.

Rip sounded almost disappointed.

"It looks like a decent runway, but nothing more. Let's see what the port looks like."

Rip started the engine while wondering if they could camp on Wakde for a week or two. That might be the safest way to keep them from being recognized. They'd return later when Gar eventually arrived.

"Rava. What do you think about buying camping gear and spending a couple of weeks exploring Wakde?"

"Heck, we already have almost everything we'll need. Let's see if we can hire a boat to drop us off and come back later to fetch us."

FOUR

CHAMBO FOUND HIMSELF DEEP IN THOUGHT and mumbled to himself.

"Let's see, where to start?"

He'd found a small aircraft company near Suvarnabhumi Airport that worked with Kevlar and fiberglass. They agreed to design and build the two canoes he'd described.

Four workers gathered around him inside their Bangkok hangar. Chambo held up a large picture of a crude canoe that resembled a hollowed-out log with a tapered front.

"Here, this rather crude look is what I'm after, but keep the structure light. The outer surface should look hand-hewn and weathered, the inside can be smoother. Let's put the fuel tank along the floor and make it big enough to run the engine for at least six hours. That would be about twelve to fifteen gallons."

He continued with various other details.

"If you can include a top covering that I can pull overhead from inside the side structures, it'll give me the option of sleeping in the canoe on rainy nights. I'll find a couple of motors and deliver them later today."

He turned to leave, then hesitated.

"And . . . I'd like two crude paddles for each unit."

Chambo sat behind the steering wheel, thinking. He eventually started his van's engine and turned the air conditioner fan on high, all the time worrying the lab he needed to provision would turn out to be a discombobulated mess. He tried to recall the equipment he'd used in high school chemistry class. Questions ticked by one after another. Can I trust Aczel? Are they knowledgeable?

His phone beeped. A text from Gar. . .

> Chambo, I have little idea of what equipment Rip needs for a lab, but he suggested among other things a microscope, a microbiological incubator, and a centrifuge. You know, all the basics. Be sure to ask the supplier for his recommendations. I'll somehow justify the cost later. Don't worry about the disposables yet. Grits has a contact who'll help us there. Have fun!

Chambo reviewed the list again and decided that it included pretty much what he would have come up with given a few minutes.

It took more than an hour before he spotted Aczel's storefront and another fifteen minutes to find parking. A young female sales attendant met him inside the brightly lit showroom.

"Sawadee ka, may I help you, sir? Ooh . . . you're as big as a giant."

Chambo laughed, his huge frame and curly blonde hair often prompted such a reaction.

"I have a list of items I'd like to see. I'm setting up a new lab and need . . . well . . . just about everything."

She looked over the list.

"I can show you most of the items on your list. We have new, and in a few cases, high-quality used equipment. Maybe we could have tea while I explain an option to order what we don't have on hand. We guarantee delivery within a week on most unstocked items."

Once Chambo had placed a rather extensive order, he asked for the girl's phone number and suggested he'd call if he needed anything more. He concluded that the brief visit went far better than he'd imagined. He also decided to order something, anything would do, later.

Smithberger called Lieutenant General Spencer, Commander of Air Force Special Operations Command.

"Hi Gene, it's Grits. I have a special request that I'm hoping you might be interested in satisfying. I'm conducting rather secretive research that includes a prototype quadcopter. Unfortunately, I don't have anyone with tilt-rotor experience, and of course, that's the crux of my request. The work will be conducted in Asia, probably in Papua. Do you have two experienced pilots I might borrow for a month or two?"

"Good to hear from you, Grits," Spencer replied. "I'd hoped you called to offer me a couple of excess CV-22s or an increase in our manning allocation. As you probably know, we're stretched pretty thin on personnel, but if you can support me on a future budget fight and maybe share the pertinent details of your research, I'll try to free up a couple of capable flyers."

"Thanks, I'll remember this," replied Grits. "Let's get together the next time you visit our crazy capital. I'll give you a more detailed update on our testing, which I think at a minimum, you'll find interesting."

Gar realized that flying internationally had changed dramatically over the past year. Rather than taking a direct flight, he'd have to connect via Singapore before continuing to Tokyo. He booked an evening trip with a two-hour layover, followed by a seven-hour flight to Tokyo's Narita Airport.

Ming pre-flighted and started one of the Raptor aircraft. He'd replace the lengthy drive to Suvarnabhumi Airport with a more relaxed thirty-minute flight and deposit Gar on a commercial ramp near the main terminal.

This would be Ming's last flight with Grey Hawk International. The time had come for him to shift gears and move back to administrative work in Washington D.C. He'd contribute his considerable intelligence and communicative skills as a legislative liaison for the Department of Homeland Security, more specifically, for General Smithberger.

As they flew toward Bangkok, Ming turned to Gar.

"Gyoza or sushi. They'll keep you thinking straight in Japan and somehow stave off the effects of too much sake."

"Has that been your experience?" Gar asked in a light-hearted tone.

"Possibly," Ming responded before a nearly imperceptible smile revealed the truth.

"I'll miss you, Ming. Hell, we'll all miss your subtle insights."

"If you find time," Ming added, "you might try a place we call Communist Gyoza near the Tachikawa train station. You get one chance to order. No sharing. No seconds. No take-outs. I think he'll let you get beer refills, but that's it.

"The real name is Gyoza Ten-go-ku, or Gyoza 10-5-9, but it literally means 'Gyoza Heaven'. The sign by the door reads 'Gyoza 1059'. Try the garlic gyoza. Like all the others, it's huge. In fact, it's like eating a handful of barely seared raw garlic. It's pretty good."

Gar awoke in his first-class flight pod an hour out of Tokyo. An attractive flight attendant stooped next to him a moment later and asked if he'd prefer eggs and bacon or miso soup, grilled fish, and steamed rice. He decided on the Japanese option mostly because he'd acquired a taste for miso soup.

His Blackberry displayed an alert from Smithberger just as his food arrived.

> Gar,
> You're cleared to proceed with acquiring two pilots–they'll be yours for up to two months. Those guys are tough and smart. I only hope they fit in with your existing group of misfits.
>
> On your way to Papua, please plan a refueling stop at Zamboanga City in the southern Philippines. Don't be surprised if an official-looking party asks you to load additional cargo. They might also give you a security team.

Rip's work is vital to our overall plan for a man-machine interface. That in all likelihood has made him a priority target by others. Be cautious.
Grits

Gar called the tilt-rotor squadron commander while processing through Narita's Immigration section. The commander suggested he catch a train to Mitake Station between Ome and Lake Okutama. Leaving the station, he needed to cross the main road and find a pathway down to the Tama River where he'd start hiking downstream. His volunteers would find him along the way. If he could wear a straw hat, it'd help.

Gar eventually exited Customs and spilled out into the general concourse. The Airport Limousine bus ticket counter caught his eye. A large display board showed the next bus would depart in ten minutes for Shinjuku Station from position number eight outside. The ride relaxed his mind. From Narita, the bus transited farmlands until being drawn into metropolitan Tokyo. Traffic moved steadily along multi-lane expressways and crossing Tokyo Bay at 150 feet provided a magnificent view of Tokyo's skyline.

After snaking its way through Ginza, the bus descended from four levels above ground to the more congested streets of Shinjuku. This area came alive at night with glitzy clubs and karaoke rooms. Upscale hotel bars and restaurants added spice to its skyscraper landscape. Even at mid-morning, the streets felt alive with noise, traffic, and businessmen scurrying to and fro.

From the street-side drop-off, he'd find his way into Shinjuku's train station, and from there, an Ome-line train would take him to Mitake.

Gar immediately realized that finding Shinjuku Station wouldn't be so easy.

"Sumimasen," he asked the first businessman walking slow enough to hear. "Shinjuku eki wa doko desu ka?" all of which meant, "Excuse me, where is Shinjuku train station?"

The businessman stopped and smiled. He pointed to stairs leading under the street. "Take those and go right. If you don't see your train line, ask the official at the entry gates. It's not too difficult."

Gar simply thanked him. "Arigato gozaimasu."

He hadn't realized that Shinjuku held the honor of being the world's busiest train station, handling over two million passengers each and every day. He soon found himself in a cramped flow of humanity, all knowing exactly where they headed. He'd thought that finding the station would end his overwhelmed feeling. The feeling only intensified until he found an official in a nearby office who spoke perfect English. His hopeless feeling of being lost in a strange world faded.

"Can you help me figure out how to take the train from here to Mitake?" he blurted.

"Don't feel bad. This station intimidates a lot of foreigners and local Japanese alike. First, do you have a Suica Card? It'll make paying your future fares much quicker."

After Gar's negative reply, he looked at a table of fares on his desk.

"The card will cost five hundred yen and you can add money to it when your balance gets low, like a debit card. All you have to do after that is swipe it at the entry and exit gates until you need to add more yen. You can use it for the monorails, vending machines, some retail stores, and almost all the konbinis."

Gar swiped his way into the inner regions of Shinjuku Station once fully outfitted with his new Suica Card and followed signs for the Ome Line. All Ome line signage came with orange trim. It made finding the right signs much easier. The station attendant told him to take a train for Ome. He'd exit the train there, walk to the parallel track, and board another train for Okutama.

He flowed amongst hundreds of other travelers with his head tilted up to read the overhead directional signage. Despite the crowds and frenzied pace, he found track No. 10 and eventually boarded the right train. His mind wandered. The trains looked immaculate. He saw no graffiti, no trash, nothing like that. Even the people looked neat and acted with extraordinary politeness toward each other. No one made phone calls or listened to music without earbuds. He found it all remarkable.

Neighborhoods passing outside the train's windows captured his momentary attention, and each station along the way appeared unique. He got the sense that his train always arrived and departed exactly on time. Inevitably, the timing had to get out of sync now and again. There seemed no good way of knowing unless a special announcement forewarned him.

Ome anchored the end of the line for the train he rode. It would reverse course at that point and head back into Tokyo. Another train segment started on the adjoining track and made multiple stops while climbing into the mountains toward Lake Okutama. One could hardly miss the connection because only one choice existed after getting off the first train.

He felt the transition from a relatively flat topography to a steady ascent. The fast-flowing Tama River flashed in and out of sight hundreds of feet below him. During the past hour, urban sprawl transformed into rural wilderness. Mitake's isolated and quiet passenger platform existed in a different world than Shinjuku. He immediately noticed a store across the main road as he exited the station. A young girl behind the counter sold him a wide-brimmed straw hat, the style a tourist might buy, and pointed him to a trail leading to the river.

The area oozed beauty. High forested mountains rose near-vertically in all directions. The Tama River tumbled its way between them. Previous landslides had left brownish streaks in their aftermath, only to have been overlaid with a concrete grid that held pine saplings. This modified reforestation would hopefully prevent a reoccurrence.

The river flowed forcibly over and between glacial-sized boulders. A team of four individual kayakers fought currents from rapids to rapids, all the time testing their technical skills. Gar wanted a closer look and wandered off the path. The rocky riverbank where he stood proved a perfect vantage point to see the water's near-perfect clarity. It made the bottom look deceptively close. He touched his hand to the river and absorbed its freezing bite, and he imagined the river turning angry after rainstorms. It seemed incredible to experience the remoteness of the area so close to Tokyo's fourteen million inhabitants.

A raft filled with six school-aged riders passed as he turned back toward the walkway. Two more rafts followed closely behind, everyone laughing and enjoying the adventure.

Wildflowers blossomed everywhere. Butterflies flitted about, and Gar found himself lost in thought as he wandered along the riverside pathway. That is until he stumbled upon a muffin and coffee shop and felt like he'd found heaven.

He'd come to an open garden where Japanese and foreign tourists relaxed at small tables while enjoying soba noodles with tea or sake. Two of the foreigners smiled and waved for him to join them.

"Hi! I'm Devon and this is Quinn. I assume you must be Mr. Gar because you're the only one we've seen with a straw hat."

"Yep. I'm Gar. No need for the 'Mr.' That's too formal for such a beautiful place."

"This is actually part of a sake-tasting area for the Sawanoi Sake Brewery across the street," Quinn explained. "You can get other drinks like juice or beer, and of course, food."

Gar placed a five-thousand yen note on the table.

"You don't suppose we might buy a bottle of sake to help us through what I've got to say."

Two devilish smiles flashed back at him. Quinn grabbed the note and started toward the cashier.

"I'll be right back."

Gar asked Devon about the river and the surrounding mountains. When Quinn returned with the sake, Gar gathered his thoughts.

"Are you at all familiar with any of the research connecting man's brain with machines? For example, a paraplegic moving prosthetic fingers just by thinking about it."

Neither had a ready answer and Gar chuckled to himself.

"It's pretty much a rhetorical question." Gar chuckled before continuing. "Don't worry. Not many people think of such things. But in part, that's why I'm here to ask for your help. My boss in Washington is directing a rather secretive effort to take machine inputs, translate them into electrical pulses, and transfer them to the human nervous network. I'm at the end of the whip, so to speak, in that I'll be testing the work of others.

"One of those others is a scientist in Papua, and he's having issues with a group of thugs trying to steal his work. My job is to make sure they don't get it. At the same time, I have a rather unique aircraft that needs field testing. That's where you two come in, and it's because of your tilt-rotor experience that you're uniquely qualified to help.

"You'll be flying in Papua, which is an unforgiving environment. It's remote. It'll feel more like camping in the jungle when you're not flying. Food will be basic most of the time and the environment could become dangerous.

"I've got you for two months if you agree to come along. It's your choice. If you decline, I'll make certain none of this reflects badly on you. Do you have questions?"

"Can you say any more about the aircraft we'll be flying?" Devon asked.

Gar sipped his sake.

"I suppose I need to clarify a bit. It's a quadcopter, a precursor to the V-22, but with ninety-five percent of it modified. Your ultimate role will be more of a mission manager than a pilot, although your piloting skills are an essential ingredient."

"When do we leave?" Quinn asked.

FIVE

RIP AND RAVA SPREAD THEIR GEAR ACROSS THE bed and onto the floor. They'd pre-positioned everything in the car, but laying it out made repacking their clothes and equipment much easier. Rava organized her stack of loose items with a look of satisfaction.

"I'm glad you thought to bring along your roughing-it gear. It'll make hiding out a whole lot easier."

"I didn't plan on using any of it," he chuckled as he spoke. "But I found the backpack to be so much easier to fill than a suitcase. Plus, I threw it around in the trunk and never worried about scratching the sides. On the other hand, what if we couldn't find a hotel? Or what if we ventured into the jungle together? It suddenly made more sense to bring the sleeping bag, a tarp, and a hammock."

"At long last," Rava sighed in a more whimsical tone, "it appears you've developed common sense. I'll hire someone at the port early tomorrow morning who can take us to Wakde. Let's leave at first light before anyone notices us milling about."

They had a week's supply of dehydrated food and enough coffee to last a month between them. Rava focused on organizing the essential items while Rip worried about what to do with their borrowed car. When it dawned on him that it could easily link them to the murdered couple, hiding it suddenly became more critical. If detectives correctly identified the victims and determined them to be using Rip and Rava's car, they'd soon be on the lookout for the tech's actual car, and might even consider Rip and Rava to be suspects.

He thought about leaving it at the airport and taking a taxi back to the hotel, but that might only make the car easier to find. The idea of leaving it at the port presented a similar risk. If he removed the license plates and left the car at the hotel, it'd lessen the risk of discovery but at the same time might invite its theft. The whole idea of hiding the car soon became an impossible balancing act between risk and reward.

In the end, he smeared grease across the license plate numbers to make a '6' look like an '8' and a 'P' look like a 'B'. He parked the car on the second level of the town's only parking ramp and moved what little lab supplies and other items they'd brought from the back seat to the trunk.

The sky loosened its grip on darkness, allowing only the faintest hint of light to radiate from the horizon. Another day came to life as Rip and Rava emerged from the hotel burdened with their large backpacks. They breathed in the cool air and started walking along empty streets toward the dock. Morning quietness embraced them to the point where they could hear their shoes squeaking on the pavement. Stretching their legs heightened the excitement of pushing further toward invisibility.

A handful of small fishing boats bobbed in the water along Sarmi's single pier. Fishermen carried large baskets of fish from their boats and spread them on nearby ground tarps in the predawn twilight. Rip and Rava passed without undue notice.

A medium-sized canoe near the end of the pier appeared barely adequate for the trip but seemed to be their only transportation choice. Its owner busied himself with untangling mooring ropes when Rava interrupted his fiddling.

"Are you open for hire? We'd like to explore Wakde Island."

They quietly eased into the ocean and soon the pronounced up-and-down motion of its hull sliced through morning waves. The droning sound of its engine produced a slow rhythm that dulled their senses. Even the lone seagull hovering overhead cawed in a soothing monotone as if to say, "I'm here with you, relax and enjoy the ride."

Rava watched the graceful seabird glide effortlessly behind their canoe. She imagined the bird's freedom and its ability to fly above the jungles and find the magical plants. Her thoughts wandered again. The island they'd first considered exploring passed to their right. It appeared to be small and the jungle thick. She couldn't imagine finding an opening large enough to camp. Beyond the island, only the ocean lay before them. Waves two miles to their right curled high enough for surfers to ride and beyond that the mainland remained only a sliver of green between the ocean and sky.

Thoughts of a new research lab occupied Rip's mind. He wondered if he'd find a place to conduct acceptable lab tests.

Perhaps Sarmi had space to lease, a place with stable power. Maybe if he and Rava ventured inland, they'd first acquire a lightweight portable lab setup. Simply too many factors existed that he didn't know. A final lab arrangement would have to wait until Gar arrived.

Wakde's two islands filled the landscape several hours later. They steered between the large island to their left and a smaller one to the right. Wakde's T-shaped pier came into view beyond a sandy beach where a quaint village hid under nearby palm trees. No one else had moored their boats near the pier, so Rava asked if the canoe could return in fourteen days. She nodded "yes" when the fisherman requested a partial payment before agreeing. Rip and Rava gathered their gear and headed toward shore. The fisherman pushed his canoe free and slowly started his three-hour return to Sarmi.

Two boys ran toward them wearing big smiles and little else.

"Hello," they chimed. "Welcome to our village. Come, have coffee." Visitors seldom came to Wakde. The children's excitement and curiosity broke the morning serenity. Rip and Rava smiled in response, an internal warmth and calm filled their veins.

One dwelling caught their attention because of several plastic chairs and a table arranged out front. Two large palm trees shaded them. A middle-aged woman smiled and pointed to the chairs.

"Please sit. I'm Grace. I'll bring hot coffee and if you like I'll tell you about our island."

Rip wanted to be cautious with his words until feeling more comfortable on the island.

"We're here to explore the old runway and hike around the shoreline. Is the runway still used?"

"Oh no," Grace laughed, "not anymore. Only during the war did airplanes land on the runway. The jungle has eaten much of the open space since then. I haven't been back there for almost a year, but I think you might still find several collapsed buildings. Are you familiar with the fighting on this island?"

"Yes," Rava replied. "We've heard about the big fight between the Americans, Australians, and the Japanese. I'm curious if we stay for more than a few days, will it be possible to get fresh water and food?"

"Yes, of course. Our food here is quite simple, fish, sago, and coconuts, but we always have enough for others. We have fresh water here too, and I think you might find a well near the airfield. You'll have to look for it."

Rava appeared surprised. "Wow, I didn't think you'd have a freshwater well here."

"It's interesting," Rip explained, "that many of these small islands have wells to augment the rainwater they collect. The water table exists at approximately sea level and since fresh water is lighter than saltwater, it often forms a lens or bubble. That's the water they pull from the wells."

He turned to the woman as she set out two cups of coffee.

"I think we'll hike to the old airfield today and set up our hammocks near there. We'll stop back here in a couple of days and perhaps have more of your coffee."

pointed them toward the far end of the village and told them they'd find the pathway to the airfield there. Rava realized as they started hiking that the village consisted of only twenty or so crude buildings along the sides of the sandy path they followed. Villagers had elevated the structures three to four feet into the air on wooden support posts. Bamboo matting covered the exterior sides. She counted the number of thatched roofs. They outnumbered tin roofs two-to-one.

Their hammocks swung gently in the warm breeze. They'd strung lightweight tarps over them, mostly for shade but also for rain protection. Most of their gear found a home inside the hammock, and thank goodness, Rava had insisted after her first jungle excursion that they add mosquito netting to the mix.

The two explored more and more of the tiny island each day, finding corroded pipes and parts of buildings. Rip couldn't help but think of those who'd been here before.

"With a little imagination, you can see how long this runway must have been. I bet those poor souls stationed here felt isolated and dreamed of their far-away families. At least they had a magnificent ocean view."

"They probably didn't have time to snorkel or swim, or even to fish," Rava added. "On the other hand, they must have cleaned themselves in the ocean and caught fish to eat.

"Let's hike back to the village today. I'd like another cup of Grace's native coffee."

Rava noticed it first when they arrived, sensing a subdued mood throughout the village. Children must have been off playing elsewhere. There didn't seem to be any kids nearby, and the neighborhood remained unusually quiet.

came out from her house.

"Good day, you two. Are you enjoying our little island?"

"Yes, it's beautiful," Rava answered, "but, it's so quiet here today."

"One child is sick with a fever," Momma replied. "It's high, and it won't go down. We're all worried.

"We don't have a hospital, and we don't travel to the mainland often. Even if we did, what could we do? This poor child is in the hands of the spirits."

Rip nudged Rava. "I still have a sampling of your miracle potion. Do you think we could give the child half? If whatever is causing the high fever interacts with the nervous system, perhaps the potion could provide relief."

Rava nodded her head in agreement and turned to .

"We may have something that can help. Do you think we could mix it with a cup of warmed coconut juice and give it to the child?"

"Let's go and look at the little boy," responded. "I'll ask his father."

The boy's house consisted of a single room with slit bamboo slats across the floor and woven matting along the walls. They'd arranged a small fire pit in the center where a single smoldering log fed a feathery smoke column. The father and his young wife knelt beside the boy and adjusted a wet cloth across his forehead.

Rava came close and motioned for the parents to raise the boy so he could drink the coconut juice.

"There, that should do it. We'll know within a few hours if it worked."

She touched her hand to the shoulder of the father, and then the mother.

Rip, Rava, and Grace returned to the coffeehouse, where Rip and Rava shared a small portion of sago bread with their drinks. Rip exhaled as he leaned back and relaxed.

"You know, this sago bread tastes like Indian naan bread. If I eat enough sago, I'm afraid I'll acquire a liking for it."

"Just remember," Rava added, "it's good for your blood pressure."

They smiled at each other, finding it difficult to laugh.

Rip added kindling to a small fire near their hammocks. He and Rava relaxed in their ultralight backpacking chairs while talking about the stars and attempting to identify southern-sky constellations. A nearby rustle startled Rip. His muscles tensed as a dark figure emerged from the brush. The young boy's father bowed slightly and grinned.

"My boy is better! No fever. Thank you, thank you."

He reached out to touch Rava's shoulder.

"Thank you, ma'am. You saved my son."

SIX

DAYS ALIGNED INTO A SIMPLE ROUTINE OF exploring, eating, relaxing along the beach, and sleeping. Island life brought with it isolation and security.

The swath of soft white sand they'd picked for tonight's conversation faced west toward Sarmi. Streaking thin clouds flashed orange and golden hues as Rava busied herself with digging a fire pit. She'd quickly grown to enjoy these moments. Rip, meanwhile, gathered driftwood and dried branches which he stacked next to Rava's pit.

The tiny flame soon grew with an energy that crackled against the evening calm.

"Brother, I've always wondered exactly how my plant extracts make such a difference in your work. I don't suppose you'd consider providing me with a layman's explanation of exactly what you do."

Rip realized that he'd never explained any details of his experiments to Rava.

"It's not so easy to explain without first giving a broad background. Are you sure you want the unabridged version?"

"Well, what else is so important that you can't entertain me with your science just a bit?"

Rip took a deep breath, looked toward the sky, and gathered his thoughts.

"Neurons are a strange type of cell. They're different, obviously, from others. Think of a colorful splat of paint, the shape of an octopus but with more fragile tentacles. Those darned things are everywhere in the body, constantly sensing input and moving it to the brain for evaluation.

"We're not sure exactly how they sense raw data, but it appears they have high fidelity."

"What exactly do you mean?" Rava asked. "Like knowing the difference between temperatures or knowing a punch to the stomach differs from being stabbed?"

Rip laughed before nodding his head slightly. "Yes, I suppose that's part of it. Responses become somewhat automated with repetition, however. For example, neurons can tell if something is between icy cold and searing hot. But the sensors aren't perfect. Sometimes ice-cold feels almost the same as boiling. Visual cues help us differentiate. That's the key. A segment of these neurons senses temperature, others are visual, and others pick up smell and even motion.

"These living sensors have incredible clarity and deliver their information along highways with relatively direct routing to the brain."

Rava sighed in jest. "It's getting complicated."

Rip hesitated for a moment. "Think of each tiny neuron as a juggler tossing three balls. Catch and toss. Catch and toss. And on and on. That's what they do. Sense and transmit. Sense and transmit. Easy, sort of.

"We don't know exactly how the sensing mechanism works, just that it does. Taking what we sense and converting it to a chemical or electrical impulse is similarly a rather complex mystery. Time and research will eventually solve these unknowns. But in the meantime, we're trying to convert our current grab bag of mechanical sensors into recognizable pulses.

"This entire process of moving and translating sensory data is a two-way street. Data exists outside our body that's sensed and sent to the brain for analysis. But there are data and ideas inside our brains that are sent through an interface to a machine. I'm looking at the first scenario where we sense raw optical data and send it to the brain.

"Have you heard about the paraplegic who can move a computer's mouse icon by simply thinking or willing it to move? Well, that's the other scenario. Interesting man-machine cooperation.

"Okay, it's your turn. How do you know which plants are so beneficial?"

Rava twisted a stick in the fire. Embers danced upward as she began.

"Well, to be honest, initially we don't know which plants are special. The natives have found them for us and tested them over years of trial and error. Once we determine exactly what part of the plant provides a beneficial result, we'll study the process by which it produces that benefit. By that, I mean we'll observe cellular interaction under a microscope. We'll perform tests to validate the data, and we'll mix other ingredients to determine the effects of dilution."

"How did you know that mixing our secret potion with warm coconut juice wouldn't negate its effect?" Rip asked. "Tell me, science or luck?"

"No, not so much luck," she responded. "In the jungle, someone seldom injects the potions. It's much more common to apply them directly to the skin or to mix them with water or coconut juice. With a sick child, they often won't drink the water but will take coconut juice. I felt fairly certain the potion wouldn't degrade so I took the chance."

"Interesting," Rip said.

Rava wanted to hear more about Rip's work. "So, tell me, how do those neurons move data? We're not made of electrical wires, or are we?"

Rip enjoyed her curiosity. She remained the only person with whom he could share more technical conversations.

"You'd think we had tiny electrical cables holding us together. There are several functional types of neurons, at least in my simplified way of thinking about them. There are super sensors and there are super transmitters. If you think of branches on a tree, all those tiny branches are primarily sensors, the larger branches and the trunk are almost entirely transmitters.

"Transmission of data happens when a chemical or electrical charge passes from one neuron to the next. The area between the neurons where all the action takes place is called the synaptic cleft. That's the area I focus on. It's where I'd like to inject machine-sensor data that I've already translated into an appropriate electrical pulse.

"What's amazing is that all this transferring of data happens so fast it feels instantaneous. Think about when you stub your toe. The pain doesn't wait. You feel it immediately, yet there are millions of synaptic transfers between the toe's neurons and the brain. It's mind-boggling."

Rava stood and stretched.

"I know you've probably tried to tell me this before, but to be honest, most of your research goes over my head. Now that I've got a basic understanding of what you're up to, how does my potion play into your research?"

Rip feigned surprise. "I can't believe you're telling me this. You actually listened to my explanations and didn't understand any of it. And, you didn't ask questions?"

In a mock heartbroken response, hand clutching his heart. "I'm devastated." And in a more serious tone, "As much out of boredom as anything else, I added a small portion of your plant juice to a solution of neuron cells. It seems your potion acted like a fast-response fertilizer. The neurons became active and clustered into what looked like neural pathways. I found it quite remarkable."

"Why does this little anomaly get you so excited?" Rava asked. "I'm not sure what I'm missing."

"Ah yes. Well, let's start with the sense of sight. Say a person has a severed optic nerve or even something as simple as faulty eyes. In either case, the optic nerve remains fully functional, but lacks visionary input data, leaving the person blind. Suppose we mount a miniaturized high-definition wide-angle camera on a pair of sunglasses. The signal could be translated into a synaptic discharge format and transferred via a short neural passageway from the head's temporal area to the functioning portion of the optic nerve. From there, the subject's existing pathways would feed the data to the brain and the blind person could once again see.

"Think of it like this, the eyes don't actually see, they sense. Their rods and cones only receive and interpret photons. They translate those inputs into chemical/electrical pulses that are passed along neural pathways. In the simplest of terms, we're building an on-ramp to that internal neural highway.

"We could eventually tweak the inputs to a higher resolution than our human eyes provide. Applications like low-light optics or infrared vision could become realities.

"Now, think about the sense of smell. Sensors in our nasal passages collect aromatic data and transmit it to our brain. We have a limited olfactory range and I think that's a blessing in disguise. Let the bears and dogs smell all the bad odors out there." He laughed. "Cats have very discerning smell receptors that let them know exactly what, or who, they are smelling. Perhaps we could capture those signals and transmit them to our brains.

"I love the potential to help a broader swath of humanity. Take the paraplegic with spinal damage. If we could short-circuit the damaged portion of their spine by capturing a signal from their lower extremity muscles and routing them around the spinal damage, perhaps the crippled person could walk again. There are a lot of good applications."

"Is that why General Smithberger funded our expedition and research?" Rava asked.

"Well, that's getting to the core of it. I think he wants to develop those areas that benefit humanity, but I think his more immediate focus is on changing the role of today's pilots. I don't see any of this as a misuse of technology, but rather a way to keep the flow of funding.

"Others, like those chasing us probably have more nefarious motives. I don't think they know anything about the neural pathway applications, but if they did, they'd want our research even more."

"What about Gar? What does he want?"

"Unless General Smithberger has explained it to him, I don't think he knows exactly what we're doing here. But knowing Gar, he'll support the General's requests and do his best to see that we succeed."

Rava stirred the last burning embers and whispered to herself, "It'll be nice when he gets here. I'd like to ask him face-to-face what he thinks."

SEVEN

MARLO'S FLUTTERY STOMACH REFLECTED A twinge of excitement. He'd soon cast off the mooring lines of his new fast support vessel and begin its first official voyage. He'd had her out two times in the past month, but the captain who'd delivered the ship months earlier had supervised those brief excursions. Today, he sailed on his own with a crew of eight Filipinos and seven Americans.

Marlo would normally address the crew in the ship's main lounge, but today he directed everyone to gather on the pier next to the boarding ramp.

"Good morning, men. I'd like to make a few important announcements before we embark on our first operational voyage.

"Just to be clear, we all work for Grey Hawk International and my boss is Mr. Gar. You'll likely meet him during this voyage, and I suspect you'll like what you see. He's friendly and quite laid back. But don't fool yourself into thinking you can run a ho-hum ship. Gar expects excellence on the job. I expect the same, so be sure to hold up your end of the operation. Don't be afraid to ask for help if you need it. And if someone asks you for assistance, please give it to your ability.

"I think it's time to name this vessel, and Gar has given me the authority to do so. Since my favorite beer-drinking appetizer is kinilaw tanigue, I hereby name this vessel the Tanigue.

"For those of you who may not be familiar with kinilaw tanigue, it's a Philippine ceviche, which in this case is uncooked Spanish mackerel marinated in vinegar and onions.

"We're about to depart for Rayong, Thailand. The voyage will take five days and once there, you can expect to assist with several shipboard modifications. For now, let's prepare to get underway."

Tanique, at 210 feet, seemed much larger in many ways and smaller in others. She rode fifteen-foot waves without undue thrashing while slicing through the ocean more like a cruise liner. Large maneuverable vector-fin stabilizers extended midship below the waterline on either side of the vessel. These protuberances looked and acted like fish fins. In anything less than rough seas, they all but eliminated any rolling motion. The ship's bow and stern thrusters provided excellent maneuverability when in close confines. Visibility from the bridge spanned 360 degrees.

Bembol, the chief engineer, had crewed an Exon supertanker earlier in his career but when he took over the engine room on Marlo's fishing trawler, everything became significantly smaller. He'd liked the trawler's tight and cozy feeling. Keeping it spotless and organized had been a relatively straightforward task. Tanigue's engine room appeared enormous by comparison. Each of the ship's four

Rolls Royce diesel engines stood almost nine feet high and stretched fifteen feet long. Several smaller engines drove generators that supported the ship's extensive electrical systems. Computer control panels filled the entire forward engine room as automation touched every aspect of starting, monitoring, troubleshooting, and securing the engines. Bembol loved the upgrades.

Marlo had the ship pointed southwest on a direct course for the Gulf of Thailand. The distance before swinging her north would be one thousand nautical miles and another three hundred and forty nautical miles from that point to Rayong. He glanced slightly right toward the master plot on monitor number five. It displayed a three-day course to the turn-point based on forecast weather and currents. Monitor number six displayed sub-surface topographical data and correlated it with the master navigation computer so that the ship would automatically steer around known shallows.

Marlo thought about how easy sailing this ship could be. He engaged the autopilot and decided to monitor the gauges for another hour before walking the ship and checking how everyone else performed their duties.

He double-checked the monitors to once again verify they displayed what he wanted. Fuel management would require thought for this trip and, to be sure, he ran through the numbers again. The fuel on board could propel them all but a few hundred of the 4,500 miles needed to cruise unrefueled to Papua. Since he'd have several days at Rayong's port, it made sense to fill up there. He'd do the same when they visited Zamboanga as it would be another twelve hundred nautical miles from there to Sarmi. Filling up at Zambo offered him the most flexibility. He thought to himself for the umpteenth time how much easier it would be sailing this ship compared to running the trawler.

Marlo tuned and set the radios. As state-of-the-art as he made his trawler, this bridge had been designed and outfitted from the ground up. It appeared complete, incredibly functional, and perfectly integrated. Even better, the area behind the captain's seat featured a fairly large lounge. A sofa with a coffee table filled an area that overlooked the entire aft section of the vessel. Large windows filled the walls and ceiling. It felt bright and airy, and the air conditioning kept it comfortable.

Gar dialed Marlo's number on the satellite phone. "Hi, hope you're making good time steaming this way. I need deck measurements if you can take a few minutes to get them. What are the dimensions of the helo flight deck? I'm trying to design a cover for whatever eventually lands on it."

"It'll take a few minutes. I'll call you back."

Marlo turned to the only other person on the bridge.

"Chief Mate. You have command of the bridge," he said in his usual jovial tone. " Everything is set. Keep an eye on the weather, other ships, and . . . you know, all that stuff you monitor. Let me know if there are any surprises."

He climbed out of the large Star Trek-looking captain's chair, stretched, and proceeded aft to the bridge's lounge.

It'd been a mess sorting out the crew duties. Everyone specialized in one thing or another, but none had experience as a basic deckhand. He imagined having to abandon the ship and it becoming an every-man-for-himself situation. What if they left him behind? He summoned Bembol from the engine room.

"Bembol, I've got a problem and I need your input to help solve it."

Bembol smiled, got up, and walked to the commercial-grade expresso machine where he filled his mug with its dark, aromatic liquid.

"Could I interest you in a cup of this sludge? . . . What's on your mind?"

Marlo slid a sheet of paper across the coffee table toward Bembol. "It's a list of our crew and their specialties. I'd appreciate hearing your thoughts after I share mine.

"The electronics technician can work with you in the engine room when he's not tending to electrical issues elsewhere. I've dedicated three individuals to the bridge and four to the engine room. Those are required, and I can sub on the bridge when needed. Unfortunately, that doesn't leave much for anything else. What do you think?"

Bembol studied the sheet of paper and thought for a moment.

"Normally, a ship of this size would carry twenty to thirty crewmen. But, during the next four days, when everything is fairly basic, this should work fine. If the weather gets bad or if we've got a lot of passengers onboard, it might get interesting.

"My suggestion would be to assign each individual a specific duty during emergencies. And beyond that, I'd let passengers know to clean up after themselves, be as self-sufficient as possible, and ask questions if they're not sure about something."

Marlo nodded his head in agreement.

"Let's do a fire drill today, a man-overboard drill tomorrow, and an abandon-ship drill sometime the following night. That'll give us time to run through the cycle again if necessary."

Gar exited Japan Airlines flight number 707 with Devon and Quinn in tow. An airport agent stood outside holding a sign with "Mr. Randolph" boldly displayed. Smithberger had requested diplomatic handling for the small group and because the Thai government held Gar in high regard ever since the work he'd previously done in the country, they'd quickly approved Smithberger's request.

The agent whisked them through immigration processing and deposited them at a door that opened to an adjoining tarmac. Gar's helicopter, Galileo, awaited with rotor blades turning.

He leaned his head toward Devon and Quinn. "This little beauty has a few of the same modifications we've integrated into our quadcopter, Icarus. It becomes nearly invisible when we engage its cloaking function and the cockpit is revolutionary. You'll have time to see it on the way to U-Tapao."

Quinn looked more closely, trying to put his finger on what seemed out of place.

"Geez, the skin looks different. It's really smooth."

"That's because it's covered with tiny cameras, and for lack of a better description, monitors. I'll explain all that when we get to the ground school sessions for Icarus."

Devon and Quinn remained wide-eyed for most of the thirty-minute shuttle to U-Tapao. The sole pilot seat didn't seem to have any controls or instruments. Gar provided Devon and Quinn with flip-down visors shortly after take-off and when they donned them, an AI-generated instrument panel suddenly appeared.

"This interior layout probably looks like a toy when the power's off," Devon commented. "It'll only have seats inside at that point. Pretty interesting."

Grey Hawk International buzzed with activity as they entered the hangar. Chambo could be heard barking non-stop directions.

"Okay, let's stack those container panels in the corner . . . Do you have the canoe engines wired yet? Well, keep at it . . . All this medical stuff needs to be organized and labeled."

"Chambo's one of our pilots," Gar explained to Devon and Quinn, "but more importantly, he's the operations manager who's riding herd on all the deployment preparations. He'll drive you to the hotel in a few minutes and get you settled in for the next few days."

Quinn looked at the hangar from wall to wall, like a kid in a candy shop.

"What is all this stuff? It's pretty impressive."

"A local body repair shop fabricated these odd-shaped forty-foot container panels over here," Gar explained. "We needed a protective cover for the quadcopter when it's not flying, something to keep it from prying eyes. There's still major work ahead, of course, like getting the panels installed and functional on Tanigue, which is our ride to Papua.

"We're bringing along our canoes so that Rava and others can penetrate even farther into the jungle from where you drop us off. The canoes have to look authentic, but they also have to be reliable. We've added a few extra capabilities, but the key is that they're lightweight. Chambo had them made using Kevlar and fiberglass and included special attachment hardware so we could fit them to the underside of Icarus.

"All these other boxes contain what we hope will suffice for a basic research laboratory. Several other toys are lying around that we might bring along, like those two electric motorcycles." Gar chuckled. "We've got a lot of unusual toys around here. After all, that's what we do . . . research out-of-the-box ideas."

"Man, I like this," Quinn said with an inquisitive look. "Can't wait to get started."

"Where's Icarus?" Devon asked.

"It's in the other hangar. We'll get to that tomorrow when we start your aircraft orientation."

Chambo had suggested convening an informal meeting at Ban Chang's Sunshine Smile Pub. Several hours later he, Devon, and Quinn finished eating individual plates of stir-fried rice noodles called phad thai. A cute young female bartender with an engaging smile refilled their large glasses with Tiger beer. Outside, the heat of the day clung to the city as skies darkened and neon lights brought life to the otherwise ordinary stretch in front of the bar. Several fans and a struggling air conditioner circulated a temporary swirl of cooled air.

"Have you ever been to one of these local bars?" Chambo asked. "I find them much less formal and more comfortable."

"Well, I remember drinking in a small soba house on a mountaintop in Japan," Devon boasted. "They served iced beer, and the outside air felt so refreshing."

"What about that place in Vietnam where I basically drank you under the table?" Quinn recalled. "I'm pretty sure it prided itself in providing a romantic atmosphere, at least until you showed up."

"Wait a minute!" Devon shot back. "Remember that house party where I had to drag you into my car so I could drive you home?"

"Whoa," Chambo interrupted. "Are you two always this competitive? Perhaps we should create a more civilized competition before measuring ourselves based solely on beer consumption."

"Great idea," Quinn agreed and half-heartedly suggested. "Maybe we could race chariots around Ban Chang's coliseum."

They laughed together. But a mischievous expression slowly came to Chambo's face.

"That's not a bad idea. What about a tuk-tuk race around the block? Oh, sorry. A tuk-tuk is our version of a motorized rickshaw. It's mostly a three-wheeled motorcycle with a single seat behind the driver."

Devon wanted to up the ante. "Okay, but make it three laps. Let's go outside and hire our chariot drivers."

"Wait, that's still too easy," Quinn protested. "We can hire the drivers, but after that let's drink a tall beer before running to our tuk-tuk . . . better yet, between each lap, let's run inside and chug another beer. The first one to finish the last beer after the third lap will be the winner."

"I'm liking this," Chambo mused, "but I think we should add a taste of Thai culture to the challenge. Let's say we each eat one of those tiny red or green peppers before drinking the beers. Four beers. Four peppers."

Devon smiled, feeling confident. "I've got this. Let's find the real man here."

They proceeded outdoors as the girls behind the bar chuckled and whispered amongst themselves. They secretly placed bets on their favored contestant and, before long, barmaids from neighboring bars joined in the betting.

Neither Devon nor Quinn spoke Thai and had to enlist the help of bar girls to pick the fastest tuk-tuk. This tactical disadvantage resulted in the choice of younger, more daring-looking drivers who unfortunately drove lower-powered tuk-tuks. Chambo negotiated privately and settled on an older driver riding atop a slightly more powerful engine. Everyone prepared for action. The three tuk-tuks lined up side-by-side in the street and awaited the crazy foreigners to come charging out of the bar after their pepper-eating start.

The Sunshine Smile Club's Mama-san clanged the bar's bell. Each of the three swallowed an inch-long green pepper. Chambo smiled, gulped his beer, and rushed outside. Devon almost choked and eventually coughed out half of his chewed pepper. Quinn turned red and squeezed his eyes shut as sweat formed on his brow. He downed his beer and ran outside.

Quinn's and Devon's drivers raced to catch Chambo, who leaned around the side of his tuk-tuk and laughed at them. Devon breathed deeply, trying to draw cool air into his inflamed throat while Quinn could barely mumble, "faster, faster."

Chambo lumbered out of Sunshine Smile Club as the other two entered. Competition masked the pain of the race. Somewhat miraculously, the second pepper and beer experience transpired with neither cardiac arrest nor undo pain.

Devon arrived an instant before Quinn at the end of the last lap. Both rushed inside, ate their last red eye-of-the-devil pepper, and tried to slosh down the beers. Devon lost to

Quinn, who ran to the bathroom and remained there for the next fifteen minutes.

Once Devon regained a minimum level of awareness, he asked the Momma-san about Chambo.

"Where is he? Did he crash or take a wrong turn, or what?"

"I don't know," she answered.

Chambo walked into the bar a moment later.

"That old guy had a flat. I had to walk back. Forget that last pepper. I need another beer."

. . . and that's how their night began.

EIGHT

MARLO MESSAGED GAR.

> Arrival time estimated at 4 p.m. tomorrow. Cleared to moor at the Mabtaphut Tank Terminal, pier number 2.

Gar and Chambo sat in Grey Hawk's SUV beside two flat-bed trucks loaded with hangar paneling, laboratory equipment, and an assortment of spare parts for Icarus. A small army of Thai workers waited nearby in a grassy area. Neither Gar nor Chambo had seen Tanigue other than in pictures taken before it left the U.S. The vessel they watched approaching the pier appeared massive. While Tanigue paled by comparison to behemoth cargo or tanker ships, when paired with the title 'yacht' it seemed incredibly large. All the rust and corrosion hinted at Tanigue being a converted liberty ship that might or might not, survive another day on rough seas.

No sooner had he secured the mooring lines than a bubbly Marlo crossed the short gangplank.

"Mr. Gar, Chambo, I present to you, Tanigue." He laughed, and added, "She's not nearly the derelict she appears. I've saved a few sips of Jack if you'd like to celebrate seeing her for the first time."

"I think we can save the celebration until later," Gar replied with a chuckle. "I'd like to see the helipad and the area we've set aside for a laboratory. That way, we can get rid of Chambo. He and his small army of workers will have their hands full getting those areas ready before departure.

"Perhaps you could give me a brief tour of your new pride-and-joy and introduce me to your crew."

The helipad and the laboratory comprised the aft-most section of Tanigue. That's where Marlo led Gar into the interior lower deck. Gar wondered how Grits came across the vessel, and how he found the vision to think of acquiring it. The entire acquisition process seemed fairly incredible. Tanigue made freshwater, processed most of the garbage into environment-friendly waste, had more power than he could ever use, and represented a technological gem. The builders had automated just about everything and made most systems redundant.

Marlo explained as they proceeded. "Here's the laundry room, and this is a small gym . . . the crew quarters are quite adequate, in fact, better than on most ships."

"Okay men, let's start with all these boxes," Chambo ordered. "Stack them along the laboratory wall . . . carefully . . . we'll open everything and secure all the equipment later."

His small army of workers sprang into action. Boxes moved steadily from the flatbed onto the ship, much like a column of ants carrying leaf fragments along a miniaturized jungle pathway.

Installing the collapsible hangar walls required far more planning and assembly work. Welders attached electrical motors below the helipad edges and ran electrical wires from them to a single control panel on the forward open deck. Its two buttons either raised or lowered the faux-shipping container panels. The hangar deployment process resembled a huge, four-sided electric garage door rising into the sky. Chambo thought of the folding panels as giant tulip petals blossoming before Icarus flew and closing after it landed.

Once Chambo satisfied himself that the construction work met his standards, he, Gar, and Marlo found a good viewing position on the pier while one of the deckhands operated the controls.

"This looks great here in the tranquility of Rayong," Gar noted. "Do you think it'll perform this well at sea?"

Chambo didn't know. "We've over-engineered the support materials and I'm sure that once we erect and secure the panels, they'll withstand whatever Mother Nature throws their way," he confidently answered. "Still, I'd suggest not tempting fate."

"Problems will be hard to fix at sea," Marlo cautioned. "I think we'll need specialized safety harnesses and maybe another roll of mesh netting."

Gar mentally reviewed the pros and cons and felt satisfied. "Well, despite our concerns, it really looks like a stack of shipping containers on the aft deck. Unless one knew better, he'd think we're a tramp steamer."

Gar and Chambo returned to U-Tapao once satisfied that Tanigue's modifications appeared to be progressing well.

Devon and Quinn experienced a similar two-headed malaise. Their bodies operated at three-quarters speed and no matter how much they brushed their teeth or gargled mouthwash, they couldn't remove the lingering taste of peppers.

Quinn committed to himself that he'd avoid any such future contests. The heat is something he'd have to consider more heavily in the future.

Devon knew Quinn had to feel the same as he did.

"I don't know about you," he confided, "but I'm ready to focus on learning quadcopter systems. And, I never want to see another one of those damned peppers again." He stifled a gag reflex and forced a muffled laugh.

Gar met them as they entered the hangar.

"Good morning, guys. Hope you had a good night's sleep because today will be a busy one."

Devon and Quinn looked at each other. They didn't share Gar's enthusiasm.

"Maybe we should start by getting a cup of coffee," Gar added more softly. "Let's go inside and sit around the conference table while I detail Icarus' background."

The air-conditioned control room offered an immediate measure of relief, and steaming coffee infused a welcome nugget of missing energy.

"That helicopter we flew from Bangkok to here had been a Bell Textron test bed for developing control surface technologies," Gar began. "We added several features that worked surprisingly well, such as low visibility. That modification works best when the airframe has smooth curves and little to no surface irregularities. When you see the main fuselage of Icarus, you'll notice it looks like a smooth, fat cigar. All antennas are conformal. Vents are flush, and so forth.

"Remember when I mentioned that the helicopter skin contained a mix of cameras and monitors? Well, Icarus is the same. Each camera points outward from the fuselage and projects that image to the monitors on the opposite side. There's a lot of image-blending and other hocus-pocus going on, but when you activate the system, the quadcopter virtually disappears.

"The inside feels magical at times. We can display those same images on the inside walls using identical techniques. You'll feel like a bird when it's engaged. We're working on a variety of alternative presentations for the inside. So far, we've included the ability to view low-light and infrared modes."

Quinn couldn't help but think this technology, like so many modern-day advances, should have been exploited before now.

"Why has it taken so long to develop this? We should have had this capability a long time ago."

"Well . . . young grasshopper," Gar teased, "painting monitors onto the skin of an aircraft took longer than overnight to invent. And think about this, how complex do you think it is to connect the camera signal to the monitors on the opposite side of the aircraft? It's a fairly complex process."

Gar walked to the rear of the room to project an image of Icarus on the front whiteboard.

"We've done a lot of work with noise suppression. Around the rotors are two-foot-high rings of honeycomb-like plastic. Their purpose is to capture the high-pitched noise coming off the tips of the rotors and shift the phase-amplitude 180 degrees. Think of a headset with noise-canceling capability. We're employing the same technology on a much larger scale."

Devon perked up. "That's got to be a tremendous improvement, but what about all the engine noise? Have you reduced it?"

"Now that gets somewhat more complex," Gar replied. "It might be best to let you experience the noise situation first-hand because we have several types of motors producing distinct sounds. The main rotor engines are electric, and they're pretty quiet out of the box. But we've also got a couple of small rotary engines that we haven't silenced yet. And there's the radioisotope generator system which is almost silent."

Quinn and Devon's eyes opened wide.

"A nuclear engine . . . what?" they blurted in unison.

Gar raised his hands as if to say 'stop'.

"I'll explain that later, but it adds another dimension to sustained operations."

Chambo and five Thai workers huddled around the two canoes on the hangar floor.

"Show me everything . . . like . . . where's the engine?"

The lead Thai stepped to the first canoe and touched what appeared to be a bag of vegetables next to a plastic fuel canister.

"Here. This is the engine cover."

He rotated the painted Kevlar shape up and forward to reveal a small rotary engine.

"This cover has quite a few little vents."

He stepped to the rear of the canoe and pulled the rudder and tiller free from their restraints.

"Here's how they snap into place along the canoe's inside and this is where we fasten them for air transport."

He pulled a semi-rigid mylar sheet from inside the left gunwale and attached it to the right gunwale.

"This arched cover encapsulates whatever you store inside the canoe, but it also makes the overall structure much more aerodynamic."

Each of the canoe's four metallic attachment rings had been positioned under what appeared to be wooden blocks. The Thai removed the covers.

"She's ready to be attached. What do you think?"

Chambo grabbed the end of the canoe and lifted it.

"Wow, this is like a feather. How much does that engine weigh?"

"It's our heaviest part," the Thai answered. "The engine is eighty pounds, but it's plenty powerful."

Chambo had known the approximate engine weight because the engines used in the canoes had been two of the spares for Icarus. He'd simply removed the generators from the originals and added shaft adaptor plates.

The informal inspection concluded and Chambo gathered his workers.

"Okay my beloved cretins, let's get these attached to Icarus." Turning to the ground crew, "It's time to get Icarus ready for its flight to the ship."

The time had come for Chambo to grab his bags and make one last trip to Rayong.

"I want you to run five cycles of raising and securing our container hangar including unlatching and storing it," Marlo instructed his deckhands. "Your goal will be to assemble and latch it in ten minutes or less. Apply the same time standard to unlatch and secure it. Once you're comfortable and proficient with the process, leave the container cover in the open position so we can land the quadcopter."

"How much time do we have before the quad arrives?" one of the deckhands asked.

Marlo looked at the sky before glancing at his watch. "It'll be tonight after we've departed and cruised at least ten miles from the coastline."

Gar led Devon and Quinn into Grey Hawk's hangar.

"In a few minutes, we'll tow Icarus outside and get it started. I'm going to engage the low visibility cloaking feature and the propeller noise reduction system and depart without running the LPs.

"The 'LPs' are LiquidPiston's X-Engines. They're re-engineered rotary engines that are significantly better than the old Wankels you might have heard about. LP eliminated the problem of high oil burn and increased fuel efficiency by thirty percent while increasing relative output power. At eighty pounds, they're lightweight, tiny, and quiet. Each engine powers a 30kW generator that charges Icarus' batteries."

Gar envisioned using them primarily inflight except for departures and arrivals when even small increases in ambient noise might betray their presence.

Standard 400 lb., 35hp diesel engine compared to a LiquidPiston 80 lb., 40hp diesel engine.

"Let's move Icarus outside," Gar ordered, "climb on board, and get going. I think you'll enjoy the ride."

He donned a visor and strapped into the single pilot's seat. Devon and Quinn settled in behind him. The startup could not have been easier.

BATTERY SWITCH to ON. Their visors came to life. A primary flight display appeared to the left of center and a multi-function display illuminated to its right. He flipped the four ENGINE switches to ON and all four rotors began turning. He set the virtual mode-select knob to Interior – Real-Time and Icarus's inside ceiling and walls instantly displayed the sky and surrounding facilities. For the ground handlers, Icarus simply vanished before their eyes when he engaged the CLOAK switch. Gar set the sound deadening system and added power.

They ascended vertically before tipping forward and gaining speed. U-Tapao's lights soon faded behind them.

Rayong to the left and Sattahip to the right similarly disappeared as they passed the coastline.

Gar keyed the radio to Marlo's pre-arranged frequency. "Tanigue, this is Icarus. Estimate arrival in fifteen minutes. Please go infrared."

"Roger. Awaiting your arrival," sounded in his headset.

Gar twisted a virtual mode-select knob to infrared. The inside walls changed to a near-black display. Within minutes, a white spot appeared off their nose, growing in size and detail as they approached.

Gar spoke in a monotone. "Icarus, fly approach."

The aircraft locked onto the ship's helipad signal and automatically adjusted power and directional inputs so that Icarus flew directly to the helipad. They hovered a moment at ten feet altitude before slowly descending to a perfect landing.

"I don't believe we did that," Devon commented. "This isn't like flying at all."

"We could use this for all sorts of missions," Quinn added, "even formation flying in the clouds."

Gar squeezed his radio transmit switch. "Tanigue, this is Icarus. Do you have us in sight yet?"

"Negative," responded Marlo.

Rava crawled out of her hammock and stretched in the predawn darkness. Rip snored nearby. It felt like a good time to stroll along the beach. She wanted to see the sunrise and she needed to consider her next jungle trek. She heated water on a tiny backpacker's gas burner, prepared a mug of coffee, and headed off through the palm trees.

Ocean sounds, barely perceptible, rose from the sandy beach as waves rhythmically rolled in and flowed out. On the horizon, a faint glow of pastel yellow grew brighter. She sat in the sand and let her mind wander.

She loved it here, maybe because it forced her into its seclusion and unknowingly blocked the unpleasantness elsewhere. She imagined being stuck here forever and wondered if she'd eventually crave a plan of escape. The warmth of the sand around her backside relaxed her muscles in the cool morning air.

Next week she'd find her way back to Sarmi and wait there for Gar. Rip would set up some sort of lab. She hadn't seen a hospital and suspected that only one or two doctor's offices existed nearby. From that, she surmised that he wouldn't find an existing lab.

It frustrated her that the potion plant grew such a long way into the jungle, but realized that its remoteness explained why no one had discovered it before. She didn't feel ready for a month-long boat trip down the Taritatu River.

Rip appeared out of the palm trees and sat beside her.

"It's beautiful here in the morning, isn't it?"

"Yes brother, we're lucky to have found ourselves in such a place."

Rip sipped his coffee before adding, "Well, there's less than a week left before we return to Sarmi. Are you ready for that, for the cars and the people and the noise?"

"And the danger. It's what it is. I prefer it here if you must know."

NINE

"We're heeere!"

GAR TRANSMITTED AS HE DISENGAGED THE CLOAK switch.

Marlo happened to be looking at the helipad when Icarus suddenly appeared out of nowhere.

"No . . . what the hell. That's spooky."

Gar stored the rotor assemblies before turning the BATTERY SWITCH to OFF. The assemblies on the right side moved upward three feet and rotated inward. The others simply tucked in underneath them. Once completed, Icarus' footprint slimmed considerably and, as hoped, fit within the hangar structure.

The after-landing procedure included strapping Icarus to the ship. The crew could easily accomplish this by fitting nylon-strapped bags over the landing gear and cinching them to locking points on the deck. Once complete, everyone cleared the area after which Chambo erected the hangar walls.

"This is the part," Devon grumbled, "where we normally drag our bags to a flea-ridden third-rate hotel and try to get some sleep."

Quinn looked around the lit portions of the deck. "Yeah, except this is nice so far . . . although I've never spent time on a flat-top hulk that I've particularly liked."

Gar climbed up the companionway to the bridge.

"Nice job getting underway," he said to Marlo. "The hardest part is always making that final decision to pull the lines and push free of the dock. I worried that you might have lingered another day finishing up the odds and ends."

Marlo laughed and gave Gar a welcoming hug. While hugging, Gar couldn't help but notice the six monitor displays. He felt satisfied knowing Tanigue had been configured into a fully capable vessel. His floating resort could carry them pretty much anywhere.

Marlo released Gar and scolded him. "You pretty much scared the bejesus out of me when, out of nowhere, you burst onto my ship. How'd you do that, anyway?"

Stars twinkled against a dark sky. Gar slid the lounge's etched-glass door to the side and sauntered onto the teak flooring outside. He and Marlo eased into a pair of overstuffed chairs and gazed into the night, content with life.

"Marlo, it's good to be underway at last. We've got an interesting and potentially dangerous mission ahead."

Chambo arose early and made his way aft to the laboratory. He congratulated himself on getting it to at least look like a lab, minus all the little necessities like test tubes and swabs. He hoped that Rip would approve. The hatch behind him moved. He flinched. His heart rate increased a notch as the hatch swung open. A deckhand entered with a smile and a mug of freshly brewed coffee.

"Thirsty?" he asked.

Chambo tried to hide his relief. "I'm liking this little voyage. Thanks."

Plugging in the electrical cables, making sure everything worked, and strapping down loose items like the small electron microscope and the burner plates would complete his laboratory setup. He imagined the first day of rough seas and all this stuff finding its way to the floor.

Satisfied, Chambo set out to find the ship's library.

Gar led Devon and Quinn to a converted mission planning room located immediately forward of the laboratory. Its walls held large maps of Papua and the South Pacific, along with an unmarked whiteboard. Devon and Quinn settled into office chairs in front of a typical conference table. Gar stood before them.

"Today, I'm going to brief you on Icarus, AI integration, and your role during this little adventure.

"In terms of aviation philosophy, the Air Force emphasizes high and fast. Detection is mitigated with airfoil shapes, energy-absorbing materials, and electronic countermeasures. Your aircraft tend to be complex and require skilled maintainers to sustain their most critical systems. You go through fuel like water and require a significant refueling plan as part of every operation. Icarus represents the polar opposite approach to getting the mission done.

"Flying Icarus low comes with fewer penalties than flying a turbine-powered aircraft at the same altitude because Icarus uses electric engines. Flying fast isn't a priority, but I have to admit, it's still nice. When it comes to stealth, we view it differently. Invisibility and low noise generation make Icarus nearly undetectable, and its all-Kevlar composite construction is immune to radar interrogation.

"During the past twenty years, the aviation industry has developed aircraft and terrain avoidance systems that have secured their place as essential equipment in commercial aviation. They add real-time precision and shared situational awareness to air traffic surveillance. But those systems add a lot of weight and rely on an Automatic Dependent Surveillance-Broadcast signal called ADS-B. Anyone with access to the internet could track our flight path along with airspeed and altitude. That's why we've decided to forego the merits of ADS-B for added electronic invisibility.

"I'll admit that we're still working on some RF issues with the electric engines. Nonetheless, design simplicity eliminates ninety-nine percent of the daily maintenance. We don't refuel . . . well, maybe once every week or two, or longer. In a nutshell, Icarus provides self-sufficient autonomous operations.

"The rotors are no more complex than those off-the-shelf commercial quadcopter blades. Rather than having multiple inter-connected linkages to change individual blade pitch and plane, an electronic control module, or ECM, adjusts rotor rpm via dynamic voltage change. That's how we control yaw, bank, pitch, and directional movement. We've got a central flight computer that grabs a variety of inputs and translates them into rotor rpm.

"Remember when I flew the approach to Tanigue? I commanded 'fly approach' and that verbal command triggered the flight computer to lock onto Tanigue's approach beacon and descend along a pre-programmed glideslope to a ten-foot hover, and then to land once the hover stabilized.

"Icarus contains a variety of sensors, many of which are used for functions other than flying, like feeding the primary and multi-function displays. I'll touch more on those inputs later, as they're designed to help you make better mission decisions.

"We hope to input artificial intelligence along with that sensory data directly into your brain. Don't worry, brain surgery isn't required. It'll be a lot more like listening to music through a headset, except it'll feed data rather than sound to your gray matter."

"I think Quinn is worried about being radiated," Devon warned with exaggerated concern. "You should know he's already filled his brain to its limit. Does that nuclear power have anything to do with thought modification?"

"My brain is fine, you over-stuffed hockey puck."

"Whoa!" Gar chuckled. "Let's go over the engines and how they're used . . . and don't worry, there's almost no chance this brain-feeding process can worsen the current state of your libido.

"The four main motors under the rotors are electric, much like Tesla's 310hp S/X. They turn at an adjustable rpm and not much more. Okay, I'm going to tell you something deceptively simple while sounding incredibly complicated–the two rotors in front turn in opposite directions and the same is true with the rear rotors. Got it so far? The front rotor on the right turns opposite the rear rotor on the right. Same on the left side. This creates a perfect balance when all are turning at the same speed. By adjusting the speed of individual rotors, you can change the yaw, pitch, and roll. That's why we have a primary and a backup computer module to sort it all out. Those little commercial quadcopters have already validated the concept and we're doing the same aerodynamic movements but on a larger scale. So basically, it's pretty simple."

Quinn thought about how automatic it all sounded, and frowned.

"You know, you're taking all the fun out of flying. But what happens if an engine fails?"

Gar drew an 'X' on the whiteboard and labeled each of the four endpoints '1', '2', '3', and '4'.

"Let's say engine '1' fails. The ECM will shut down '1' and '2' so you'll end up with the front two engines or the back two. It's not ideal, but it'll allow you to continue to a place where you can land.

"Let's move on to the batteries . . .

"The four main batteries are the key to sustained flight, and the LP engines recharge them if you're on an extended mission. By the way, the fuel required to run the LPs is our only expendable commodity. That's why we burn it with discretion. One battery will power two motors for two hours, so typically two batteries will power the four motors at any given moment. The ECM automatically switches to the reserve batteries at approximately the two-hour mark, which provides another two hours of flight.

"They'll recharge the spent batteries until the ECM switches back again if both LPs are running. This progressive switching cycle can extend the flight time up to approximately ten hours.

"The pair of two-foot by two-foot advanced Stirling radioisotope thermoelectric generators are four times more efficient than the one powering the Perseverance rover on

Mars and they use half the radioactive material. By the way, we use Americium-241 because we can get it much cheaper than Plutonium-238. The only drawback is that it requires additional shielding. The systems have free-floating pistons that move continuously inside the engine, but they don't contact other parts, so there's no wear. Even better, there's little need to worry about getting radiated after a hard landing because we've added a fair amount of crash-resistant padding around the whole works. Those darned reactors will produce a constant electrical charge for a thousand years. It's the primary charger whenever Icarus isn't flying.

"Icarus contains the four main batteries and one accessory battery. It takes at least six hours to recharge a pair of them using only the radioisotope thermoelectric generators. Depending on the time between flights, it may be sufficient to recharge everything without needing LP help.

"But if we do need the LPs, there's enough Jet-A fuel on board to run the two of them for approximately three days non-stop. Nonetheless, we need to conserve that fuel.

"In summary, Icarus can operate off the grid and without refueling for a very, very long time . . . and remain invisible for most of it.

Low gray clouds hung over a calm sea as Marlo approached Zamboanga's western port extension. At 6 a.m. most of the city remained asleep and this section of the port appeared equally quiet. Marlo could see only two stevedores smoking cigarettes near its lone office building. Gar stood behind Marlo toward the rear of the bridge.

"If all our cargo is ready, we should have the loading done before noon. How long will the refueling take?"

Marlo remained focused on maneuvering the bow thrusters. "Hopefully, we'll be ready to sail by early evening. I've got two or three friends here who'll make sure we get adequate refueling priority."

Gar gathered the Chief Mate, the Chief Engineer, and the Emergency Medical Technician.

"I've got a special assignment for us today. Follow me."

He led them to the cargo office where he asked the agent about their load, specifically, boxes with "fragile" labels plastered all over the sides. Two young Filipinos appeared from the back storage area.

"General Santana, our Regional Police Commandant, sent us to help you today," one of them announced. "We've got a vehicle with your boxes already in the back. Would you like to inspect them before we go?"

"Perfect," Gar replied. "Please pass my best regards to General Santana. If we have time, I'll thank him personally."

Gar joined the driver in the cab. The others found room in the back next to the boxes. Zamboanga's unique architecture revealed its mix of Spanish and Muslim origins. Congested streets slowly gave way to pockets of urban modernization, but at its core, Zamboanga remained a fishing community with a growing maritime trade. Within minutes, they lost themselves in the rustic beauty of it all.

An elderly Canadian missionary approached their vehicle after they'd parked in the yard of what appeared to be a small school.

"I'm so happy to see that you arrived safely. Your friend General Smithberger said you'd be coming for a visit.

"Welcome to Saint Francis House. Our orphaned and abandoned children are eating breakfast, but they're all excited to meet you."

The boxes they'd delivered contained a variety of foodstuffs, including ten cases of spam and several large bags of rice. Gar distributed enough toothbrushes and tennis shoes for everyone, along with several soccer balls and basketballs. General Smithberger had suggested that the adult family members of the staff be present, as he'd included a solar charging panel and a new iPhone for each family. These would keep them connected during the numerous power outages they'd experience each year.

Tanigue had been refueled by the time they'd returned to the port. Deckhands hoisted several pallets of goods onto the deck and lowered them into the ship's relatively small cargo hold. Chambo busied himself with distributing the goods to their ultimate storage locations onboard.

Marlo pushed free of the pier in the early darkness and Tanigue slowly disappeared into the southeast, headed toward Papua.

Gar stood before Quinn and Devon in the briefing room.

"There are two training objectives left to check before we arrive in Sarmi. One is to get you guys flying Icarus. We'll do that today. I'd like each of you to fly a fairly simple profile, and accelerate to at least 180 knots before slowing down for a landing on Tanigue. Make multiple landings until you're comfortable with the process. I'll ride along in the back and be available should you have questions or need my help.

"The other objective is to get you started with our data-to-brain research. I've concocted several fun exercises to help you develop the process. But that's for tomorrow. For now, let's get ready to fly."

Devon climbed into the pilot's seat and methodically ran the abbreviated checklist. He eased the throttle forward, feet flat on the floor, right hand barely touching the control stick. Icarus eased straight up and drifted aft off the helipad.

"It's stable," he commented, "the controls have a good feel . . . okay, let's take it for a little spin around the neighborhood. Do you think we'll see any whales at this time of day?"

The rotor assemblies rotated from horizontal to sixty degrees vertical as they sped up. Most of the thrust pushed forward at this angle while leaving enough to hold altitude. The movement happened automatically without pilot input. Devon flew a large box-shaped pattern around Tanigue before approaching it from the rear. Today's quartering tailwinds would normally have dictated an approach from a different direction, but Gar wanted to demonstrate Icarus' ability to overcome all but the most severe wind issues.

Devon commanded. "Fly approach." Icarus locked onto the helipad beacon and started its descent.

Devon and Quinn hand-flew numerous approaches, ventured away from Tanigue and engaged Icarus' autopilot, played with a variety of verbal commands, and adjusted the displays appearing across their visors.

Quinn flew his last approach to a perfect landing on Tanigue. A look of satisfaction spread across his face.

"And one more thing, this baby is the quietest plane I've ever flown, hands down."

Sarmi sits on a finger of land surrounded by the ocean on three sides. The town and port look southeast into the ocean. Two miles to the north is an isolated island. Marlo had suggested anchoring Tanigue on the far side of that island, as it would effectively hide the vessel from curious eyes. The ground party could use their thirty-foot rigid hull inflatable boat to transit the two miles to and from shore.

Marlo ordered the anchors to be lowered. Tanigue quietly arrived at its new home, where it would hopefully remain unnoticed.

TEN

RAVA WATCHED RIP AS HE READ A MESSAGE on his phone. His blossoming smile foretold the good news.

"They've arrived and anchored behind that island north of here. Gar's asking about a quiet place to meet."

Rava shared the emotion. "Why not have him meet us at that little hole-in-the-wall bar two blocks in from the pier? It's the one that looks like a converted garage with everything painted ugly blue inside.

"We could get there early and have an evening coffee."

The area appeared dark and isolated. Rip's nerves jittered, cold for no reason. Too dark, too isolated. Before he could suggest moving somewhere else, an indistinct shadow transformed into a tall Asian.

He approached their table and spoke in a villainous tone. "I've been looking for you two. Do as I say or I'll hurt the girl."

Rip sprang to his feet in protest. Who is this brute, and how did he find us? A large bolo knife flashed in the light.

"Another step and I start carving you to shreds."

Rava grabbed her purse. Anything to use in defense. The fact that he seemed to be alone didn't help.

A large black man appeared from the darkness behind the assailant and swung a baseball bat into his head. A sharp thud preceded his collapse. The native lifted the aggressor without speaking or so much as making eye contact and just as quickly disappeared with him back into the night.

Gar had been less than a block away when the commotion started. He arrived to find Rip and Rava in their seats, shaken and nervous.

"What happened?"

"To be honest," Rip answered in a confused tone. "I'm not exactly sure. Another Oriental appeared out of nowhere and threatened us with a large knife. I don't know if he wanted to rob us or to steal our research."

"Out of nowhere," Rava added, "this large black man came to our rescue and disappeared as quickly as he'd arrived. I didn't see his face clearly, but honestly, even if I did, I probably wouldn't have recognized him."

The black man reappeared with a satisfied smile exposing his white teeth.

"Sir, Ma'am, are you two, okay? You saved my son, and I will protect you."

Rava recognized the boy's father from Wakde. "Thank you. Thank you so much."

"I know how to survive in the jungles and how to communicate with many of its tribes. Take me to help find your plants, and I will protect you."

Gar smiled. "Please sit with us. Would you like a cup of coffee?"

Gar pulled out his smartphone and tapped a series of numbers on the screen.

"Chambo, we've had a minor scuffle here. It's all under control, but keep a sharp eye out for strangers around the pier."

Chambo had piloted their rubberized tender and stayed with it when Gar left to meet Rip and Rava. The pier area emanated little noise beyond the constant lapping of waves against its barnacle-encrusted concrete structure. Salt air that mixed with the sweet aroma of algae added another layer of calm. Gar's alert couldn't have been timelier.

Chambo thought it odd when he noticed several middle-aged men snooping around the dock area. He didn't want them asking him questions and decided to curl up on the hull of the boat. He'd pretend to be asleep, but not so asleep that he couldn't keep an eye on things.

He counted five of them. They acted with a focus, as though looking for someone or something important. It didn't look normal. Once they'd visited the food stalls and market area, they continued onto the pier where several small boats separated them from his RHIB. Chambo eased to the bottom and remained still.

"Hey, you!" one of them called to a boat owner moored not more than fifty feet from Chambo. "Have you seen an American man and woman traveling together in the past weeks?"

Chambo recognized his oriental intonations and decided that he and his accomplices must be the ones giving Rip and Rava such a hard time.

The boat owner said nothing.

"If you have information, I will pay for it," added the thug.

"Well," the boatman slowly responded, "I seem to remember taking such a couple to Wakde Islands two weeks ago."

"Where are they now?" the other demanded.

"How do I know? You ask a lot of questions."

"I'll pay more. Here, take this. I'll double it if your information is good."

The boatman hesitated before answering. "Well, I might have returned them here last week. I think they're still somewhere in Sarmi."

Satisfied, the group departed, like dogs on the hunt.

"Do you have any idea why we're being hunted by these men?" Rip asked. "It's been pretty persistent, and that makes me think there's more to this than I first thought."

Gar leaned in slightly and spoke in a soft voice. "I've received a series of updates from the General, and he's convinced the source of your trouble is coming from a single Asian country.

"They've been experimenting with biological weaponry for several years, but fortunately, with a relatively poor track record. By that I mean, they've created several deadly viruses, but to our knowledge, haven't yet found effective antidotes. They won't employ a virus as a weapon without the ability to immunize their soldiers first.

"Their goal is to infect whoever might be an enemy while providing immunity to friendly troops. In the past, they've stolen research touching all aspects of virology, and I think they've been watching you ever since General Smithberger came into the picture."

Rava felt empty. The thought of that creep stealing something so good and turning it into a biological weapon put a sour taste in her mouth. Rip shared the feeling.

"Do you think they know about the neurological effects of this new potion?"

Gar couldn't be sure of the answer.

"I don't think so, at least from what you've told me. It sounds like you've been able to keep your hands on all that paperwork. But I suppose it doesn't really matter in terms of the immediate threat.

"Let's find a path forward, one that keeps you two safe."

Rava listened to all that Gar said while mostly sitting in silence. She could see his concern for her and Rip. At least he listened and took charge at the same time. She didn't think "interesting" described him adequately. She sensed there to be a lot more.

Gar couldn't help but notice Rava's subtle vulnerability. Her mussed hair gave her a mysterious, sensuous appearance. She looked beautiful in the dim light.

Rava turned toward the black man with a concerned, but grateful look.

"I've never asked your name. What do people call you?"

The Wakde native smiled proudly. "I am Diah Setiawati Saturdawati Permata. My son calls me Saturday."

"Then I shall call you Saturday as well," she added and looked to Gar, "I'd like to take Saturday when we go into the jungle. Will that be okay?"

Gar nodded his head. "Will the man who threatened Rip and Rava be a problem?" he asked Saturday.

"He won't bother anymore. My friend is taking him to the fishes now."

Gar turned to Rip. "Tomorrow morning, drive to the airport and buy two tickets for Jayapura. Drive your car somewhere north of Sarmi and park it. I'll rent a motorcycle and join up to get you back here.

"We'll leave the hotel tomorrow after dark and go back to our ship. You can plan your jungle trek from there. In the meantime, I'll join Chambo at the pier. We'll maintain a low profile and keep an eye on port activity."

"It's about time you got back here," Chambo whispered as though scolding Gar. "I thought I'd be up all night waiting for you."

Chambo had thought to add a couple of rolled foam mattresses before launching the tender from Tanigue. They stretched across the boat's bottom.

"Welcome to home sweet home," Gar said mostly to himself,

"It gets better," Chambo added.

He pulled a rope from over the side of the craft. At its end, a six-pack of beer appeared.

"Care for a nightcap?"

"I'm glad I brought you along," Gar responded.

ELEVEN

CHILLED GUAVA JUICE QUENCHED RAVA'S morning thirst. She'd taken the last spoonful of fried rice when Saturday entered the dining room and approached the table.

"If you have large items for the boat, I'll take them in a bajaj."

"What on earth is a bajaj?" She asked, "I haven't heard that before."

Saturday chuckled. "It's a tuk-tuk, but we sometimes call them bajaj. My friend has one."

Rip emptied the car's trunk and stacked its contents in Saturday's mini-cargo-hauling bajaj. Cleaning out the car brought a feeling of freedom from haunting thoughts of the previous owner's demise. Rip still bore the quilt of having changed places with him the night he died. He turned to Rava after loading the bajaj.

"I hate to leave you behind, but at least you'll have the afternoon to get us packed for tonight's departure. Try to stay out of sight until I return."

The same agent sat behind the business counter at Sarmi's airport operations building.

"Hi," Rip said. "We took your advice on Wakde Island and had a great time exploring the old airport. We seemed to be the only visitors there."

The kid looked up and smiled.

"Oh, I'm glad you went. There's a lot of hidden history waiting to be revisited. What can I help you with today?"

"We're ready to fly back to Jayapura and take care of several business issues. Can I buy tickets in advance?" Rip asked.

"It's unnecessary, but sure. I'll prepare them if you want."

Rip thought for a moment.

"We'll be hiking north and west of here for the next couple of days, but we'll be back for the weekend. I'll check in and purchase the tickets then."

Rip again noticed the airport lacked any kind of activity as he left. It surprised him that the airport generated enough business to keep the poor kid employed.

Rip's phone rang. Gar.

"Rip, I'm sitting on a rather frail motorcycle that has seen better days, but I think it'll get me to you and carry us back to the hotel. Where are you?"

"Just follow the road toward the airport until you see the Amsyur Elektonik store. Make a right turn there. If you cross a small river before turning, you'll have missed the turn and gone too far.

"That road is under construction and has sections of new concrete. Anyway, keep going straight until you cross another small river. I'll be a little way beyond that. I'm not there yet but will be in about ten minutes.

"I told the agent at the airport that Rava and I would hike west of there."

"Okay, got it, on my way."

Gar laughed to himself, thinking how comical he and Rip must look as they wallowed along the road, headed back toward Sarmi. The small motorbike strained under their weight, but to the few locals who paid notice, they appeared entirely normal.

A gentle rainfall cooled Rip's and Rava's faces as they walked out onto the pier. Two deckhands wearing international orange raincoats held out similar slickers for them to don. Only when Rip took the orange suit did he recognize the deckhands as Gar and Chambo. Saturday appeared moments later and boarded the rubberized boat. He and Rip sat immediately forward of the covered captain's console. Gar and Rava sat in padded seats at the bow.

Chambo flipped several switches and the twin Suzuki 140 hp outboard motors came to life, their low purr blended with the patter of the rain. As their tender eased away from the pier, Rip and Rava relaxed as they watched Sarmi separate behind them. Chambo added a twitch of power and they soon slipped away from Sarmi's nighttime glow. He shifted focus to the GPS display panel so he could intercept its course back toward Tanigue. In the dark of the night, it'd keep them from straying blindly into the vastness of the ocean.

"Are you okay in the rain," Rava asked Gar. "You know, it rains here almost every day. It's sweltering hot or steamy wet . . . and if you're clawing your way through one of those tangled jungle pathways, sticky mud and slick vines steal all the enjoyment of the rainfall. I suppose you'll get used to it . . . oh, I'm rambling."

"I enjoy listening to you," Gar responded with a sense of curiosity, "so please don't worry about boring me.

"And you're right. I'll get used to the rain, but for me, it feels good. I enjoy the solitude that comes with heavy showers."

"How long do you intend to protect us?" she asked.

Gar chuckled before answering. "I guess it depends on how much time it takes to find your miracle plant and to complete whatever field analysis you'll need to do."

"I hope you can get us near the mountains. It's a significant distance and the rivers have so many turns that it's disorienting when traveling for days on end."

"I think we'll set aside time tomorrow to thoroughly plan your trek," Gar replied. "Once we decide on an initial starting point, we'll figure out the easiest and safest way to get there. I've brought a quadcopter and two canoes, so maybe they'll do the trick. We'll see."

The rain intensified as stiffening winds flattened the angle at which it struck them. Waves grew in size. Rava instinctively squinched her arms into the dry regions of her sleeves and leaned against Gar. He absorbed her warmth and together they shared the sense of security that huddling brought.

Their rubberized boat crashed through several waves before momentarily floating in the air after a swell beneath them dropped away. Gar and Rava wrapped their arms around each other until they smacked the ocean a moment later. It felt like having flown through a down-draft in an airplane.

Rava quickly released Gar and he slowly loosened his arm from her waist.

"Tell me about your plant. How did you find it? Where does it grow? What about all the cannibals in Papua? Did you find them more friendly than hungry?. . sorry, that's probably a poor joke."

"Speaking of hungry, I'm famished. I hope your galley is well-stocked."

Gar couldn't suppress a broad smile.

". . . Well," Rava continued, "about the plant. A native gave it to me, so I'm not one hundred percent sure what it looks like in the wild. He told me that it grows along the Taritatu River near the mountains. It's a close relative of the Dendrobium Atroviolaceum orchid, which is somewhat unique to that area. I'm afraid that's all I've got.

". . . And the natives, I've come across several native tribes and thankfully, they've all been really friendly. But, I've never explored the Taritatu River."

Her facial expression shifted to feigned concern. A hint of a smile curled the sides of her mouth.

"I suppose there may be a few unsavory types running about that neck of the woods. We'll have to be cautious."

She laughed.

The rain and the wind slackened as quickly as they'd worsened thirty minutes earlier. The ride smoothed and Gar drifted in thought. Rava seemed to be a lot more than an egg-headed botanist, full of life, smart, and humorous. He thanked Mother Nature for the well-timed rainstorm.

Chambo maneuvered the tender against Tanigue's aft boarding platform. Several tiki torches flickered in the dark, highlighting the ship's teak deck. Rip and Rava had expected to board something akin to a cargo ship and a somewhat disoriented sense of location filled their minds. Rip couldn't help but voice his confusion to Rava.

"What the heck? This isn't at all what I expected. I think we're on a yacht."

Gar led the group down broad steps into an equipment storage room where a deckhand collected their rain suits.

"This is so clean," Rip noted, "and organized. I have to say that you run a tidy ship. What kind of ship is this?"

Before Gar could respond, Marlo appeared from an adjoining passageway and greeted them.

"Hi. I'm Marlo, the Captain. Mr. Gar keeps me around because I seldom get lost and I tell interesting stories of the sea."

He chuckled before continuing, "Damen Shipyards originally designed Tanigue as a luxury yacht support vessel, but the U.S. government got their hands on it and made several modifications. We're still figuring out its best use. If you'll follow me, I'll play tour guide along the way to the library. We can relax there while the cooks prepare dinner."

Rava didn't know what to expect when they entered the engine room and asked herself why they had to walk through what she anticipated to be a loud and cramped space. She hoped she'd fit between all the pipes and air ducts.

The quietness immediately struck her as odd. Then she realized the engines didn't seem to be running. No wonder it sounded so quiet here. Marlo read her thoughts.

"We've only got one generator running to power all the systems on the ship. It gets slightly louder when the big engines are running, but not nearly as loud as you might imagine. . .

"This room is where we do our laundry . . . and here is our gym . . . these refrigerators and the freezer keep us stocked with enough meats, poultry, seafood, and dairy goods to last a month.

"Please follow me up the companionway to our library."

The cleanliness, and more noticeably, the quality of the passageway walls and flooring suggested to Rip that they'd boarded something more akin to a luxury liner. As he exited the companionway into the library, he gawked in near-disbelief.

"Oh my. This isn't at all what I expected."

The library, or more accurately, the lounge, resembled a cozy nook at London's exclusive Soho House. An overstuffed leather love seat faced an electric-powered fireplace and several winged reading chairs lined either side. The intimate library filled the forward half of the room. The walls toward the fireplace consisted of ornately carved wooden bookshelves and the ceiling featured a patchwork of wooden beams. A large oriental rug covered most of the polished wooden flooring.

The aft half of the lounge consisted of a single circular dining table on one side and a long wood-carved stand-up bar along the other wall. Windows allowed ample sunlight through the aft walls during the daytime and offered wrap-around viewing of the stars at night.

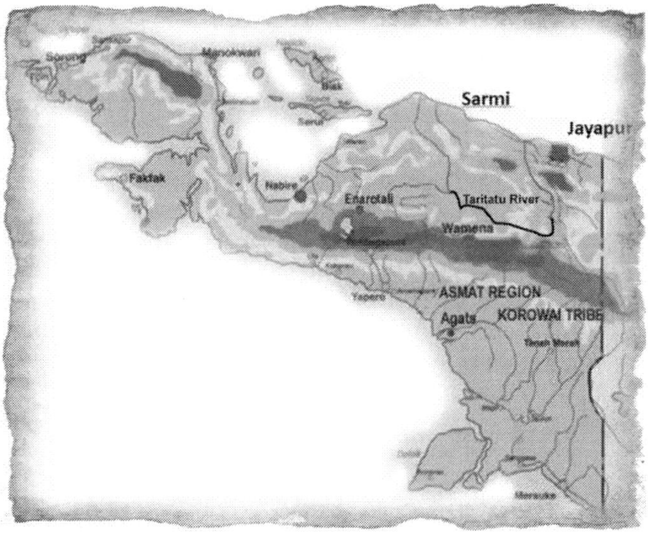

Papua with Taritatu River

Gar had asked Chambo, Rip, Rava, and Saturday to join him for coffee in the morning. They gathered in Marlo's upper lounge immediately aft of the wheelhouse.

He greeted them one by one. "Rava, how do you envision tracking down your plant?. . maybe I should be a little more specific. Do you have an idea of where our search should begin?"

Chambo's well-worn map of Papua laid flat across the coffee table, a brownish coffee cup stain testament to its previous use. Rava pointed to an area south of Jayapura.

"This first section of the river, here, consists of narrow rapids. It's mostly impassable by canoe or even raft. I'd like to start south of that area by searching the swampy areas that border the river. If that doesn't bring results, we can continue westward along the more navigable Taritatu."

"Okay," Gar replied, "We'll have to see if there's a way to offload the team and the canoes somewhere near the river. Besides yourself, who else will you need?"

She thought for a moment.

"We'll plan for a one-month trek. I'd take Saturday and at least one other strong-bodied guy to help carry our gear."

"What about you, Rip? Will you need to go along to research in the field or would you feel more productive working here on Tanigue?"

"I'd like to look at your lab first before giving a definite answer. My top concern is for Rava's safety. If she's in good hands, I'd probably prefer to stay and work here in a more stable research environment."

"How about this," Gar suggested. "The search party could include Rava, Saturday, our EMT-certified cook, and myself. That would give us plenty of muscle for backpacking everything, and an EMT is always good to bring along. We could hire one or two local natives to work with Saturday and to help with navigation, cooking, and general situational awareness.

"Devon and Quinn will share Icarus flight duties, and when not directly supporting the search effort, they can fly several test profiles. Chambo will stay with them to launch and recover their flights, and he can handle any maintenance issues that might come up."

"Marlo, starting tonight, I want you to post two crew members on overnight security watch. You can run the surface radar all night or anything else to keep intruders off Tanigue. You have my permission to take whatever action is necessary to make that happen up to and including shooting them. There are a lot of things I want to keep secret and this ship is one of them.

"If you should have an incident, I recommend moving a safe distance down the coast."

TWELVE

TANIGUE CAME TO LIFE AT 3 A.M. AS DECKHANDS scurried about the aft decks. Their early start came as a result of Gar planning a pre-dawn departure. He'd hoped to gain additional concealment during the transit across built-up areas.

In his words, "Why should we let anyone see which way we're headed?"

The straight-line course to the river island on which they intended to land angled southeast across Sarmi and Jayapura regencies. Heavy jungle growth shared geography with river basins and swamps along the entire route, and a three-thousand-foot-high mountain range extended east to west through the central region. Several miles inland marked a transition from coastal habitation to a vast, undeveloped, and mostly isolated wilderness.

Chambo moved with purpose about Tanigue's deck while directing various one and two-man work crews. A mechanical mate rotated and clamped the end of a coiled refueling line to its orb-shaped storage tank. A second worker uncoiled the other end toward a canoe fuel tank.

After servicing each of the canoes, he verified Icarus' onboard fuel level and eventually stowed the fuel lines.

"Where are those darned tarps and hammocks?" the cook mumbled to himself. "They should be here on the shelf."

Nearby, two deckhands inspected the area around the hangar siding, moved a mooring line out of the way, and prepared to unfold the container-looking structure.

Before anyone climbed into the back of Icarus, Quinn extended the large-diameter rotor housings while Devon removed the wheel covers. Quinn flipped a virtual switch to begin the process . . . nothing. He tried again, and again. Nothing happened.

"Are you having fun in there?" teased Devon. "We're all ready to board once you figure out how to get the rotors deployed."

Quinn cut him off. "I can't get them to move. There must be something wrong with this damned switch."

Devon stifled a laugh.

"Did you remember to de-arm the safety first?. . like Gar so clearly instructed?"

"Hey dung-breath, I know what I'm doing in here," Quinn snapped.

He flipped the de-arm switch and tried again. It worked.

Saturday stood next to Rava, somewhat in awe of the technological world before him.

"Is such a ship normal?"

"Well," she replied, "this one is unusual. Highly trained engineers have created mechanical parts over many years. Those guys spend most of their time in rooms without windows solving technical issues."

"I think it is good, but outdoors is better."

Devon and Quinn squabbled about who would fly Icarus to the river island.

"Look," Devon insisted, "it's a short one-hour flight, mostly at night. You wouldn't like anything about it, so I'll take the pilot duties this time and give you the better flights starting tomorrow."

"Not so fast. I'm much better suited to fly when we have a full load of fuel, the canoes, and passengers. You can schmooze with Gar while I monitor gauges through the boring nighttime cruise. Besides, you'll have more fun that way."

"Nope. Nope. Nope," Devon snapped, "maybe we should flip for the pilot seat."

"Well, okay . . . but . . . Saturday will toss the coin."

Rava and the med tech settled into their seats with cold-skinned claustrophobia. Icarus had no windows or anything other than seats.

"This feels like sitting in a large drainage pipe," he complained. "It kinda gives me the creeps."

"Well, yes, I agree. To me, it's more like being inside a large plastic tube. Why would they design it like this?"

Quinn flipped several switches before a low hum breathed life into the rotors. Moments later Icarus lifted off the deck of Tanigue and tilted forward as it accelerated. Quinn set the internal lighting to artificial intelligence mode. He adjusted the time of day to 8 a.m. and the sky condition to CLEAR.

The interior walls and ceiling flickered an instant later before transforming into what appeared to be a huge glass window. They could have been birds soaring in the morning skies.

"Wow, I get it," Rava remarked. "This is quite magnificent."

"It's so weird," the tech agreed. "I know it's still dark outside, but everything says it's mid-morning and clear. I don't think I'll leave my seat during this flight."

He laughed with a worried inflection.

"I could fall out."

Before long, he couldn't help but fixate on the terrain passing beneath them.

Saturday's face tightened with fear. His eyes grew bigger and it took several minutes before his grip on the seat loosened. He eventually looked left and right and slowly became fascinated with his godly view of the jungle below. A faint smile came to his face.

Quinn found himself five miles northwest of the river island, following a narrow squiggly section of the Taritatu River. Less than a mile off his right rotor assemblies, mountains abruptly rose to nearly two thousand feet. The entire area appeared remote and impassable. Another river joined the Taritatu east of the island, and together with converging rivulets, left the entire area resembling a jumbled intestinal track.

Quinn liked the shore area he'd looked at earlier, but all that scrub brush would mess up the landing. He concluded that landing on the island seemed a better idea.

Quinn engaged the exterior stealth mode to mask their arrival. Miniature cameras captured the view before them and transmitted the image to the opposite side of Icarus. In an instant, Icarus disappeared.

Quinn dragged a "Landing Zone" icon across his virtual display and positioned it on the island's western sandbar. He flew a mile to the east and reversed course.

He commanded, "Fly approach" and Icarus began a controlled descent toward the virtual icon, stabilized, and gently landed.

"Rava, why don't you take Saturday and explore the island for a place to set up camp," Gar suggested. "We'll download all the gear and move it to the campsite once you find one."

"Good idea. I really need to stretch my legs … Saturday, let's get started."

Chambo walked around the quadcopter to Gar.

"Keep a close eye on her. She's something special. Anyway, I think it might be best for us to stay here for at least a day or two. That way, we'll be sure you're okay before we depart for our staging field. Besides, it'll take time to get the canoes into the water."

"I agree. Why don't you guys stick around at least until we explore the local area and find a couple of tribesmen to help Saturday."

The following morning Gar approached Rava and Saturday.

"Where would you like to start the great plant-finding expedition?"

"As Icarus approached the island, I noticed a confluence of rivers close to here," she said. "I'd like to start there. That mixing of currents often brings more nutrients to the surface and ultimately to the surrounding area. It's a long shot, but what the heck, you asked."

Her interesting analysis surprised him.

"Yes ma'am, you're wise to consider such an area," Saturday added. "I may have friends in this region. Maybe we'll run across one or two of them."

Gar felt lucky having Saturday around. The guy seemed to have friends everywhere. Interesting native.

They would paddle a single canoe, as it had ample space. This end of the island eased into the river with a sandy beach. Gar gazed downriver, breathing in its delicate, ethereal presence. Fresh jungle aromas wafted between the tranquil river and a low-hanging misty overcast. Wispy reeds and low-hanging branches obscured less-defined shorelines. It felt so remote, so pristine.

Saturday boarded last after pushing the canoe into the river. Since the distance for today's venture would be short, Gar and the tech paddled rather than running the engine and wasting fuel.

"Over there looks good," Rava said as she pointed toward a spot on the far shoreline.

They pulled the canoe partially onto the shore and tied it to a nearby vine. Saturday looked over his shoulder and motioned for Rava to follow him into the jungle. The others fell in step close behind.

Gar immediately realized that Saturday knew his way around the jungle. His every step appeared effortless, yet Gar sensed his awareness of what dangers lurked on the ground and in the bushes and trees.

Saturday momentarily stopped and turned to Gar.

"Do you want snake meat tonight?"

The question caught Gar off guard. He instinctively scanned nearby branches to see if one had slithered its way within reach. He saw nothing.

"I think it'd be a great addition to the rather bland porridge we have on the menu. Do you have a particular snake in mind?"

Saturday laughed, knowing he alone had spotted the reptile.

"Well, there's one to your left. After passing it, I thought you might enjoy its full flavor."

They all looked left.

"There, geez, it's a big one," the tech gasped.

Saturday pulled a long stick from the undergrowth and came back to them. He loosened the snake from its perch on the branch and lowered it into a bag he had tied to his belt.

"We'll keep him alive until later. That way, he'll stay fresh."

"There, see that?" asked Saturday. He pointed to the tops of trees on the far side of a jungle opening. Several fragile-looking treehouses appeared totally out of place.

"We'll talk with the natives who live there and get information."

Several natives approached Saturday as they neared the structures and talked in a dialect none of the others understood. Saturday turned to the group.

"Follow us. We'll go to their house and talk more."

Rava thought Gar might find her knowledge of the unusual houses perched fifty feet atop clusters of leafless trees interesting.

"Tribes still occasionally fight for more territory, and these high houses provide safety and a good vantage point. I suppose it keeps them away from four-legged predators as well, to say nothing of being above all those pesky mosquitos."

"It's hard to imagine hauling all their food and water to such heights," Gar added. "I don't even want to think about the bathroom situation."

They sat around a small fire pit at ground level. Saturday intermittently spoke firmly, laughed, and chatted.

"The chief will line up those who will help us," Saturday explained. "You'll pick two. In gratitude, we'll give him that bag of rice I packed with our supplies.

"When we're done with our voyage, we'll bring the natives back here. Is that okay?"

Six tribesmen stood shoulder to shoulder minutes later. All wore calf-length cloth skirts. One pot-bellied native dangled a cigarette from his mouth, another sported a scar across his side. Most stood with arms crossed. They all looked strong.

"Which two will be the best?" Gar whispered to Saturday.

Saturday rose, reached down, and gently grabbed Gar by the arm, subtly asking him to rise. Together, they inspected each native front and back. Saturday leaned close to Gar's ear after returning to the firepit.

"The one on the end and the kid."

Gar looked to the Chief. "Thank you for your offer of help. These are all good workers. I will look one last time and decide."

He arose again and stood before each man, nodding toward the one on the left and again toward the kid.

"Do you know of the orchid I seek or the plant that grows with it and provides good medicine?" Rava asked.

"The orchid is not common here. If you have a wound, I'll show you what we use. If you have fever, we cook bark."

Rava listened to this and more but concluded they didn't know of her plant. Still, she'd search for it.

Saturday instructed the two new tribesmen to gather food for the night. The group headed to the canoe when they returned. Saturday sat in the front for the short paddle back to the island. The two natives and the tech squeezed behind him. Rava and Gar sat toward the rear.

A welcoming party composed of Devon and Quinn greeted them at the island's shore. Saturday climbed out of the canoe and walked ashore when something inside his cloth sack moved. Devon's curiosity got the best of him.

"Saturday, what's that?"

"It's for dinner," Saturday responded.

He upended the sack and out fell the large green snake. Devon and Quinn simultaneously jumped back as Saturday stepped forward, and in a quick move, grabbed the snake behind its head. He held it high.

"It's a good one. Will taste good tonight."

Early the next morning Chambo approached Gar.

"It's time for us to leave and establish our base camp farther up the river. The distance will be short, but the terrain below us will be rugged. We'll follow the river and send a message if we spot large rapids or other dangers."

"I agree. It's a good time to move. Besides, we need to pack up and continue our search farther south. We'll rejoin you in a week or two."

Devon maneuvered Icarus above the Taritatu River as it flowed through a meandering mountain gorge. Flying in this environment required constant attention to the terrain. He became lost in thought as Icarus silently banked left and right. It appeared to be incredibly remote, with no canoes, no smoke from village fires, and no natives. Devon knew the clouds built into storms every afternoon and decided he'd fly in the mornings as much as possible.

Chambo verified their position by comparing major bends in the river with those on the map. He moved his finger along the route with each new identifiable feature. If he noticed any dangerous sections, he marked them for later transmission to Gar.

Beauty existed everywhere. While the river carried a light brown, almost milky sheen, it brought contrast to verdant green foliage everywhere else. He silently wished he could have been in one of the canoes.

A primitive bridge crossed the river where the Taritatu turned westward. Chambo marked the location on the map. Two children played nearby, the first humans they'd seen since the treehouse natives. The road continued from the bridge as it cut a path through the jungle roughly parallel to the river. He imagined driving on such a remote, rutted pathway, and how vulnerable he'd be.

THIRTEEN

Do Not Enter

DEVON FLEW LOW ACROSS THE RIVER TO THE runway's end.

"See that wide spot to the right. That's where I'll put her down. Chambo, can you make out what looks like a blue-and-white building at the far end? Let's stay out of sight."

The grass runway had been carved out of jungle growth by whoever used it. Once Icarus landed, Chambo directed Devon and Quinn to cover the aircraft with the lightweight ghillie-type mesh he'd stowed in one of the onboard compartments.

Chambo viewed the overall area and thought it looked pretty good.

Quinn looked at the river and wondered what fish he could catch for dinner.

Devon began pulling out his camping gear and wondered how often airplanes landed at the strip. It seemed important information to know so that they wouldn't be around when one did.

"Okay boys," Chambo said. "Let's hike up the runway and make sure there's no one around who'll bother us."

Quinn swatted his hand at several annoying flies.

"Perfect. It'll give us a chance to evaluate the runway condition. But let's walk in the shade. It's fricken' hot here."

The runway's central surface consisted of hard-packed reddish dirt that looked firm in its dry state. Chambo felt certain that that afternoon torrential rains would turn this into a mess. Thank goodness they had Icarus because with her it didn't matter.

Chambo unexpectedly held up his hand.

"Ssh! Do you see that guard up there in the chair? Looks like he's got a weapon … I think he's bored."

"This way. Let's slip into the jungle," he added in a hushed voice.

"Here's a path," Quinn half-whispered to the others. "Looks like it leads toward the hut. Come on."

They followed one behind the other, stepping quietly, on high alert for any sign of human activity. The trail drew them deeper into the jungle and they questioned whether it led to someplace completely different. Eventually, it spilled out of the foliage onto an open pathway that led to the far side of the hut.

Chambo never considered simply exploring the area. Normally, he wouldn't be so cautious. Even now, that guard could be a nice dude. But little of this excursion had been normal. Better to be safe and hidden until getting a better feel for the lay of the land.

The guard appeared to be sleeping, and fortunately, he sat motionless thirty yards away on the far side of the small shack. A previously unseen one-room building between them and that outhouse-sized structure appeared vacant. Boarded windows concealed most of the interior, but allowed enough visibility to confirm the darkness inside and its lack of occupants. A tattered sign on the door displayed a red circle with a horizontal white line through the middle, warning 'do not enter'. The Hanzi characters below the symbol said as much. Chambo's curiosity instantly piqued. He wondered why they used a Chinese sign. The fact that it said, "keep out" made him all the more determined to slip inside.

Quinn slowly turned the doorknob. To his surprise, the door opened. All three quietly entered, pulled out smartphones, and turned on the spotlight feature.

Chambo directed them in a hushed tone. "Be careful, we don't want to alert the guard. Snap pics of anything interesting or unusual."

A large cabinet with locked glass doors occupied the far wall. Chambo squinted to read the labels on several bottles and noticed an almost imperceptible poison symbol on several of them.

Another floor-to-ceiling shelf arrangement contained thirty to forty plants, each set in a jar of water. It appeared to be a crude field laboratory.

Devon found a stack of papers with notes neatly scribbled on them. He quickly snapped pictures before returning the papers to their original position on the table.

Chambo's internal clock told him they'd been inside long enough.

"Let's make our way back outside before we're discovered. Move carefully."

He looked back as they slipped into the jungle. The guard remained asleep but from the other direction, he heard voices coming their way. They crouched.

A group of four scruffy Orientals appeared, walking single-file toward the laboratory from the open pathway. Raindrops muffled their conversation, but it seemed they spoke in an East Asian dialect. Chambo noted that all carried rifles slung over their shoulders. An eerie feeling shot across his skin and he wondered what could be so important that it required rifles.

"Let's get back to Icarus and decide what we're going to do next. I don't think this isolated airport will work as our operating base."

Raindrops splatted against the jungle canopy above them. Its sound filled the air as they withdrew. At the same time, water droplets generated a rich smell of moisture after mixing with more earthy aromas. Previously dormant scents of tree bark and mosses from the jungle floor revealed their nuanced composition to those perceptive enough to interpret it. The rain's intensity increased. They made a beeline for Icarus, slipped under the ghillie net, and climbed inside. It provided a welcome refuge from the drenching storm.

Chambo gathered his thoughts and tried to prioritize their next moves.

"Let's start by translating any text we captured in the pictures. That should give us an idea of what's going on here. After that, we can discuss our next step."

Devon displayed a picture of the notes he'd snapped with his translation app. It read, 'Plants from 3 41 50.5 S 140 13 42.10 E. Sample #231 neg for exanthematous A, B, and C viral. Sample #235 neg for . . . Sample #301 pos, needs re-sample test'. . .

"This looks like a crude lab testing for viruses. I suppose it could be legitimate," he added.

Chambo translated the text from one of the small bottles he'd photographed in the cabinet. The label included 'SARs adv'd,' which seemed unusual.

"I think we should assume the worst and keep ourselves separated from this group."

Quinn plotted the coordinates listed on Devon's picture.

"It looks like that sample came from the swamps southwest of here. If we're gonna find a new operating base, I'd suggest heading in the opposite direction along the river. I noticed several interesting islands not far back."

"If this rain keeps up," Devon added, "we'll be stuck here tonight. We could move in the next few hours, but to be honest, I think we'd be a lot safer waiting until morning."

"Let's not tempt fate in the middle of this muddy morass," Chambo interjected. "It's unlikely the group we encountered will venture this way after dark, and between now and then it'll be so muddy they'd have a hard time doing it."

All three endured a restless night inside Icarus. Each took a shift sitting outside in a camping chair while holding an umbrella overhead and drinking hot coffee. They'd watch for anyone coming their way, and alert the others if they noticed anything unusual.

Chambo awoke before dawn and joined the others with a steaming mug of coffee in hand. Devon and Quinn began pulling the ghillie net clear, eventually folding and stowing it. Chambo checked the battery charge levels and inspected the area around the aircraft for any obstructions that might interfere with their imminent departure.

They found seats inside Icarus as Quinn unfolded the rotor housings. A dull electrical hum preceded the muffled swooshing of the rotors. Quinn engaged the sound-deadening feature along with the cloaking cameras.

Icarus lifted and eased out over the river as the first light of dawn crept up from the horizon. Quinn added power, and they quietly disappeared along the river. The only person within possible earshot of their departure remained asleep in the same chair he'd occupied earlier.

Three miles to the east, the Taritatu River made a ninety-degree turn south and meandered in that direction for another five miles before intersecting a major tributary to its right. That's where Quinn had spotted a potentially suitable river island.

"Yep, that's it," he said, mostly to himself. He followed the tributary a short distance before reversing course and hand-flying Icarus to a landing.

"If this location satisfies you guys," Chambo announced, "let's get back in the air and fly a little recon around that airport. I'd like to know if there are more surprises in the nearby jungle." His comment caught them off-guard, but the thought of flying again stirred enthusiasm.

This time Quinn climbed to a thousand feet before overflying the airfield. It appeared isolated. Even the open pathways remained hidden under towering trees.

Look, over there to the east," Devon said. "See that small riverbed? There's a building or something alongside it."

They orbited over the point when Chambo noticed another building.

"It almost looks like a bunkhouse arrangement. This could be a mining operation, or it could be something else. Seems like a lot of activity for such a remote and isolated location.

"Let's head back and set up camp."

Icarus sat alone on the sandy point where Quinn had landed. The ghillie-net concealed its symmetrical form but failed to convince them it could be a bush or clump of trees. Fortunately, anyone flying overhead would be hard-pressed to notice anything out of the ordinary.

Each of the three set up individual dome-shaped tents and strung a large tarp between them for protection from afternoon showers. It provided a dry venue for dining and socializing. Chambo surveyed the overall campsite while thinking about catching edible fish and gathering a couple of fresh coconuts.

Devon and Quinn tied medium-sized hooks to the fishing lines they'd brought along. Quinn surprised Devon when he pulled out a small container of beetles for bait. As the two talked about their fishing techniques, Chambo became interested and joined the little fishing adventure.

Devon stopped before casting his line into the river.

"Wait! Since catching fish requires as much skill as luck, it only seems right that we should have a contest for, let's say, most keepers and biggest fish."

"But we don't even know what kind of fish are here," Quinn suggested. "Let's only count fish we can eat."

"I agree," added Chambo as he joined in their spirit of competition. "But what would be the prize? Maybe we could make a plaque with the winner's name etched onto it. We'd hang it in Tanigue's library. Or, we could exempt the winner from cleaning up after dinner."

"What about a points system?" Quinn added. "We could have a daily tally. Each fish would be worth so many points based on size. The largest fish would be like a bonus category worth ten points."

Devon took in the discussion and slowly displayed a somewhat devious smile.

"The contest will conclude when Gar's canoe touches our island. Whichever of us has the most points, including the bonus points for the biggest fish wins. The losers will pay for the plaque, and it can't be a cheapo piece of crap. It needs to be … to be, honorific."

They hiked off in different directions, each looking for the most favorable location. Quinn sat in a folding chair several feet back from a rocky drop-off. Shade blocked direct sunlight from his chair but did little for the oppressive heat and humidity. He dosed before long and began dreaming of flying Icarus amidst towering thunderstorms. Slow-moving currents lapping against island rocks in a rhythmic pattern slowed Quinn's normally active metabolic rate.

He opened his eyes and randomly focused on movement along the far shoreline. Another movement, a crocodile.

"Devon, get over here! I need you to see something."

Devon and Chambo came to Quinn, worried he'd seen more Asians, attacking cannibals, or something worse.

"Over there," Quinn pointed as he spoke, "do you see that croc on the far shore? We need to make sure it doesn't come out to our little island."

His line went taut. The first fish had taken his bait.

Predictable afternoon rains began as light showers before intensifying into gully-washers. All three took shelter under the tarp, exchanged fishing stories, and prepared an early dinner.

"We should ferment the coconut juice into something we can enjoy during the afternoon rains," Quinn wondered aloud.

"I've got a rudimentary setup that might work," added Devon. "We'll need to gather wood for a fire. If we get that, I think we can distill the juice into something tastier. Why do you think I brought that bag of sugar?"

Chambo pulled out the satellite phone to call Tanigue.

"Hello, this is Marlo," sounded after several clicks and a tone. "How are you guys doin'?"

"We're fine," Chambo responded, "but we've discovered a few interesting tidbits along the way. At our planned staging airport, we ran across a couple of buildings with an armed guard nearby. It seems to me that whoever is occupying the buildings is conducting plant antidote research. I'll forward the pics we took. You might have Rip take a look and pass his opinion to Gar.

"I think the Asians are already here looking for the same prize that we're after. Because it looks so suspicious, we've moved to a river island several miles east of the original airport. That's where we'll meet Gar and Rava."

Devon and Quinn each piloted a series of test flights during the following week. They focused on systems performance, which tested the quality of onboard software. Devon programmed a mildly complex route on one such flight that departed and returned to their island hideout. After takeoff, Icarus climbed to three thousand feet and flew a predetermined route to an arbitrary landmark, delayed there for fifteen minutes, and flew another route back to the island.

Devon touched nothing, allowing autonomous flight. The capability could be useful but frustrated the pilots who wanted more control of the flight profile.

"At first," Chambo said, "this autonomous flight regime will feel unbearably frustrating. But once we prove it works, we can move on to fill your idle time with dynamic mission management. I think you'll find that even more challenging than simply manipulating a quadcopter."

The mission proceeded without a hitch. Icarus landed itself two-and-a-half feet from the sandy tire impressions left after its departure.

Quinn flew a three-part stealth mission during which he departed in the pre-dawn darkness and flew repeated low passes over the island. Initially, he didn't engage any of the stealth features. Chambo and Devon observed from the ground while busily jotting down notes on recorded decibel levels and visual anomalies.

The first series of passes established a baseline. He flew Icarus several miles south and engaged sound phase-shifting to deaden the noise of the rotors and powered the mini-cameras for the outer surface display. He returned to the island, made several low passes, hovered at five hundred feet, and eventually landed. A flip of the switch disengaged stealth mode and allowed Icarus to appear in full view.

"It's about time you came back," Chambo remarked. "Where'd you go?"

"You really heard nothing?" Quinn asked. "I landed a minute before appearing."

"In the dark," Devon added, "and even as the sky lightened, we couldn't see anything. I thought I heard the trees rustle and a faint whooshing sound. I could feel the air pulsing. It felt strange because I didn't hear any sound even though I suspected you hovered about nearby."

The mid-morning and evening iterations of the same profile returned similar results. Knowing Icarus' true stealthiness would come in handy down the road. For now, the flights complimented their ongoing fishing contest.

FOURTEEN

MORNING SERENITY EMBRACED THE JUNGLE as it had every day since their arrival. The Taritatu River slept. Miniature water bugs flitted across its otherwise undisturbed surface. Dense fog clung to every treetop bordering the river, creating a low ceiling that transformed the river passageway into a mysterious natural tunnel. Cool, moist air rose from the ground with crisp aromas and the welcome taste of overnight oxygenation. Into this tranquil world of Papua, Gar, Rava, and the others silently pushed forward.

"We'll paddle until the waters extend into the jungle," Rava advised. "That's where we'll find the orchid."

She shared the first canoe with Gar and one native while Saturday, the tech, and the older native paddled the second one. Gar could feel the life of the jungle. It seemed foreign here, yet so inviting. He found it amazing that such an inaccessible wilderness held the answers to so many of the world's issues. Here, time existed as day or night. For many, each day balanced life and death. The environment appeared almost magical, so different.

The shoreline soon merged with adjoining marshes. Foliage thinned, and the river extended its reach farther inland.

"Let's paddle into the brush a bit. I'd like to look for our plants over there."

"Watch the branches for snakes," Saturday called softly to Gar's canoe.

The mangroves existed in a world apart from the open river. Tangled tree roots grew into single trunks. Branches intertwined, creating a latticework canopy that filtered light and often made passage impossible. Mangroves slowed progress but tickled their curiosity with their vast array of hanging plants.

Rava soon spotted a clump of interesting flowers. They'd taken root along vines that had wrapped themselves around the gnarled trees.

"I'm going to wade into this jumble. I think it's the only way to get those plants."

Saturday glanced directly into the dark waters. "Yes ma'am, I think the level is low here. I'll come with you."

They slid out of their canoe. Water reached their upper thighs but no higher. Rava pushed forward, careful to ensure her footing remained secure.

"Here, this one looks interesting."

She meticulously separated the plant's outer roots from the tree's bark and from between several vines. The process warranted explanation as she worried that Saturday might damage the plant structure if not careful.

"It's important to get as much of the root system as possible without overly traumatizing the plant. That way it'll have a much better chance of survival."

She carefully placed it in a plastic bag after she'd worked it loose from the tree and vines and filled the bag with enough river water to keep the roots wet. A rubber band sealed the bag around the upper stem. She labeled it with a sample number and location code before placing the plastic bag in the canoe.

The process repeated itself throughout the remainder of the day. Billowing clouds turned dark and ominous late in the afternoon. Lightning flashed from cloud to cloud and Gar thought it time to seek shelter - but where? Bushes lined the sides of the river, leaving no place to beach the canoes.

"Sir, that tree ahead will hold us in place," Saturday suggested. "We can stay in the canoes until the rain goes away."

"Yes, I don't see a better alternative. Let's tie ourselves to it and pull the covers from the sides of the canoes."

The native in each canoe lashed a line around the tree while Saturday tied the other end of the canoes together. They extended domed coverings from the gunwales and attached them to the far side. Everyone scrunched down inside what now amounted to a relatively waterproof floating tube.

Rain began pounding them and the sound of large droplets resounded inside. Gar and Rava stretched head-to-head along the bottom of their canoe.

"Is this at all what you had in mind when you started this adventure?" he asked Rava.

"Are you kidding? I thought we'd ride larger rafts and friendly natives would meet us every afternoon. They'd introduce us to their Chief, and we'd feast on exotic foods each night."

Gar laughed along with her.

"My mother always told me to keep an open mind and find happiness in even the most dire situations," he confided. "This isn't so bad. After all, I've met you and we're here in this uniquely isolated canoe getting to know each other better."

"You're too serious," she shot back. "My mom told me to be careful about setting expectations. It eliminates spontaneity from life. On the other hand, she totally expected me to become a doctor."

"She must be a special person," Gar said. "Sometimes our mothers know more about life than we realize.

"Now that we're getting to know each other better, there's something I feel compelled to point out. We attract leeches when we venture into the mangroves. Those little buggers are mostly a nuisance but can cause infections. It's best to remove them by scraping a knife along the skin where they've attached themselves. We'll all need to check each other for them."

"Wait a minute," Rava responded. "I'm not getting undressed so you can check me for leeches."

"It's your decision," he countered. "I'm just saying that someone should check the parts you can't see. It doesn't have to be me."

A worried Rava pulled her pants leg up, and to her dismay, spotted a single leech above her ankle.

"Yuck. I've already got one on my leg . . . okay, I'll let you check my back, but nothing more."

After two days of negotiating relatively open waters, the group approached the only section of the river Chambo had marked as dangerous. It existed in an area where mountainous cliffs on either side of the river squeezed together and formed a series of rapids.

Gar gathered the others at the side of the river to explain what the day held in store for them.

"We'll have to portage the canoes over a distance of a quarter-mile, give-or-take a bit. Once the current increases, we'll use the engines to propel us as far toward the rapids as possible."

They heard the rumble as they approached the danger zone. Everyone scanned for a place to begin the portage. The kid spotted a good landing place first.

He pointed ahead. "There. Excellent spot."

Gar followed Saturday along a makeshift trail that climbed around several large boulders before leveling. They hacked the vegetation, hoping to clear a path wide enough for the canoes. They'd gone nearly half a mile when the river came back into view.

"This will do," Gar huffed, "but it'll take a bit of work."

The canoes weighed next to nothing when empty, but with the engine, fuel, and supplies, each approached two hundred pounds.

"Two trips are best," Saturday suggested. "Go slowly and be safe."

"I'd suggest getting two long sticks and lashing them across the front and rear of the canoe," Gar said. "Use them for lifting and carrying and you can even pad the sticks with extra clothes. They'll help when climbing between the rocks."

An impromptu coffee break at the river's edge proved to be the perfect reward for their dogged efforts.

The beauty of the river repeated itself from one breathtaking view to another. Several days ago, two long hollowed-out canoes had passed in the opposite direction. Natives sat one behind the other with large sacks of vegetables between them. They looked with curious eyes, said nothing, and disappeared around the next bend.

The river eventually led them into the western mountains, where the current remained negligible. Terrain along the shoreline rose sharply upward. Monkeys scurried from branch to branch in the overhanging trees, while high above, birds glided along warm updrafts.

After another day, they paddled free of the mountains and the river straightened noticeably. Another canoe passed in the opposite direction. Rava noticed the man-made structure first.

"Gar, look there. It's the bridge we've heard about. I wonder if we'll see any natives along the road?"

"I think we should go ashore regardless," Gar responded. "I'd love to talk with the locals and hear what they know of others who've traveled here recently."

A group of women washed clothes on rocks below the bridge. Children played farther upriver along a sandy area near one of the support pilings. Saturday and his two natives climbed the slope to the road where they met two tribesmen.

"Praise to you," Saturday said in greeting. "Your land is rich in beauty and appears fruitful. You are lucky."

One of them nodded. "You are not from this area. Where do you travel?"

"We search for good medicine," Saturday answered. "We have come from the north and will continue toward the sunset. Have you seen others exploring this region?"

"The road brings miners once in a while," the native answered. "It felt peaceful here before. Now foreigners roam about with guns and threats. They moved west, but I think they remain somewhat close. They are evil men."

"What do they do that makes them bad? We've had unpleasant experiences with them, too."

"They bring disease," he said. "They carry it in a tube. When our people got sick and didn't get better, they left. Bad men."

"Thank you for the warning," responded Saturday in a low tone. "We'll try to avoid them."

Gar studied the bridge while Saturday talked with the natives. The structure consisted of several cables that engineers had strung between large wooden posts on either shore and which they anchored with large buried concrete blocks. A single-lane roadway rather precariously hung from the overhead cables via three-inch-thick rope lines. The surface consisted of short wooden boards affixed crosswise with parallel longboards laid on top to support vehicle tires. He conceded that the layout might be structurally adequate, but he'd never want to test it. He couldn't imagine walking across it, much less driving a truck over it, and instinctively looked to the river for fallen vehicles. Nothing. But he imagined a pile of them hidden in the bottom mud.

Saturday approached Gar and Rava.

"I understand only a little of their language. Others have been here and are ahead. They tested diseases and made these tribesmen sick before they left without providing a cure. The natives called them foreigners. That means they are not natives, maybe Asian. They are bad … no … evil men."

Taritatu's headwaters fed both rivers beyond the bridge. Waters at the junction swirled before dividing and flowing either left or right. What little current existed would work to their advantage.

Gar periodically looked toward the high ground to his right in an attempt to follow the road that cut through the jungle in that direction. Nothing associated with it caught his attention, yet he couldn't resist looking, regardless. Several hours later, and as clouds gathered overhead, they approached the tributary Chambo had told them to follow.

The area comprised a broad lowland valley. While the river set a distinctive path, broad swaths of swampland extended beyond its shores.

"Can we take one last look for plants along this section?" Rava asked Gar.

"Sure, we're almost home, and a little time looking won't hurt anything."

Saturday led the way, pushing through an area of reeds and into an open body of standing water. Something splashed.

Gar also noticed it and told Rava, "Don't jump into the water until we figure out what's already in there."

"It's a small crocodile," warned Saturday. "Nothing to worry about, but stay in the canoe here."

"I win" Devon cheered as Gar's canoe touched the island shore.

Quinn busied himself with cleaning the six largest fish they'd caught during the past two days. He pondered his conundrum of what to do with the entrails. If he threw them in the water, the crocs would come. Maybe Devon could drop them out of Icarus in the morning.

FIFTEEN

GAR ASKED CHAMBO, RAVA, AND SATURDAY to join him early the next morning on the far end of the island.

"Let's have coffee and discuss our situation before the oppressive heat and humidity show up."

Saturday instructed the two natives to keep everyone's coffee cups filled during the discussions. Devon, Quinn, and the tech slept late.

"Let's talk about whether we should continue searching for the orchid east of here," Gar said, "and more importantly, for the miracle plant. The Asians, unfortunately, are only a stone's throw away and that presents something of a problem.

"As I see it, we can overfly them and continue looking farther west, or we can take the plants we've already collected and head back to Tanigue."

"Quit looking?" Rava protested. "No, not yet. After all, we still haven't found the right plants, and I'm not ready to give up so quickly."

"As far as Icarus goes," Chambo added, "it's passed all our tests to date. Probably the biggest plus is that our batteries are fully charged. We have full tanks of fuel, and there aren't any maintenance issues.

"We'll be good with whatever you decide."

"What do you think? Gar asked Saturday "Will your natives fly a short distance on Icarus?"

"I want to avoid the Asians because they are evil. We will fly ahead. Okay."

"Well, that settles it. We'll continue the search. I wanted us to be of a single mind on this."

They stacked backpacks, tents, a duffle bag filled with foodstuffs, and other sundry items under the trees near Icarus. Devon surveyed the cargo and mentally computed the flight profile.

"We shouldn't carry everything on a single flight. It'll put us close to our weight limit. The good news is that we can do it in two shuttles. I'd suggest taking five passengers on the first run. Once I drop them off, I'll return for the others and the cargo. It shouldn't be over two hours before I'm back."

Gar had anticipated the likely need for two shuttles and had considered who would go when.

"Besides myself, Rava, Saturday, and the two natives will go first. That'll give us time to survey the area, find a suitable campsite, and contact any tribesmen in the area."

Chambo and the tech, with the help of Devon and Quinn, attached the canoes to the bottom of Icarus. Each one required two heavy-duty bolts to be inserted through fuselage brackets and a gunwale-to-gunwale support tube. Devon and Quinn lifted opposite sides of the canoe to align the front bolt holes.

"Up, more, more, okay … forward, there," directed Chambo.

He and the tech slid in the bolts, added washers, and wrenched the nuts until tight. The work went relatively fast with everyone sharing a portion of the process.

Devon engaged the sound-deadening and cloaking features before adding takeoff power. This precautionary move reduced their appearance to little more than a blur as they followed the river westward.

Gar and Rava had selected their destination on an old map where it appeared as a dry, open area surrounded by endless swamplands. It seemed suitable for a campsite.

The Asian airstrip and the primitive lab came into sight shortly after takeoff and appeared quiet.

"There, see that." blurted Devon. "I'll be. There's an airplane on the ground."

Gar stared in that direction and as they passed the runway's end, he realized the plane had begun its take-off run.

"Thank goodness we're mostly invisible to them. Let's stay low along the river until they fly away."

A mile later several canoes appeared in the river.

"Well, lookie there," Devon said, "those aren't natives. Wonder how far they're headed?"

"Keep an eye out for them on your return trip," Gar added. "I'd like to know where they're going, but don't waste time looking for them. Just keep your eyes open."

The encampment existed as more of a jungle anomaly than a natural clearing. Perhaps early explorers or miners stumbled across the high ground and used it as a base camp, although neither buildings nor signs of human occupation existed.

Most of the clearing consisted of low grass and gravel. The end nearest the river dropped off ever so slightly into a mushy pathway that led to the river nearly half a mile away.

Detaching each canoe from Icarus required a slightly more deliberate approach. Gar and Devon removed the fore and aft attachment bolts while supporting the weight of the canoe. Once detached, they lowered it to the ground and proceeded to the second canoe. Saturday and the natives moved the canoes to the side once Gar and Devon had completed their bolt removal efforts.

Gar and Rava spent the last two hours swatting away annoying jungle horse flies, while Saturday and the natives appeared to be immune to their attacks. Rava wondered if they simply had learned to ignore the flies or had actually gained immunity.

She commiserated with Gar. "Are these little man-eaters driving you insane? I can't focus beyond trying to kill the lot of 'em."

"That pretty much sums it up for me, too. Tomorrow, it'll be pants and long sleeves. I feel like the river gods have cursed us or at least put us under a weird kamikaze insect spell.

"Hopefully, the rains will shoo them away. At least I hope so."

Devon returned with the second group minutes before scattered raindrops announced the onset of afternoon showers. Chambo and the tech worked quickly, stretching two large tarps over a grassy area at the side of the clearing.

The others stacked gear underneath and began setting up their tents.

The rains intensified and individual raindrops became much heavier. Everyone found a place under the tarps. Some sat in camp chairs while others sat directly on the grass.

"Did you guys find any cannibals while Devon returned for us?" Chambo joked. "It looks pretty isolated here," he added in a more serious tone.

"Saturday left with the natives to survey the area," Gar replied, "but they didn't find anyone. Even the river remained quiet. Maybe once we move around a bit, we'll come across others.

"We did find swarms of flies, however. I don't know how we're going to search for plants if those little monsters continue their blood-thirsty attacks."

"I agree," Rava added. "They'll make it challenging. Saturday enjoys a degree of natural immunity, but even he seemed bothered by their constant biting.

"I'm not an entomologist, but I know a little about these guys. First, only the females bite. I guess they relegate the males to flying around their quarry as a distraction while wives and girlfriends press the attack. And technically, they don't bite at all.

"They've got these tiny dagger-like blades that hurt to the high heavens when thrust into your skin. It's not like they're sucking your blood, but creating a laceration and letting your blood flow into their mouths.

"These swarms aren't normal, or at least they shouldn't be a constant occurrence. I'd guess that in a couple of weeks, they'll return to pollinating plants. In the meantime, we're stuck with them."

Quinn ventured from his tent before the others. Cool morning air and fresh jungle aromas greeted him. It felt peaceful until the first of the horse flies buzzed around his head. He felt momentarily thankful that only one came to bother him.

"Hey Devon," he called as Devon crawled out of his tent. "Let's have a contest to see who can kill the most horse flies. Only the dead ones that we collect count. That way, we can use them as fishing bait."

"Don't tell me they're already out?" A look of disappointment crossed Devon's face. "This is gonna be a painful couple of days . . . okay, let's get Chambo involved before we officially start. Maybe we can hang a little brass plate under the fishing plaque that says something like *Winner–Horse Fly Executioner King*."

Gar and everyone else wondered if they could explore effectively with all the hideous horse flies. He decided they'd try today and then decide if they could continue on this part of the river.

"Let's get an early start," he said. "We'll scoot across the river into the mangroves and swampy area. Hopefully, the flies will be elsewhere and we'll be okay. If they're unbearable, we'll return to the safety of our tents."

Constant swatting overshadowed the beauty and peacefulness of their hike to the canoes. The team wasted little time in pulling them from the tall grass to the water's edge and pushing them into the open river. The flies temporarily abandoned their attacks.

The river stretched fifty yards between shores as it coiled in a winding path westward. Its main channel had changed course over the preceding centuries, leaving defunct channels as narrow waterways into the mangroves. The entire area transitioned into a maze of twisted, tunnel-like avenues through the trees.

The flies returned with a vengeance as soon as the canoes entered the foliage.

"Look there!" blurted Rava. "And over there. We've found the orchids."

A smile forced its way through a grimace on Gar's face. He'd killed a large horsefly who'd stabbed his ankle.

"Do you see anything that looks like your medicinal plant?" he asked.

"Yes, they're here, but I'll need to get out of the canoe and slosh through this mess to get to them."

Rava and the older native pushed through knee-deep waters while bending low and twisting this way and that to maneuver through the trees. The plants grew in tree bark higher up where the sunlight hit them more directly. Their challenging position required Rava to climb several feet before she could carefully remove the extended root system. She again demonstrated the process to the native while gently pulling individual roots free from the cupped-like bark.

"See, like this," she said. "Try not to break any of the roots. Pull gently."

Horse flies residing in the unusual bark struck her as odd. She thought they must live there with the orchids and medicinal plants.

They worked individually for the next twenty minutes.

Suddenly, a tree branch snapped, followed by a short but painful moan. Rava looked at the fallen native only to see him wincing in pain and holding his leg.

"Oh no, he's fallen onto those gnarled roots." She called to Gar, "Bring the med-tech! The poor guy has hurt himself."

Gar and the tech slid out of their canoe and waded to the native. He floated sideways in the water when Gar turned him onto his back and held his head.

The tech examined his legs. "This looks pretty bad," he concluded. "His right leg is broken below the knee . . . there could be more damage. For now, let's get him back to camp and I'll see what I can do."

Gar decided it would be easier to keep the injured native lying in the canoe and carry the entire works back to the campsite. Rava gathered together the five plants they'd bagged and followed the others with a worried sense of concern.

Saturday talked with the injured native and assured him he'd be okay. As they talked, the younger tribesman returned from the jungle with leaves to deaden the pain. He and Saturday ground the leaves between rocks and then applied them to the native's lower leg. They wrapped his leg and the goopy concoction with banana leaves.

"I've stabilized his broken leg," the tech told Gar, "but it's only a temporary solution. He'll need to get a cast and I'm not sure where to get that done other than on Tanigue."

"We'll have to consider our options and get him treated properly. It's my responsibility to return him home in one piece."

"Tell me about the plants," Gar asked Rava. "Are these the ones you're after? Did you get enough or do we need to come back for more?"

"These appear to be the real deal. I'll know after comparing their structure to the others under a microscope.

To answer your question whether this is enough. In a word, no. We'll need something like twenty-five plants to regenerate enough for a garden. Five plants are, fortunately, more than enough for my initial research.

"One other consideration and this is pretty much conjecture for the moment, I noticed horse flies sleeping in the tree bark, lots of them. It made me think that perhaps they have a symbiotic relationship with the medicinal plants or the orchids. They're pollinators after all. Just a thought and perhaps a coincidence worth noting."

Gar considered his options and decided on a course of action.

"We'll pack everything early tomorrow morning before the flies become a nuisance. The load will be heavy, but we'll try to get airborne with all of us onboard Icarus. We'll fly directly to Tanigue so our broken native can receive proper care and start mending.

"Rava and Rip can conduct their initial research on the plants. Devon and Quinn can proceed to phase two of their training and Chambo can restock our supplies for the next excursion to this fly-infested swamp."

SIXTEEN

ONE OF GAR'S MORE INTIMATE ENCOUNTERS each evening involved checking Rava's back for leeches. What started as a nervous peek-a-boo look soon strengthened into a trust-building exchange. Gar knelt close behind Rava as she unbuttoned the top half of her shirt and lowered it off her shoulders.

She turned her head toward him and mouthed the words, "Be good," then more emphatically, "and don't get any ideas."

Gar laughed, as he'd heard the same admonition every night for the past two weeks.

"Don't worry," he responded in a deep voice, "I'll only look at leeches, nothing else."

Gar enjoyed looking at her smooth dark skin and wondered if she bathed in lotion every night. Her shirt lowered to waist level when Gar noticed a leech attached to the small of her back.

"Rava, you've got one at the top of your butt. Can you remove it? Or do you want me to cut it free?"

Rava shuttered within herself. She twisted around but couldn't see it with her hands holding up the front of her shirt. She let out a breath of resignation.

"I suppose you'll have to help with it this time."

"Can you loosen your pants? You probably won't need to lower them, but I'll need more space to get at that little bugger."

"Damn," she muttered.

That tingly feeling of nasty delight flashed through her once again. She noticeably relaxed while reaching to loosen her belt. In the process, her shirt momentarily fell free.

Gar looked away and fumbled with his pocket knife while opening the large blade.

"Sit still, this will only take a second."

He pressed the knife blade flat against her back next to the leech and slid it across its attached mouth. The leech fell into his free hand.

"There, that didn't feel so bad, did it?"

Rava tingled again. She didn't want him touching her but at the same time craved it. She considered having Saturday do the checks, but Gar's hands touching her back felt so warm.

The older native spent the night on his back in the canoe. The med-tech had laid a sleeping pad along the bottom and immobilized his lower leg with a folded blanket and several short aluminum braces. He secured this arrangement in place with three wrap-around Velcro straps. Gar silently thanked him for bringing the larger emergency medical kit.

To offset the added weight of the two natives, Quinn suggested pouring out all but an emergency supply of water.

"We'll still be on the heavy side, but as long as we're flying relatively low, I think we'll get back to Tanigue okay."

The sun hadn't yet reached the horizon on its daily ascent, but the skies above it had illuminated their campsite sufficiently well to load Icarus. They attached the canoes, one fully configured with its top cover secured in place. The other canoe with the native inside had mosquito netting temporarily strung across the top, in part to provide light. It would become dark inside once they pulled the top cover into position.

Everyone shared a concern about the native panicking from claustrophobia during the flight.

"Any ideas?" asked Gar.

"I'm going to give him my smartphone and show him a couple of games," the med-tech responded. "Hopefully, he'll find one he understands and likes. I'll give him a couple of Valium pills before closing up his canoe. If the games don't work, the meds should do the trick."

Quinn eased Icarus' single power lever forward and as they lifted off the gravel, he tilted forward. What appeared to be two floating canoes eased toward the river while slowly accelerating and gaining altitude. Control response felt heavier than normal because of the weight, but fortunately, Quinn seldom felt a sense of urgency during these situations and considered this to be no exception.

"Today," Quinn stated, "will be a salute to south-of-the-border Carlos Santana and Selena. Sit back, relax, and enjoy my idea of cultural immersion."

He broadcast a mix of female Latin singers interspersed with Santana guitar solos.

Lush green rolling hills came to life as morning sunshine climbed their darkened slopes. Beams of sunlight reached the slope's crest and shot toward the next rise. Between the music and the scenery, Icarus felt alive and invigorating.

After a mesmerizing hour of flight, the coastline came into view and brought a refreshing look compared to that of the growing heat below. Quinn keyed his radio switch.

"Tanigue, this is Icarus, inbound for landing. Say your position."

A moment later he heard. "Icarus, welcome back. We've moved sixty nautical miles east and are fifteen miles offshore. Do you copy?"

"Roger, twenty minutes out," Quinn acknowledged.

He located the origin of Tanigue's call and adjusted his heading to the vessel.

"Tanigue, I've got you in sight. See you shortly."

Rip and Marlo stood together on the open deck forward of the landing pad.

"Do you see anything yet?" Marlo asked.

"Nope," responded Rip, and then, "Wait, I see the canoes floating in the air. That must be them, over there, about half a mile out."

"Dang," mumbled Marlo, "I never see those guys coming. It'd be nice if we could make Tanigue disappear like that."

Hand-flying Icarus to Tanigue's helipad always demanded the pilot's undivided attention. Lining up the quadcopter for an approach to the tiny target seemed easy enough, but holding it steady before settling to land often became impossibly difficult.

To save time and to sidestep the associated embarrassment of struggling to land, Quinn and Devon usually opted to let Icarus land itself during operational flights. They'd practice doing it themselves on training flights when others occupied themselves elsewhere.

Gar called Chambo once the deckhands secured Icarus to the deck.

"Would you mind joining Rip, Rava, and me for an update from Marlo? The others can help carry the native to our infirmary. We'll all meet in the library for refreshments once he's treated."

Devon unlatched the canoe's top cover and found the native asleep inside. The med-tech, who'd temporarily scurried away to the onboard clinic, returned and took charge.

"Okay, let's ease this portable stretcher under him and, together, lift him onto the gurney.

"Ready, set, lift. . ."

The native reclined on the clinic's stainless steel examination table. Saturday and the younger native stood near his side, watching and wondering what would happen next.

They'd never seen a medical facility or anything else as foreign-looking as Tanigue. From their perspective, the entire undertaking comprised white man's medicine. The younger native considered the med-tech to be their medicine man. Both he and Saturday worried because everything here felt so different from their world.

The med-tech huddled with the others to explain the process.

"Devon and Quinn, you two will be in charge of keeping him still and comfortable. Devon, why don't you stand behind his head and support his back? Quinn, I want you to hold his ankle still while I wrap his leg with the cast materials. It's going to hurt during this part, so do your best to keep everything still.

"Saturday, you and the kid can watch from there, or even get closer if you like. Maybe you should explain to the native that we're going to lift his leg so I can apply the cast. It'll take about ten minutes and it'll hurt until I start getting it wrapped. But this is the only way to give him full use of his leg once it heals."

Saturday nodded and spoke as best he could to the injured native. The kid added a few comments and the older native nodded his head.

The med-tech filled a bowl with warm water after he'd gathered the necessary materials. He began by fitting a specialized sock over the foot and pulled it to below the native's knee. He then wrapped several layers of inner material around the native's injured leg from knee to toe and dipped a roll of hardening material in the water, squeezed out the excess, and wrapped it over the previous materials. The process continued for several minutes and ended when the med-tech slid a pillow under the native's ankle.

"Let this set for ten minutes. I'll fit a special shoe to his foot."

"He'll need to stay off this leg for two weeks," he explained to Saturday. "I've got a pair of crutches he can use and I'll show you how they work. I'd suggest we keep him in bed for the next week. Can you teach him about the crutches?"

Saturday acknowledged with a nod.

Marlo led the others to the upper lounge. They sat down and a deckhand appeared with bottles of beer, a carafe of wine, and a pitcher of iced guava juice.

"I'll leave these here," he explained. "If you need refills, just call. Do you want anything to eat?"

"I'm curious why we're located sixty miles from your original anchorage," Gar asked Marlo.

"It all started with an interesting first week back at Sarmi," Marlo explained. "The second day, a boat filled with six light-skinned occupants passed less than a mile from Tanigue, heading north. Later that day, they reappeared even closer, as if surveilling our ship.

"They didn't look like locals. We could tell by their features and their light skin. That night, a boat approached in the dark. We first spotted it on radar and tracked it using night vision goggles.

"The bastards appeared to be armed, and it seemed to me they planned to board and seize Tanigue. You know I wouldn't let that happen. I had the boys fire a volley across their bow and that turned them around. We probably should have sunk their damned speedboat and chummed the waters for sharks.

"Anyway, we pulled anchor later that night and moved south. And now, here we are."

"There's more to the story," Rip added. "I queried my friend, the missionary, who shared a few interesting tidbits about sick passengers he and the other missionaries flew back to Jayapura.

"He says the natives are fearful of the Orientals in the jungle because they always bring sickness. Several natives they pulled from the jungle had symptoms of SARs and one or two other more exotic diseases I'd never heard about. Medical authorities in Papua seemed similarly puzzled by the occurrence of these viruses.

"I think the foreigners are using the natives as guinea pigs for biological experimentation. It's scary."

Gar listened with concern.

"I'm going to contact General Smithberger later tonight and get his perspective on all this. In the meantime, I think we should spend our time analyzing the plants Rava found yesterday."

"Tell me about them, Rava," Rip asked. "Did you find the same kind the natives gave you?"

"Yes, These are the same ones. They're hard to pull from the trees, but I think there's more than enough of them back on the river for us to start a full-fledged garden.

"But, we'll have to go back to get them."

"How are we doing with provisions?" Gar asked Marlo. "Do we have sufficient fuel, food, and other supplies to remain here for another month?"

"Whoa . . . I'm not sure about a month. Actually, I'm pretty sure we don't have enough food. Our fuel is good for the time being, but we're not in a position to embark on a voyage of any distance. Before much longer, I think we'll need to replenish everything, maybe at Jayapura or around the tip of Papua New Guinea at Lae.

"Another possibility would be Rabaul in New Britain. That'd be an interesting destination and only slightly farther. It became a household name during World War Two because it had been the Japanese Navy's main harbor in the South Pacific. It's where they hoped to launch the invasion of Australia."

"We'll have to consider all the alternatives," Gar replied. "Rabaul is definitely an interesting option, perhaps beyond the reach of the Asians. Let's see. . ."

He looked to Rip and Rava. "Our native will have that cast on for the next six weeks, and during that time, he won't be of much use to us.

"I wonder if he'd feel more comfortable with Momma Grace on Wakde Island. We could fly Saturday and the natives there before re-provisioning Tanigue. Once we're ready to head back into the jungle, we could pick up Saturday and the kid, and leave the injured native to keep Momma Grace company. We'll eventually return to get him, cut off his cast, and return him to his village."

"I like that," said Rip. "He'd at least be eating food he's accustomed to and he wouldn't have to worry about doing any work for us. I think Momma Grace would enjoy the company. If we offered her rice or coffee beans as a token of our appreciation, I think we'd all feel good."

"I agree," added Rava.

Gar prepared a message for the General and hit the send key.

Dear Grits,
The expedition to Papua has not been without its surprises and intrigue. Rip and Rava are safe and in good

hands, and I'm happy to add, are making progress on their research.

We've explored several sections of the Taritatu River and have located the prime medicinal plants Rava seeks. During the coming week, she and Rip will analyze the five plants we brought yesterday.

You might be interested to hear that we came across more Asians in the river region and have heard stories of what sounds like biological experimentation on resident natives. This alone is troubling, but they continue to be hellbent on stealing Rip's research. Shortly after we left for the jungle, an armed team approached Tanigue in the dark of the night. Marlo sprayed a pattern of bullets across their bow before they withdrew.

This group is unscrupulous in its abuse of natives and its aggression toward competitive research. They're bad actors.

We plan on returning to the river in another week or two and in all likelihood will again encounter them. Do you have a preferred method for us to handle such an occurrence?

I'll remain aboard Tanigue while we sail for replenishments (port to be determined). By the way, your decision to acquire such a vessel will stick in my mind as yet another of your all-time brilliant moves.
Gar

General Smithberger's response appeared on Gar's smartphone an hour later.

> Gar,
> Thank you for your update. After not hearing from you in so long I thought that maybe you'd lost your way deep in the jungle. For now, continue as planned and try to avoid the Asians as best you can. I'm working on a better solution but will need time to fully coordinate it.
> Grits

Devon departed with Saturday and the two natives on board Icarus the following morning. The injured native had arrived at Icarus on a stretcher and hobbled into one of its seats. Saturday placed the stretcher and a pair of crutches alongside him.

Impressions of Icarus' wheels appeared in an open area along Wakde's old runway forty minutes later. The three passengers exited, waved, and started carrying the older native to Momma Grace's hut.

Devon added power and disappeared back into the morning sky.

SEVENTEEN

RAVA EASED HER WAY ALONG THE PASSAGEWAY from the galley back toward Rip's laboratory. The mugs of hot coffee she carried necessitated a kick on the hatchway to alert Rip of her presence.

"Ah, thanks for thinking of me," Rip said after taking a mug. "Come on in so we can look at your plants and see exactly what we've got."

"Remember the last test series you performed in Jayapura?" Rava asked. "I'd like to compare the tinctured concentrate of these plants against your original to set a baseline.

"And I'd like to evaluate potencies with an infusion process for the leaves, and a decoction of the stems and roots. What do you think?"

He'd been thinking along the same lines.

"There's a lot to evaluate. I want to determine if we can successfully culture our plant cuttings and propagate the darned things.

"I'll analyze the water in the bags to determine its composition. That'll go a long way toward optimizing new plant growth."

Rava opened a cabinet door in search of a magic marker. "Let's get started by labeling everything,"

Gar wandered to the bridge. Marlo sat in the captain's chair while scanning each of the fifteen different system displays on the secondary monitor. His seemingly tedious review had long ago become routine because noticing subtle rpm or pressure nuances often saved time and effort by avoiding future problems. Marlo sensed Gar behind him and spoke without shifting his focus from the monitor.

"On a ship like this, it's never good to discover mechanical issues while at sea. Better to find them early and address them when in port."

"You often surprise me, Marlo," Gar responded. "In a good way. I agree, knowing your equipment inside out is wise.

"Let's point our nose toward Rabaul and replenish Tanigue there. It'll give us a couple of days to explore the city while not having to worry about being tracked by others. I'd like to get started this evening. Twelve knots should be okay."

"Aye aye sir," Marlo responded lightheartedly. "I'll have us ready to get underway as soon as the crew completes their pre-departure checks."

Gar found Devon and Quinn in the library discussing scuba diving equipment over morning coffee. He sat on the sofa and listened as their conversation wandered.

"I think the plaque should hang above the fireplace," Devon argued. "It needs a place of honor. Or maybe we could laminate it into the coffee table or the standing bar."

"Yeah, yeah, the fireplace seems okay," Quinn agreed. "The horsefly contest . . . is it concluded, or should we extend it for our next trip into the jungle?"

"You only killed ten flies," Devon argued while chuckling. "That'd embarrass the winner by listing such a miniscule total. Besides, it'd detract from the fishing contest I won.

"I think we should continue the count until our next return from the jungle."

"I suppose we should let Chambo know," Quinn suggested. "Or, maybe we could forget to update him until we've swatted and scooped up a few more of those little monsters?"

They laughed. Gar stifled his reaction.

"Guys, we're heading to Rabaul. It'll take several days to get there and during that time I'd like to start phase two of your training.

"When you finish your contest discussions, would you mind joining Rip and me in the training room?"

They'd rearranged the training room with a partitioned cubicle at each end. A small table with a computer and monitor comprised their testing workstation. The area between the cubicles consisted of two long white tables with chairs that faced multiple sliding whiteboards.

Rip's smile turned serious. "Okay. Good morning, guys. For the next several weeks, I'd like to run a series of tests to determine if I can translate electronic images into impulses that your minds can decipher. The process is fairly simple, but the technology is, to say the least, evolutionary.

"Are you with me so far?"

"Is this going to affect our ability to fly or anything like that?" Devon wondered.

"I don't think so. We'll monitor your vitals and mental state and make adjustments if necessary."

"Is this one of those experiments where we have electrical probes everywhere?" Quinn asked.

"Nope, not so much. I have a very lightweight headset that fits over your temple. That and a blindfold are all you'll need.

"My background is fairly broad in a scientific sense. For example, I'm doing a lot of molecular evaluation on Rava's plants. But I also have a great deal of experience in neural engineering and in conducting tests like what we're about to run.

"Without explaining my objectives in too much detail, I'd say that what we're doing is totally safe. You should be no worse for the wear and might actually end up with superhuman powers you never knew you had.

"I'll work with one of you at a time. The other one will work with Gar on quadcopter systems.

"Devon, you're first."

Rip handed Devon a blindfold and a small plastic headphone-like setup.

"Here, put these on. The headset pads should fit over your temples . . . is everything comfortable?

"I'm going to turn on the computer, translate what it sees into a very low electrical impulse, and try to project that image through your headset to your brain.

"I'll ask what you see. It could very likely be nothing. Give it a few seconds and tell me whatever image appears in your mind.

"Over time, I'm hoping we'll start connecting with the images but we'll have to see. Okay, here we go. . ."

Rip turned on the computer and selected a red card from a table of options. "What do you see?"

"Nothing," responded Devon.

"Okay, no problem," Rip replied. "Let's try another one . . . and now, anything?"

"Nothing . . . wait . . . it's an apple . . . did I get it?"

Rip laughed which brought a look of confusion to Devon's face.

"Not quite. It displayed a glass of beer, but you're doing fine. Shall we try again?"

Gar projected a schematic of Icarus' electrical system. He hoped to keep Quinn busy with something positive while Devon struggled with image recognition.

"Let's say that Icarus has batteries and battery chargers . . . and a few incredibly complex electrical systems like Icarus' contoured surface projections and all of its projected flight data.

"I'll cover the prop motors later, but for now, think of them as lightweight state-of-the-art Tesla knock-offs. They're fueled with battery power. Once they deplete the charge, the props will stop spinning. Simple as that.

"The Defense Advanced Research Projects Agency has been working with scientists at Harvard's Office of Technology Development, the Japanese government, Toyota Motor, and Murata Manufacturing to fine-tune custom solid-state lithium-metal batteries. That's what I'd like to cover today.

"Questions so far?"

"Nope, but I'm curious about them," Quinn admitted. "Let's get started."

"Up to now those small lithium-ion batteries we all use probably came to mind when thinking of battery power. You might have also conjured up an image of several lead-acid car batteries daisy-chained together.

"Well, forget those images for the time being. The problem with the liquid electrolyte lithium-ion batteries is three-fold. They're heavy, they take too long to charge, and they come with safety issues.

"On Icarus, we're using solid-state batteries that are more compact, lighter, and much safer. Unfortunately, they're still quite expensive and until the cost comes down significantly, you won't see them in electric vehicles.

"Okay, I'm going to ask a question. If you get the answer right, I'll give you the short course . . . ready?"

"Alright, let's see what you've got."

"Here we go . . . this is true or false . . . the three parts of a battery are the anode, the cathode, and the electrolytes."

"True," answered Quinn with confidence.

"That's correct. Pick one of them."

Quinn hesitated momentarily. "Electrolytes."

"Alright," said Gar, "I'll start there.

"All the battery problems in the past focused on liquid electrolytes and in particular, lithium-ion batteries. Think of those batteries as a glass of water with two plastic straws, one on each side. The water in this case is the electrolyte. One straw is filled with lithium-carbon and we call it the Anode. The other straw is filled with lithium-sulfur. We call that one the cathode. Here's the problem. The lithium-carbon anode develops needle-like growths called dendrites during each recharge cycle. They force their way through the electrolytes and eventually puncture the cathode's protective covering. This shorts the battery, overheats it, and often explodes the whole shebang.

"Liquid electrolytes are the problem. To solve it, DARPA evaluated many solid electrolyte options, none of which came without flaws. The polymer electrolyte required an operating temperature of 140 degrees or higher. Solid ceramic-plate electrolytes tended to develop small fissures with even small vibrations or physical jolts. Each option introduced unacceptable drawbacks in place of the problems they eliminated.

"In the batteries on Icarus, the electrolyte consists of wooden cellulose nanofibrils infused with copper ions. The copper additive drastically improves the conductivity issue by creating ion superhighways that are up to a hundred times better than other polymer ion conductors. At the same time, it prevents dendrite penetration.

"Are you still with me?

"The solid electrolyte section is much, much smaller than the liquid version, maybe the thickness of heavy paper. Coupling the reduced size with a lithium-metal anode and a lithium-sulfur cathode, along with several binders compresses the working components and eliminates the dendrite threat. This makes the batteries vastly more efficient, and safe."

Quinn raised his hand to interrupt.

"What are the binders? I don't quite understand that part."

"Think of it this way . . . Binders are like spices added to your spaghetti sauce. They're tiny compared to the whole bowl of sauce, but their flavor permeates throughout it.

"Carboxymethyl cellulose and glucose binders regulate the polysulfides and control porosity. I know that's a mouthful, but basically, they stabilize the recharge cycles while minimizing battery swelling and contraction."

"Oh, okay, got it," mumbled Quinn, sorry he'd asked.

"Don't worry, you won't need to remember any of that. I'll try to keep the rest simple.

"Imagine driving down the interstate highway in your electric vehicle and stopping to recharge the car's batteries. Today it might very well take you all night, but with these solid-state batteries you'd be looking at ten to twenty minutes."

"Are you kidding?" Quinn interrupted. "Is that how we seem to always have fully charged batteries in Icarus?"

"Sort of," responded Gar. "It's not like we have an industrial-strength recharger. It'll take several hours to recharge Icarus's four main batteries because of our relatively low-output radioisotope thermoelectric generators."

"Are these batteries self-sufficient or do I need to inspect them? Do they ever fail?"

"Right now," Gar answered, "I have Chambo visually inspect them once a week. We track the discharge times and the time to recharge them. If I flag anything out of the ordinary, we'll look at it more closely. Once every three months Chambo connects an analyzer to get a better sense of component health.

"They're all rated for a thousand recharge cycles, but until we establish a longer track record, I plan to replace the battery packs every year."

"Rava, come over here a minute and I'll show you something interesting."

Rip had been analyzing samples of the swamp water to determine its composition.

"It's obvious the water isn't saline or even brackish based on where you obtained these samples. I'd bet the total dissolved solids of a sample from mid-river are somewhere above a thousand milligrams per liter. But look here. They're really low in the mangroves even though I'm seeing concentrations of iron and silicon."

Rava pretended to be interested. "So, does any of this strike you as other than what you expected?"

"It's pretty much normal for swamp water," Rip acknowledged, "and I guess mangroves mostly fall into that category. We'll need to recreate the organic substances I'm finding and use them in our hydroponic lab."

"I'm curious," wondered Rava, "why the orchids and medicinal plants are so localized to certain areas. Maybe it's those devilish horse flies that pollinate the plants, or maybe it's something else. Do you think we should catch flies?"

"I planned to save this little tidbit for later, but since you asked, I think the uniqueness of the area lies in the elevated levels of ammonium ions. I don't know why they seem to concentrate here, but they do. In general, they tend to maintain our human acid-base balance and that may have something to do with their unique medicinal properties. But to be honest, I don't know.

"I can hear myself getting geeky. Suffice it to say, the water composition may well be the key to the benefits of this plant."

"The next time we trek back into the jungle," Rava mused, "I'd like to find another location with orchids. I think comparing water composition would validate your hypothesis. Hopefully, the part about the flies is wrong and we won't encounter any more of them.

"Brother, let's explore Tanigue and find a suitable location for our hydroponic garden. Do you think there's enough room here?"

Rip looked around the room as though mentally redesigning it.

"There's not really enough room and there's so little outside light. I'm sure there's a better place, and hopefully, Gar and Marlo will let us use it."

"This is the system I've got in mind," Rava explained. "Since the plants and their root systems are mostly exposed rather than buried in soil, we could set up a nutrient film technique system.

"We'll need a large reservoir for each row of plants. It'll contain water with the same composition, salinity, and pH we've found along the Taritatu River. We'll probably need an airstone to oxygenate the water and a pump to move it to a feeding tube. If we install an electric valve to control the water exiting the tube, we can set it to close if there's an electrical failure. That should keep the plant roots dangling in the water until we fix the problem.

"We can hang lights above the plants and set them on a timer.

“I think we should size the entire system for two to three hundred plants. What do you think?”

“Let’s make a list of supplies,” Rip responded with a tinge of excitement in his voice. “Hopefully Rabaul has a good hardware store and well-equipped aquarium shop.”

EIGHTEEN

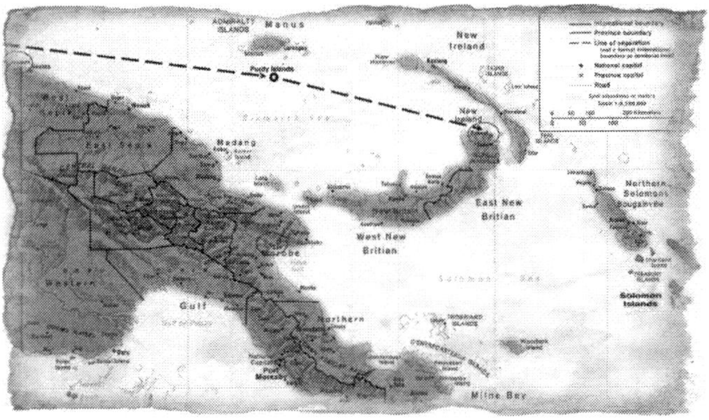

Tanigue's route to Rabaul

MARLO LAUGHED AT HIS WEATHER RADAR screen. "This pile of diodes thinks it's raining. Do you see any clouds? May the gods forgive whoever designed this expensive radar contraption. He'll never make it as a meteorologist."

Gar laughed with him, but not for the same reason.

"Have you looked at the skies behind us? You might notice that it's raining back there."

Marlo turned and broke into more laughter.

"Well, I'll be. Maybe I should give the radar guy more credit, but what fun would that be? Anyway, we're about ready to pull anchor and start churning toward Rabaul. Let me know when you're ready."

"Marlo, I've been thinking. The Purdy Islands sit atop isolated coral reefs about halfway to Rabaul. Why don't we point ourselves toward them? We'll delay there for twenty-four hours and let your crew take a break.

"I think they might enjoy scuba diving and sunning themselves on an exotic beach. We can all let loose at an evening barbeque and pick up where we left off the following morning."

As Gar explained the stop, Marlo busily plotted a course to the Bat Islands, which comprised the westernmost specks of the Purdy group.

"The distance looks like 380 nautical miles and it'll take us a day and a half to get there."

"I'll time our arrival for 6 a.m. That way, we'll have a full day to play on the beaches. Is that okay?" Marlo asked.

"Perfect."

Moderate seas forced Rip and Rava to brace themselves as they explored open passageways and interior rooms. The search for their botanical garden site required more balance than raw curiosity.

"Whoa," blurted Rava when the vessel suddenly lurched sideways. "I like calm seas infinitely more than this chaotic thrashing."

"But this is chaos theory at its best," declared Rip. "The random nature of reality makes life interesting. Let loose of your organized world for a few minutes. You'll find it's a lot more fun. Go ahead, try it."

Their first greenhouse candidate, the training room, looked good but had already been requested. They ventured into a sizeable open section between the training room and the library. It had been designed to store large speedboats which Tanigue didn't carry. However, the rigid hull inflatable boat and two jet skis occupied a small section of the opening. Rava envisioned their hydroponic plantation filling the remaining space.

Rip walked from end to end, stopping to think before continuing to the far corner.

"There's enough space, but I'm not sure about the open ends. Salt air will constantly spray the plants and I'm worried that might skew the chemistry enough to affect a controlled growing environment."

Rava gave thought to what he'd said and reluctantly agreed.

"Yep. Let's keep looking."

The only suitable areas for their hydroponic garden boiled down to Rip's lab and the dive-gear storage room below it. They agreed the dive room would be the better choice.

Rava stood to the aft of the room, forefinger curled around the bottom of her chin.

"This lovely room has no windows or portholes, so we'll have to plan for adequate lighting. I think there's room for three long tables and we'll have plenty of electrical outlets. Heck, the generators are right here and there's good access to fresh water.

"What do you think?"

Rip shared the same thoughts.

"I like it. This will be nearly perfect. I'll be right upstairs in the lab, so it's convenient. Let's see if Gar agrees.

"Would you mind finding him and discussing it while I conduct another training session with Devon and Quinn? After that, I'll catch up so we can start planning."

"That shouldn't be a problem. I wonder where he's wandered off to."

She found Gar and Chambo seated on the sofa and loveseat near the library's fireplace.

"Do you mind if I join you two for a few minutes? I'll sit quietly and try not to interrupt."

Both Gar and Chambo stood and smiled. Chambo nodded almost imperceptibly. Gar motioned toward an open space next to him on the sofa.

"Hey Rava. Of course, please join us. We've been talking about our mini-voyage to Rabaul. You might find the conversation interesting. And, I'd love to hear your thoughts."

Rava couldn't help but wonder what he was planning. She'd make sure he didn't stray too far away from her mission.

Gar summarized the conversation for Rava's sake. "We've been discussing how best to spend our time in Rabaul. Along the way, I'd like to stop for a day in the Purdy Islands. I've asked Chambo to research the area and help us determine if a stop might be workable.

"So Chambo, what did you find?"

Chambo fussed with a pile of loose papers on the coffee table before placing a chart of the area on top.

"The Purdy Island archipelago consists of five coral islands, the Bat, the Rat, the Mouse, the Mole, and the Alim. These guys are all isolated in the middle of the Bismarck Sea. No one lives there, but occasionally visitors show up to record giant sea turtles as they bury their eggs along the beaches and again as the baby turtles hatch and find their way to the ocean.

"There are shoals and reefs throughout the area. Marlo will need to exercise caution so he doesn't run us aground on one of them."

Rava suddenly filled with curiosity and looked to Gar.

"Why do I feel you have a hidden treasure map tucked under your pillow? Is there a long-ago buried trunk filled with jewels on one of these islands, or is there some other adventurous reason for stopping?"

Chambo laughed but caught himself when he realized Rava might actually be right with her off-the-wall query. Gar laughed.

"I wish, and who knows, maybe we'll find treasure.

"My purpose in stopping is vastly less exciting, I'm afraid. I wanted to give the crew a break at a location free of outside eyes and ears. But it's exotic and who doesn't like a beach party."

"The best beaches appear to be on Bat Island," Chambo continued. "It's two islands connected by a thin white sandy isthmus. Way back in 1944, the Aussies constructed a radar station on the island. It turned out to be an unhealthy decision, however, because of a rat infestation on South Bat Island.

"The little critters carried mites which spread Scrub typhus. They ended up killing most of the Aussies. Years later, another group returned to dismantle the radar site and eradicate the rats.

"Still interested in going ashore?"

"How on earth did rats find their way to such an isolated island in the first place," Rava asked Gar.

"That's a good question, and how did they survive with such a limited food supply?

"We'll have to keep our eyes open, but I think we can safely restrict ourselves to the isthmus, spend most of our time swimming, scuba diving, and relaxing on the beach.

"If we detect any rats, we'll beat a hasty retreat to Tanigue."

The conversation wound down.

"Rip and I have found a suitable location for our hydroponic garden, and I want to get your blessing before we do more planning.

"Do you think we might commandeer the dive gear room aft of the engine room? We'll keep our mini-plantation clear of all your gear along the walls."

The tender shuttled from Tanigue to the shore and back again. Multiple trips later, the crew, the pilots, Chambo, and Rip stood on the sandy isthmus. They'd been stacking coolers filled with enough food to feed a small army and had opened large umbrellas and placed beach chairs. Once they'd completed the basic setup, crew members wasted little time in donning available snorkels, masks, and flippers and venturing out to the coral reefs. Quinn got his boom box blaring a mix of pop and heavy metal tunes.

Marlo took the first shift watching the bridge. Bembol, the Chief Engineer, remained to monitor the ship's systems. Gar wandered aft from the bridge while inspecting the ship one last time before joining the others. All remained quiet until he heard a noise emanating from Rip's lab.

Could someone have stayed behind? In any case, it seemed strange. He entered and noticed Rava holding up a large penciled schematic of her proposed hydroponic garden.

"Rava. What are you doing here on Tanigue? It's time to relax and let go of time for at least one day. Why don't you join me on the last shuttle to the island?"

"I guess I'm one of those people who has to complete the job at hand before relaxing. I want to design the garden as thoroughly as possible so we don't overlook any critical components. I've already found a much easier way to manage water levels, especially if there's a power outage.

"Sometimes a little added effort brings unexpected dividends, but I suppose you're right. I should join the group and enjoy all that Rat Island offers. Or should that be Bat Island with all the rats?"

The two laughed together.

"I need a few more minutes to complete my brief inspection," Gar confessed. "I'll come back to get you and we can ride together. It'll be fun."

Gar and Rava slipped off the RHIB into the warm ocean waters near the picnic site. Devon, Quinn, Chambo, and Rip appeared in the waves a short way off as they stood to walk ashore. They'd been snorkeling along nearby coral reefs.

"Sis," Rip called to Rava, "you've got to snorkel here. There are tons of blue damsels, clownfish, and a million other varieties swimming in these corals. It's stunning."

"Will you snorkel with me?" Rava asked Gar, "I can't wait to explore such a pristine area."

"Only if you'll share a bottle of wine with me when the sun settles against the skyline," countered Gar.

"Well, we'll see."

Devon, Quinn, Chambo, and Rip shared space on a large beach towel, each with a beer in hand.

"Quinn and I conjured up a little wager," Devon announced, "guessing the exact time we dock in Rabaul. Chambo, Rip, are either of you interested in joining?"

"Of course," answered Chambo.

Rip thought for a minute.

"Who'll be the judge? You'll need someone who's impartial and who can't be bribed. Personally, I can think of only one such person and it would be me."

"Good point," said Quinn. "I can't trust these guys with a friendly bet. Do you want to be the one who determines the winner?"

"Okay, here are the rules," responded Rip. "Each of you must submit a date and time before boarding Tanigue later tonight. You must have submitted your guess to me before your hand touches Tanigue tonight or you forfeit your chance to win.

"The closest guess wins. I will measure your submission against the time we dock, either before or after. And, the exact time of docking will be when the first mooring line touches the wharf. Is all that clear?

"Now, what are the stakes?"

"I don't want a money bet," Devon chimed in. "Let's make it for a service to be rendered."

"Oh, like that chariot race that got us all sick," recalled Quinn.

"Wait a minute," interrupted Chambo. "That pepper-eating debacle seemed to be a lot of fun, to say nothing of the entertainment value it brought to half the town.

"This time, why don't we pay for the winner to get a full body massage in Rabaul? Rip can choose the place. The losers will have to wait outside and drink beer for as long as the massage takes.

"And one more detail, the losers will pay for Rip's beer since he so graciously agreed to be the judge."

The deckhands gathered wood, snapped dried branches into smaller pieces, and used a knife to split one of them for starter materials. Laughter and light-hearted banter blended with Quinn's music and the crackling fire.

Gar and Rava found a beach towel and spread it over the sand slightly apart from the others. They sat together, knees tucked toward their chests, shoulders leaned against each other. Gar poured two glasses of wine.

"Here's to a wonderful day together. It's good to see you so relaxed."

Rava sipped his wine. "I didn't know quite what to expect when you first mentioned a beach party. I thought it might be vastly more raucous and less … um, less fun.

"Thank you for pulling me away from Tanigue. I'm enjoying it here.

"How did someone as young as you ever come to have his own airline and super yacht? I find it almost unbelievable."

Gar laughed softly before answering.

"Life can be pretty amazing. It offers plenty of pain and disappointment, but it provides opportunity and challenge. The strange thing is that the extremes often come wrapped in the same package. The secret is to know which part of the package to embrace.

"I've been very lucky to have been raised in a way that opened my eyes to opportunity and consequence. It helped me make what turned out to be life-changing decisions, even though at the time they didn't seem to be so significant.

"How about you? What brought you, a skilled botanist, exploring ways to improve the lives of so many others, to this remote corner of the planet?"

Rava held her empty wine glass for Gar to see.

"May I have another? And then I'll tell you about myself.

"I'm a poor Indian girl born in Patiala, just over a hundred miles north of Delhi. It's where Punjab's high mountains start their ascent into the sky. I moved to the United States with my family as a youth. My focus in life had always centered on family and school. After graduating from Stanford with an undergraduate degree, I enrolled in a master's program followed by doctorate studies. Rip and I have always been close, and when the opportunity to mix our specialties presented itself, I jumped at it.

"I suppose that's why I'm socially awkward and nerdy at times. As I grew up, I never found time for dating or playing online games. I'm not sure exactly what I missed, but nurturing such a focused career path paved my way to Papua.

"I'll be honest. Since you showed up, this excursion has differed from what I'd imagined. I'm having fun and still applying knowledge to my work. It's the best of both worlds.

"Better yet, you've taken my mind off the Asians. I still fear the worst with them."

NINETEEN

TANIGUE'S PASSAGE INTO HISTORIC SIMPSON Harbor came with magnificent views. Marlo steered the vessel into an ancient caldera measuring six miles across at its widest point. The dominant feature to their right, Tavurvur volcano, slept under ash-laden slopes. It overshadowed six additional cone-shaped sub-vents that stood guard over the interior harbor. The entire landmass resembled Jurassic Park. Flying pterodactyls and grazing dinosaurs would have appeared quite normal.

Gar couldn't help but think that Rabaul's great beauty came with great peril. He supposed, in a larger geological sense, that this entire area remained a ticking time bomb ready to erupt at any moment.

"Marlo, no wonder this is such a prized deep-water port. Look at those slopes surrounding us. They dive almost vertically into the depths."

"You know, boss," he responded, "that big volcano with all the ash on its slopes is still active. It buried Rabaul under several inches of soot and cinders back in '94. I'm pretty sure it erupted again after that."

"We'll keep the crew onboard at night," Gar thought out loud. "No need to fuss with limited hotel space and I'd like them back by midnight. We'll start back toward Sarmi once we're refueled and replenished and leave this intriguing little piece of paradise to the locals."

"Exactly 10:47 a.m.," Rip called out while stretched across the mid-ship railing. He'd sought the best possible view of Rabaul's Puma terminal wharf to capture the exact moment a deckhand tossed the mooring line.

"I'll announce the winner this evening. It's gonna be close."

The Harbor Master approached as Gar stepped off Tanigue onto the wharf.

"Welcome to the devil's doorstep," he bellowed as he neared. "My name is Gustaf and I'll help you with whatever you need."

"Thank you, Gustaf. I'm surprised at Rabaul's compact size. I guess I expected to see a major city wrapped around this incredible port area."

"You're not alone," Gustaf responded. "A lot of visitors say the same. Over the years, our community has repeatedly endured the extremes of growth and devastation."

He looked into the distance and continued, "In the early 1900s, our population exceeded one hundred thousand, mostly Germans and Australians." He pointed toward the volcano. "The principal city flourished over there. That area is currently pretty much a wasteland.

"Back in '37, Tavurvur buried everything. Over eighty percent of our buildings collapsed. Everyone evacuated and few came back. Those who did, rebuilt here away from the volcano, sort of. We slowly started growing again …

"Until the Japanese came, 110,000 of them, and the war followed. They imprisoned most of those who'd remained and built their military base near the volcano. The buggers even built the old runway over there."

"What happened to all the Japanese and their buildings?" Gar asked. "There doesn't appear to be anything left."

"Maybe the gods paid them back for their cruelty. Maybe fate played a role," Gustaf mused. "The Americans bombed their buildings pretty heavily but didn't invade Rabaul. They never needed to physically take control after most of the surrounding airfields and encampments had been seized.

"They found it easier to simply isolate it. Japanese resupply ships no longer had a reason to sail here, and as a result, many of their soldiers starved.

"Well, here we are, living inside an ancient caldera on what used to be a mangrove swamp. We've gone from being the capital of Papua and New Britain to being an isolated port with less than four thousand inhabitants.

"So, we're once again a small community, but we have a good life. You'll have to visit the yacht club and meet our more colorful locals."

"It's an amazing story," Gar said. "We're happy to be here if only for a brief visit."

Gustaf smiled after having recounted the history of his city. He shifted to the business side of things, knowing that this large ship might need more than they realized.

"Now you know why we're such an underpopulated city. We cater to larger ships, however. Besides having ample fuel storage, we maintain a ship repair and refit capability and always have a good supply of foodstuffs. I'm afraid there's not a lot more than that."

While Marlo and Bembol coordinated the lengthy refueling process, Gar, Chambo, and the chef set out for a couple of grocery stores and the local market. Rip and Rava headed for the first of two construction supply outlets.

They dressed in what appeared to be ragtag clothes. The outfits had been tailored for that appearance. Rip found the 'local look' made shopping easier and bargaining somewhat more advantageous, while Rava simply enjoyed the loose fit.

She thumbed through the pages of an equally tattered notebook until finding an itemized list of PVC pipes, fittings, and lighting fixtures. The following page contained Hongland Hardware's address and beneath it a hand-drawn map of the port area.

"We can walk to this place. Hopefully, they'll deliver what we buy, but if not, we'll have to lease a small truck."

"It's a good plan," Rip acknowledged. "How far to your second shop?"

"It's on the opposite corner of the block, maybe ten minutes," she added. "The local market is along the way so maybe we could wander inside and look for rambutans and other local fruits."

The setting sun illuminated puffy orange clouds across the width of the horizon. Gar, Rava, and Marlo gathered outside the upper lounge aft of the bridge while the crew showered. Cool air drifted in from the ocean. Glasses of Chianti Classico and the birds-eye view of the harbor tempted all three to simply drift along with the breeze and forget everything else.

A beep from Gar's phone broke the tranquility. It came from General Smithberger.

> Dear Gar,
> Hearing from you and knowing that your mission is progressing according to plan has been the good news. The work of Dr. Siraj and his sister remains a priority, and I want you to continue providing a layer of security for them. With the Asians percolating turmoil throughout the jungles, your presence is doubly meaningful.
>
> I've contacted our defense attaches in Australia, Indonesia, and Papua New Guinea. Each one substantiated disturbing reports of biological anomalies occurring in Papua. Follow-up conversations with government representatives ultimately confirmed my fears. Papua, in particular, has recorded numerous incidents of unusual viral outbreaks. The Indonesian Coordinating Minister for Political, Legal, and Security Affairs reached out for help in getting to the source of this unexplained illness.
>
> Government investigators started visiting remote villages and found an entire community had died from a sudden illness. In one case, they found three surviving children starving after everyone else fell silent. The missionary flights you mentioned earlier carrying infected natives have come to the attention of government officials as well. Medical staff are at a loss trying to pinpoint the cause, although they suspect a group of Asians are complicit.

Other Agencies here on the Hill are preparing to intervene, which is good because I'd rather you continue supporting Rip and Rava. There's a real possibility, however, that I'll ask you to airlift a specialized team to and from a couple of remote locations, but that's it.

More to follow. . .
Grits

Rip joined Chambo and the pilots on the wharf, ready to explore Rabaul's limited nightlife.

"Let's rent a car and driver for the night. Our first stop will be the Rabaul Yacht Club. I'm not sure if they still raffle off a meat tray on Fridays, but I'm told the club still draws a friendly group of local business owners most nights. We can buy temporary memberships when we get there.

"For your drinking pleasure, I recommend South Pacific Export beer. If you want something richer, try a Bottle of Britain Spitfire brew. The guy at the hardware store highly recommends both."

Quinn polished off a second Spitfire. "Drum roll please, let's get to the winner announcement."

"Okay, okay," responded Rip. "First, no one got the exact time, except me. I entered a time just for the fun of it.

"And the winner is … Chambo, with a total deviation of only forty-eight minutes."

Devon spoke up.

"I'll drink to that," and called, "Waiter, another round of Spitfires, and bring shots of that liquid fire you call Rabaul Whisky."

"It's time we head over to the Kalvuna Resort," Rip announced an hour later. "My new friend, Felix, is the manager. He called in a special masseuse for Chambo and he assured me he's got an ample supply of ice-cold South Pacific Export."

Felix appeared several minutes later with Mua, a 230-pound full-figured girl from the central highlands.

"She has the strongest fingers in New Britain. There's never been a kink she couldn't work out and never a customer who didn't bellow with pleasure. Yep. She definitely deserves her five-star rating."

The look on Chambo's face suggested a somewhat fearful premonition of her fingers digging into his back. Devon subdued a laugh and challenged Quinn.

"Five dollars he doesn't last twenty minutes."

"You're on," Quinn responded, "but it won't go much more than that. Rip, you're brilliant."

Another message. . .

> Gar,
> Please delay another day or two until I coordinate the team logistics. I need you to transport them. Expect a pre-dawn pickup at Lae Airport as soon as I can get them there. I'll let you know the exact pickup location and date soon.
> Grits

Xi-han Wu sat alone in the dimly lit apartment along Jayapura's poorest section of the waterfront. He required scant support to live. A hammock, a table and chair, and an electrical outlet satisfied his spartan needs. After all, he wouldn't stay here much longer.

He'd normally call his contact in Hong Kong directly but today he'd transmit a typed summary of recent activities. He configured his cellphone to become a mobile hotspot, identified the network ID from his laptop, and connected to the internet. Little did he suspect that someone else might be listening.

Wu's pot-marked teenage face and sloppy stature invited relentless after-school teasing. Isolation became his refuge, anger his predominant emotion. Deep within, he imagined physical confrontations during which he'd take his revenge.

Wu had earned an undergraduate degree in chemistry before enlisting in the People's Army. This background pointed him toward the biological corps, where he gained experience mixing infectious concoctions. He later experimented on dogs and monkeys, measuring their response to his drug combinations.

Where other technicians held compassion for their subjects, Wu did not. His harsh upbringing and bullied past brought quite the opposite perspective. He felt an evil pleasure in observing his animal's painful and often fatal reactions.

Wu began typing, "Monthly summary of Papua activities regarding biological testing . . ."

General Smithberger's classified computer beeped after an urgent message appeared on the screen.

"General Smithberger, we intercepted and decrypted the following message. It originated through a service provider in Jayapura, Indonesia and I recommend you read it. Some of this may sound familiar." Agent Smith.

> Monthly summary of Papua activities regarding biological testing
>
> I have three teams deployed south of here. Each of them remains mobile, infecting isolated villages with specific viruses and experimenting with immunizations several weeks later.
>
> Our Hulu Atas team has exposed two tribal communities with a ninety-two percent infection rate. Inoculations haven't occurred. This team plans to move westward within the next several weeks to avoid further highlighting their presence.
>
> The Kwerba team continues to operate near the juncture of the Taritatu and Mamberamo rivers. They've infected one village and will administer a partial inoculation next week. This is the same team whose previous viral infection project killed an entire village. It forced them to incinerate and bury everyone in the hope of removing all evidence of the outbreak.
>
> The last team continues to make progress near Elelim Airport. Their experiments with viral enhancement and serum virus neutralization assay are moving forward slowly. The team quietly poisoned several locals after they became curious about the field lab. The situation appears to have stabilized.

I continue to be vexed by the secretive work of Doctor Siraj. My team discovered them hiding in Sarmi after I'd eliminated who I thought to be him and his botanist sister. Unfortunately, they've disappeared again. I'm convinced they're developing antitoxins, and as such, present a threat to our success. I'll eventually find them and neutralize their efforts.
Xi-han Wu

Rava decided to propagate at least one of her miracle plants.

"It's now or never," she announced to Rip. "Let's see if we can propagate fresh growth before we head back out to sea."

"And I'd like to take one plant and use it to create two separate potions," he replied. "I'll extract antitoxins from the leaves into a tea and reduce that liquid to a more concentrated form.

"I'll mash up the stems and roots of the same plant and dilute the pulp in alcohol for a second potion. The potions will be tested and compared under the microscope.

"I'll set aside samples of each to see if they improve Devon's and Quinn's ability to blindly identify my image cards. Heaven knows it can't hurt. Those two have guessed rather poorly during almost every session."

Gar's phone displayed another message from the General.

You're clear to depart Rabaul. Plan to pick up a team of six individuals three days from now at the new Lae Nadzab Airport. There's a small aviation hangar at the northeast corner. The team will meet you there at 3 a.m. on Tuesday.

They'll provide further instructions once you get them onboard Tanigue.

TWENTY

Tanigue's return to Sarmi

GAR POINTED TO A LOCATION ON MARLO'S chart off the tip of Papua New Guinea.

"This is where we're headed and from where I'd like to launch Icarus. How long will it take us to get there?"

Marlo ran a quick check.

"At fifteen knots, we'll get there in twenty-six hours. We could go slower to save fuel if time isn't critical."

"Slower is fine," Gar replied. "It looks like we're gonna have to delay once we get there anyway, and I'd much rather save the fuel."

"Chambo, grab the chef and a deckhand, and see if you can buy a week's food for six more people, maybe another butchered pig and twenty pounds of fresh veggies."

Devon, Quinn, and Rip joined Gar in the training room a few minutes later. They instinctively pulled chairs from under the conference table and sat down. A picture of New

Britain and Papua New Guinea projected onto the front whiteboard.

"Boys, we're making a little deviation along the way back to Sarmi." Gar instantly had their attention. "On the surface, it seems pretty simple, but I want you two to think through as many contingencies as possible. Better to be prepared for the unexpected.

"You'll have a couple of days to plan the flight. Here's what I've got so far …"

"Rip, I want to remain focused on Icarus' systems training, and more importantly, on your neurological testing.

"Can you provide a tentative schedule for next week? What is it you want to accomplish before we disappear back into the interior?"

Rip stood and walked to the whiteboard.

"I'm convinced that these two don't think like normal people." He directed his next comments toward Devon and Quinn. "After correlating your imagery responses, I've found each of you to be well below statistical averages and that includes several primate studies."

"I'm pretty sure that miracle drug I took here in Rabaul is going to make a difference," Devon interjected. "At first, it gave me mental clarity before my thoughts turned fuzzy, but today I'm feeling even better than normal."

"And what drug would that be?" Rip asked.

Devon feigned shock at Rip not knowing.

"Heck, you drank more of it than me. It's that mental accelerator they call Bottle of Britain Spitfire."

He and Quinn laughed. Eventually, Rip joined in the laughter.

"Yes, I'm afraid to see what that sludge did to your mental capacity.

"Once you complete the Lae pickup, I'd like to swab your temples with a few drops of plant potion. I should have enough of it processed by then and hopefully, it'll be compatible with all that Spitfire juice in your veins."

Gar awoke shortly after midnight and wandered forward to a covered observation deck at Tanigue's bow. This secluded part of the vessel had become his favorite nook for gazing out to sea and letting his mind wander. The middle of the night had proven to be the time when it refreshed him the most.

The darkened sky and a three-quarter moon shrouded themselves in wispy white clouds. Clear cool air rested upon smooth seas and Gar could taste its briney sea-smell with every breath. Tonight's mission had been for the pilots to plan and fly, but it remained a challenge for Gar to step aside and let others do it.

Envious thoughts flashed of Devon and Quinn flying into the dark on a challenging and relatively safe mission.

"Gar, I didn't expect to find you here," Rava announced in a low voice. "It's a perfect night for star-gazing. Got room for another observer?"

Her low, sensuous voice warmed Gar's heart. The unexpected companionship filled a void that had suddenly materialized with her arrival.

"So, you've found my secret middle-of-the-night observation deck. On nights like this, it really does my soul good to lean against the railing and throw thoughts to the wind."

She nudged closer, hugged the railing with folded arms, and gazed outward.

"Did you know this part of the Solomon Sea sits atop a large subduction zone? It's where the Pacific and Indo-Australian tectonic plates converge. The water here is really deep as a result and that's why there are so many volcanoes in this region. All of them seem at rest tonight. The shimmering moonlight and still air must have conspired to suppress the unknowns below the surface and have provided us these moments of divine solitude."

"Rava, I love the way you blend scientific and spiritual perspectives. It's a rare talent."

As he spoke, Rave noticed the moonlight glimmering off his smiling white teeth.

Nadzab endured as a peaceful community along the Markham River Valley twenty-six miles northwest of Lae. Its airport had become, by far, its most significant municipal entity. Nadzab's airport authority had prioritized strengthening the runway to accommodate full-sized jet aircraft. They completed that initial work and moved to their next priority, the terminal facility replacement.

The airport authority had recently limited commercial flight operations to mid-day take-offs and landings. The reduced hours lessened interference with ongoing construction while bringing the added benefit of allowing airport employees to leave early each day.

A general aviation hangar at the end of the runway housed a handful of privately owned aircraft. In addition to the limited airport operating hours, late afternoon weather build-ups coupled with the area's mountainous terrain discouraged their pilots from flying much later than noon.

At 2 a.m. on Tuesday, the only airport activity consisted of crickets chirping at one another.

A darkened MC-130 aircraft originating from Australia descended through several cloud layers as its crew began referencing their terrain-following radar. Upper-level turbulence subsided and the flight profile smoothed before the ghostly chariot of Armageddon descended through one thousand feet.

Six commandos silently double-checked their gear in the aircraft's cargo compartment. The plane crossed the Erap River at one hundred feet and touched down at the beginning of the runway. It quietly rolled out to the far end, made a U-turn, and lowered its ramp. Commandos hauled their Pelican cases clear of the aircraft and hunched in the nearby grass.

Engine noise increased. The aircraft rolled down the runway and quickly disappeared back into the darkness. The commandos began a five-hundred-yard hike to the general aviation tarmac as the quiet of night returned. They settled and waited.

Soft thumping air and the barely audible whir of its rotors comprised the quadcopter's only hints of arrival. Devon sat in the pilot's seat. Quinn slid open the cargo door and exited to help with loading the team.

He appeared out of nowhere before approaching the team lead.

"Hi, we're your ride to Tanigue. Can you give me an approximate weight for each of you and for whatever cargo you've brought?"

"Where's your aircraft?" the team leader asked.

"It's invisible most of the time. Don't worry, I'll lead you to the door in a minute."

The team lead expressed disbelief and puzzlement.

"Each of us should weigh in at approximately 250 pounds. We've got a variety of toys in the Pelican cases. Let's say they're two hundred pounds each and we've got eight of 'em."

Quinn mentally computed the weight and cube of everything.

"We can barely make the weight, but beyond that, I don't think we've got room for everything on one shuttle. Can you split your team and cargo? We'll make two quick trips. It won't take more than an hour before I'll be back again."

"Let's get four of us on the first shuttle along with as much cargo as you can manage," the team lead suggested.

"Okay, let's get started."

Quinn clicked his mic and asked Devon to turn off the cloaking system. Icarus appeared fifty yards in front of them. The team loaded several Pelican cases without asking questions, after which the first four climbed onboard.

Rava and Gar felt the low-frequency vibrations at the same time.

"Icarus is getting close," Gar announced. "I'm going to head back toward the aft deck to greet our visitors. Care to join me?"

"Nah, I'm heading back to bed," Rava answered. "I'll need to get a couple of hours of sleep before Rip starts hounding me about building our little hydroponic garden."

Gar walked out of the main dining area toward the landing pad and watched Icarus rise and depart back into the darkness. Four commandos approached him.

"Sir, I'm Mac. I've got five others, two of whom will arrive on the next shuttle. Our equipment necessitated two trips."

"I'm Gar and I'm directing our ship's operations. The captain is at the bridge. His name is Marlo. We've got room for your equipment on the deck directly below us. It's an open space with room for you to bed down if you like. We've also got several spare crew bunks."

"The open space will be fine," Mac responded. "Would you like a full briefing on our mission, or can it wait until morning? We're good either way."

"Let's get you settled," Gar said, "and you can provide an update after you've slept a few hours. I'll make sure we have plenty of hot coffee in the morning."

Mac, the commando team lead, followed Gar into the library where late-morning coffee awaited them.

"If there's anything you need while aboard Tanigue, please ask.

"Sometime tomorrow or early the next day, we'll anchor south of Sarmi. From there, we'll insert you wherever you need to go. It might take a bit of planning to determine the safest way to do it without being seen."

"Thank you," Mac replied. "We'll stay out of the way as much as possible. Our current location on the covered deck is perfect for our needs. We're not used to such accommodations. Anyway, here's what I can tell you.

"The bad guys have been operating out of a field lab in the mountains near a small town called Elelim. They have an airport and we'd appreciate a drop-off under cover of darkness. The airfield is only fifteen hundred feet in elevation, but there are mountains up to four thousand feet to the north.

"After four or five days, we'd appreciate a lift from there to Hulu Atas airport along the Taritatu River. Same routine. Night time preferred. A couple of days and another hop to where the Taritatu feeds into the Mamberamo. Any problems so far?"

"None that are obvious," Gar responded. "We'll be in the general area for most of the time, so our response time can be pretty quick should you need us.

"Are you going to need any of those extra supplies you brought along?"

"Not initially, but maybe as time moves forward. For now, I'll label each Pelican case with a large single letter. That way, it'll be easier to request exactly what we might need.

"I'd prefer to leave them on the ship. How long would it take you to fly from your operating site to the ship and back to us?"

Gar thought for a minute. "Well, it's around an hour's flight back to Tanique. Let's say it takes fifteen minutes to load the cargo and a little more than an hour to transport it to a drop-off point. Maybe two-and-a-half hours."

"That'll work."

Rip stood before Devon and Quinn.

"Boys, today we're going to try something different." He held up a modified plastic headset and explained, "I designed this rig to sit over your temples rather than your ears. I've conducted preliminary tests on two variations of the same potion that I'm about to smear on these pads.

"For today, I want to set individual baselines for each of you. Devon, you'll get potion A, and Quinn, you'll get B. In a couple of days, I'll swap the potions and measure the change in your mental reception. Got all that?"

"I hope your card deck contains new pictures," Quinn responded. "I keep seeing the same colors each time."

"Let's see what you see," Rip replied. "If I told you what I'm going to show you it'd be cheating. Ready?"

Devon donned his blindfold and adjusted the headset until it felt comfortable. Rip progressed through a series of twenty-five cards and initially, Devon couldn't formulate complete images in his mind. Towards the end, however, he began perceiving images more clearly.

"Take a ten-minute break," Rip announced. "I'm going to tweak the impulse algorithm before we run through the next set of cards."

Devon turned toward Quinn. "I'm getting the hang of this perception thing. I can almost feel my brain trying to build a data bridge from my temple to somewhere farther inside. It's weird."

"Okay, let's try this one more time." Rip loaded a new file of visual cards. This time, the complexity of the images became more difficult. The first image depicted a boy tossing a ball to a dog.

"Sorry, I see a dog getting ready to catch a ball," Devon responded. "I'm trying to focus and visualize your color, but I can't get rid of the dog. Let's try the next one."

"Take your time, young Einstein. Here, what do you see?"

"Well . . . nothing.

"I can feel a low-grade headache coming," Devon advised. "You know, the kind you get after thinking too hard on one thought for too long."

"Okay. Quinn, your turn," Rip announced with audible disappointment in his tone.

Rip smiled to himself. Devon and Quinn had registered minor improvements over their previous dismal responses. New empirical data suggested the potions performed better than wishful telepathy or simple guesswork. The minor software tweaks he'd made seemed to have improved the outcome.

He decided to study the potions under the microscope to see exactly how they differed. The guys would have a day or two to flush existing mental images of the test before he swapped potions and ran the tests all over again. But damn, he wouldn't have time before they flew back into the jungle.

TWENTY-ONE

GAR WONDERED ABOUT THE FEASIBILITY OF landing at Elelim. "Chambo, what do you know about Elelim other than it's in the mountains south of here?"

"Um, never heard of it. But since you asked, I'll dust off the encyclopedia and dig up a few nuggets known only to the most inquisitive minds."

Chambo found Gar later that afternoon relaxing in the library.

"Mind if I join you? And, a beer would surely taste good about now."

"Did all that encyclopedic dusting expose Elelim to be more interesting than you thought?"

Chambo sighed as he lowered himself onto the settee across from Gar.

"It's an interesting place, all right. Think of a mixing bowl where you squish the sides together. Well, Elelim would be at the bottom, surrounded by mountains on all sides. But it's not exactly isolated.

"Narrow valleys extend in all four cardinal directions. The southern valley is the widest and climbs into the high mountains. Those peaks reach nearly ten thousand feet before descending again into Wamena, which is one of Papua's mountain cities. It surprised me to find that Elelim Valley is wide enough to support an airport. That and the crisscrossing roads have created a natural gathering point that six thousand natives call home. Hell, I don't think there are that many humans within a hundred-mile radius of Elelim's city limits. Anyway, it became the capital of Yalimo Regency which seems kinda weird for being so remote.

"While I've found the Papuans to be generally quite friendly, in Elelim they tend to be feistier. They've re-cast their last provincial election three times, each followed by increasingly violent protests claiming election fraud. They've burned buildings, blocked roads, and destroyed a bridge. If we ever have the chance to visit, I'd recommend talking about the weather or local food rather than the governor or politics." He chuckled and continued. "Again, it's not exactly a sleepy hollow in the middle of nowhere."

Gar listened for anything that might affect Quinn's late-night commando insertion. Everything seemed to be in order so far.

"Anything else?"

"Well, the weather might be worth noting. It gets cold at night and, more importantly, it rains almost every afternoon. Can you imagine blindly descending through those buildups into a valley surrounded by mountains? No thanks."

"I suppose getting in and out before dawn is fine and it's definitely preferable." Chambo continued. "And one more item I found, there are three direct commercial flights each week between Elelim and Jayapura.

"I haven't accessed passenger records yet, but I bet I can find one or two Asians who rode on those flights."

Wu had reserved five seats on each of two flights from Jayapura to Elelim six months ago. Seven of the passengers had arrived in Jayapura off a tramp steamer from Australia. The other three had flown to Jayapura from Hong Kong via Jakarta. Wu kept them holed up in a well-stocked apartment he'd leased next to his. He used it to brief them on their mission and how to contact him once they moved to Elelim. In a separate session, Wu instructed them on how to handle curious locals.

Their orders included conducting gain-of-function research on locally created viral concoctions and others that he'd receive from Hong Kong and then forward to them. He wanted the Elelim field lab to remain a clandestine operation.

The concrete building they'd converted into a laboratory appeared neglected from the outside and that suited their needs perfectly. They secured the doors and windows and sterilized the interior tables and cabinets. In reality, the furnishings appeared incredibly unsanitary when compared to other laboratories conducting similar research.

"If Icarus' batteries won't recharge during flight, where would you land to nuke 'em back to life?" Quinn asked Devon.

"I've plotted a couple of options, but the most interesting one is south of Sengbo. It's isolated and has several good landing zones. Here are the coordinates. I think it's an old mining operation that might still be active. The good news is that I don't see any sign of recent activity on these satellite images."

"Oh yeah," Quinn agreed after reviewing the imagery. "I like this area by the river. Heck, if that isn't acceptable, there's a big sandbar that should work. It's unlikely I'll need to go there, but if I do, it'll only be for an hour or two."

A high overcast obscured the stars, leaving the sky dull black. Tanigue rose and fell in a slow rhythmic motion as though it had fallen asleep on an endless ocean. That would soon change. Floodlights suddenly illuminated, bringing the shipping container facade into a well-lit focus.

Mac and his team stood on the open deck forward of the landing pad. Their loose-fitting trousers and variety of well-worn long-sleeve shirts blended with unshorn faces. Rather than wearing sandals, they'd opted for hiking boots. Mac wore a straw hat, and all carried dark backpacks. They'd tucked low-profile night vision goggles, Glock 19s with silencers, and a variety of additional odds and ends inside.

Quinn and Devon climbed the companionway rising from the lower deck after the sides of the hangar retracted and folded.

"I'll get the inside if you can release the wheel tie-downs," Quinn suggested.

Quinn walked to Mac once he'd prepped Icarus for flight.

"Okay guys, the flight will take an hour. Relax and enjoy the ride. The weather should be perfect and I'll get you on the ground roughly three hours before sunrise. Let's hit the road."

"Roger that." Mac looked to the others. "Time to climb on board."

Icarus slowly lifted off the deck and turned toward Papua's interior while climbing to four thousand feet.

Quinn engaged the cloaking mode even though the darkness of the night already left them relatively invisible to anyone on the ground. He also projected flowing colors along the interior walls to complement his somewhat unexpected musical selection.

Quinn thought his latest playlist seemed vastly more appropriate than the alternative, which didn't exist. Vivaldi's Juditha Triumphans caught the commandos off guard. They'd expected something more akin to pop-rock, definitely not an oratorio celebrating the defeat of the Ottomans during the Siege of Corfu. Its vibrant instruments and soprano vocals highlighted one of Quinn's out-of-the-blue musical perversions.

ZZ Top thankfully flowed into the stream, followed by a mix of heavy metal and Stevie Ray Vaughan. Several commandos stopped thinking of ways to kill Quinn and eventually fell asleep. They awoke during his last selection, Chopin's Military Polonaise, an enthusiastic piano solo that Quinn always felt added an element of pre-combat inspiration.

He'd replay the compilation on his return flight.

Quinn deviated west of course rather than fly directly to Elelim so that he could overfly the point at which the Taritatu joined the Mamberamo River. He half-twisted and looked over his shoulder toward the passengers.

"Hey Mac, I'm over the Taritatu and Mamberamo. I'm gonna orbit one more time for you. How does that look?"

Mac tried to orient himself and saw little that helped.

"Thanks, Quinn, it's nice."

Elelim lay asleep under a blanket of darkness ten miles ahead. Quinn engaged the cloaking cameras and the rotor noise reduction system. He decided to let Icarus fly the approach autonomously and commanded, "NVG camera." The image projecting onto his visor changed to a low-light black and white display. Without sufficient moon illumination, however, everything remained shrouded in darkness. He needed to try something else and commanded, "IR camera." His view changed slightly. This time, the residual heat of the runway provided enough infrared contrast for him to identify it. Quinn quickly realized their current trajectory would take them several thousand feet right of the runway. He touched a landing zone icon with his left-hand index finger and slid it across the keypad until it centered on the runway. When he commanded, "Fly approach," Icarus smoothly redirected itself back toward the runway.

Mac and his five commandos jumped to the ground and ran into the grass, where they crouched to orient themselves before moving further. This time an eerie quiet engulfed them, unlike other aircraft infiltrations where the noise level remained deafening. They'd left an invisible aircraft and couldn't imagine it still existed not more than a stone's throw away. The soft thumping of the air, more than anything else, reassured them that Icarus had not yet departed.

Before he activated the return flight plan, Quinn wondered how Mac and his team would manage to get around. They couldn't possibly walk everywhere. Maybe they'd sleep in the fields. The thought made him feel much better about returning to Tanigue. He wished them luck.

Ten minutes into the flight, an automated voice sounded.

"You do not have sufficient power reserve to reach your planned destination."

"What the heck?" Quinn mumbled. "Ficknish, I never started those danged rotary engines . . . and that damned deviation didn't help."

He placed an LZ icon on the landing zone Devon had recommended.

"Re-route," he said in a monotone.

Icarus rolled into a fifteen-degree bank to the right when the automated voice returned, "Proceeding to new destination."

"Start number one rotary engine," Quinn said into his mic. "Start number two rotary engine."

His only way to verify that they started required him to call up the system diagnostics screen and verify that two of the main battery packs were, in fact, charging.

He radioed Tanigue. "Icarus enroute to alternate landing site. Will delay approximately one hour to recharge batteries. How copy?"

Marlo and Gar heard the call from the bridge.

"Copy all," Gar responded.

Quinn opted to land on the river's open sandbar and Icarus flew a perfect approach to touchdown.

He commanded, "Shut down motors all," and the rotors free-wheeled to an eventual stop.

He'd remain in the cockpit seat for the time being and monitor the electrical system screen. Based on the overall charge being applied to the batteries, he concluded the two radioisotope thermoelectric generators and the tiny LP rotary engines that powered a pair of 30kW generators all worked. Not that it particularly mattered as he'd be gone within an hour. He took the opportunity to explore more of the river.

The air remained cool and refreshing. A few stars twinkled above and the sound of water lapping against the shore created a peaceful ambiance. Quinn skipped a stone. The water shimmered ever so subtly in the dark.

Something moved to his left.

An icy shiver shot up his back for no particular reason. Something felt wrong. He climbed back into the cockpit and called up the IR camera. He'd see whatever moved, one way or the other.

"Ha, you won't get past me," he challenged the display.

Two logs appeared where he'd sensed the movement. One of them pushed into the river.

"Crocs! I nearly skipped a stone across a sleeping croc. Holy bejesus … think I'll stay here for the recharge … should have got a video of that for Devon"

Wu pulled up a chair toward the back of a dimly lit whiskey bar along Jayapura's seafront. He sipped a glass of rot-gut bourbon and smoked a rolled cigarette. The cheap, cluttered nature of the place suited Wu just fine. Working as a go-between occasionally frustrated him and tonight felt like one of those times. His contact in Hong Kong had demanded more feedback on several new viruses.

"How am I supposed to get feedback in this godforsaken corner of hell? he grumbled under his breath. "It's not like

I can pick up a phone and call for the results . . . I'll get results when I get results, and not sooner."

An informant had planned to join him one night this week with news of Elelim's progress. He hadn't appeared last night, or the night before. Another customer entered and took a seat toward the front of the long, narrow room. Wu looked up. A female. She showed no interest in him.

He rolled a second cigarette with his yellow smoke-stained fingers, lit it, and waited.

"Hey, another whisky."

The girl looked in his direction, without expression.

"Your friend is waiting across the street … in Chu's Bar. He asked me to let you know."

She stood and walked out the door without another word.

Wu disliked being given instructions but couldn't think of an alternative. He slid 140,000 Indonesian rupiahs across the bar and waited for his small amount of change, took it, and walked across the street.

Chu's consisted of a narrow bar up front and a partially hidden room with a single table in the rear. Rather repugnant Orientals occupied two of the chairs.

"Whisky," Wu called in the direction of the bartender before joining them.

He drew on his rolled cigarette one last time.

"I want an update on your experiments."

The one across from him placed his forearms on the table and leaned closer. "The laboratory has been running slowly because five workers are out infecting tribes. They need more time to test the potency of their current strain.

"Those two curious natives we poisoned have died. I don't think anyone connected their deaths to the lab, mostly because the political riots diverted everyone's attention. Good luck for us."

"When will I get results?" Wu demanded. "I need something soon."

The first Oriental exhaled smoke. "I'm going back tomorrow. I'll get something for you soon."

Wu harbored little patience. The others sensed his anger and hoped they could finish this meeting before his control snapped.

"I questioned many natives who travel along the Taritatu River and I may have come across something of particular interest to you," the second Oriental revealed more softly.

"And what might that be?" Wu asked with renewed interest.

"One of the canoes saw a foreign woman gathering plants in the mangroves. I questioned them further and they described someone who sounded like that Siraj woman. It happened pretty far west of Hulu Atas, but it might be worth a closer look."

Wu smiled and wondered how they'd gotten there so quickly. They must have hired a missionary plane or another fly-for-hire outfit. Interesting.

"I need to think about this. Meet me here tomorrow night and I'll have instructions."

TWENTY-TWO

QUINN PRAYED TO HIMSELF, "PLEASE LET ME land unnoticed. The fewer people to whom I have to explain these uncharged batteries, the better."

Unfortunately, Gar and Chambo stood together on the open deck, looking every bit a disgruntled greeting party.

"Welcome back, my wayward traveler," Gar announced in greeting. "I hope Icarus' systems all worked properly."

Quinn had expected the question but knew it would be unwise to make excuses.

"I forgot to engage the LPs after take-off. By the time I realized my error, landing and recharging at the site that Devon and I had analyzed seemed to be the safest option. I made a mistake. It won't happen again."

He noticed a figure behind Gar and Chambo in the main dining room while doing his best to sound contrite. Devon silently mimicked a doubled-over belly laugh. *I hate him.*

Chambo excused himself.

"I'll make sure we have a full charge before today's flight."

Gar knew Quinn had learned his lesson but didn't want to let him off the hook without a sentence or two of fatherly comment.

"Look Quinn, that kind of mistake can happen to any of us. I suspect it's made you and Devon eager to learn more about the batteries and those quiet little high-efficiency hybrid cycle X engines. Get a bite to eat, find Devon, and join me in the training room."

"The secret to making Icarus work has a lot to do with the batteries. I've already explained their chemistry, so today I'll go over the basics."

Gar wanted to stretch the presentation to over two hours, which he thought might be rather brutal. It would, however, leave enough time for Devon to prepare for his flight to Wakde later in the afternoon.

He picked up a rectangular electrical component from the table. "This gadget translates control inputs into rpm changes for specific rotors. In essence, it controls the direction of flight."

"By the way, there's a backup controller that automatically engages if this one becomes erratic."

Rava stood, arms crossed, with a satisfied look on her face. She'd plugged a handful of electrical cables into a specialized twelve-port power strip in preparation for a full-function test. A computerized control module that she and Rip had programmed minutes earlier could power ON, or OFF, specific ports. Lights activated based on the schedule they'd set, the same with water pumps.

"Ah, this is progressing well," she muttered to herself, "I can't wait to set up a fully equipped hydroponic garden in an old warehouse. I'll have all the nutrients and LED lights. Someday I'll grow thousands of these little beauties."

Rip felt more anxious than satisfied. He worried about mixing essential nutrients into his soaking solution.

"I hope we can get the water mixture right," Rip confided to Rava. "You know, the plants you found grew out of tree bark, not actually in soil or directly in the water. My initial root-soaking water is going to be little more than a best-guess concoction.

"Next time you're on the river, could you chop a few chunks of bark? I'd like to know how much tannin they contain. I suspect it's a lot."

Rava looked puzzled.

"I rarely think of tannin when it comes to my plants. Why tannin?"

"Did you know," Rip teased, "that tannin can be a strong anti-carcinogenic? It removes microbes from the body and fights against harmful viruses. My sixth sense tells me that the bark plays a big part in the medicinal effects of your plant."

"So, how are you going to formulate the water for our little garden?" she asked,

"I've measured the total dissolved solids and measured most of the key minerals like bicarbonate, calcium, magnesium, potassium, sodium, iron, and zinc. We've got probes to give us a constant readout of most levels, and we can manually check the others every couple of weeks.

"We can alternatively collect a supply of river water. But the tree bark interests me the most. I'll have to research it more and come up with a plan. For now, bringing back samples of the bark will be a big help."

It soon became obvious to Gar that Devon and Quinn had reached their absorption limit on batteries. Gar decided to explain something more interesting . . .

"Remember the Wankel engine?"

"Sure, it made Mazda famous," Devon proudly answered, "The RX-7, right?"

"Yep. But the Wankel story goes back further than that. A German by the name of Felix Wankel patented the engine way back in 1929. There have been various other applications, including a Wankel-powered Norton motorcycle.

"Do you recall the advantages it offered?"

This time Quinn perked up. "I know they ran smoother . . . quicker, and I think they took up less space."

"That's absolutely correct. Here are a few more advantages. They have a far higher power-to-weight ratio than traditional piston engines. There are no reciprocating parts, they're rotary and that means less wear. The elimination of opposing parts eliminated engine knock. Another advantage is that Wankels run equally well with a variety of fuels.

"Anyway, you get the point. They bring a lot to the table. But they're far from perfect. Why did Wankel fail to dominate the market? Heck, you hear nothing about them these days."

Silence . . .

"Okay. The biggest problem seemed to be rotor sealing. The original Wankel employed a three-sided rotor inside a two-lobed oval housing. The rotor had rubber seals on each of the rotating nodes. They wore out quickly, caused high oil burn, and slowed combustion. And that resulted in poor fuel economy.

"Enter the rotary X engine. We call it the LP. This engine has a redesigned rotating chamber where the seals are part of the housing. In other words, they don't rotate, lose compression through blowby, or burn oil. What we've got is a small, lightweight, quiet-running rotary engine with only two primary moving parts, the shaft and the rotor.

"With Icarus, we carry a near-limitless fuel supply, which is our battery power. It's one of our greatest advantages, but can also be our Achilles heel. You must manage this resource wisely." He stomped his foot on the floor twice to emphasize his point. "Got that?"

A two-man chorus of "Yes sir" sounded.

Chambo relaxed in the lawn chair he'd brought to the lower aft deck. This seldom occupied part of the vessel functioned as an embarkation and disembarkation point when using Tanigue's tender. He overheard Rip and Rava discussing their plant garden and later visualized Gar, Devon, and Quinn belaboring the intricacies of battery technology and power management. He enjoyed these moments when he could relax in his world and let others do the work.

His world currently consisted of two fishing lines leading to two plastic bobbers that drifted hither and yon in the waves. Dark shadows beneath the surface soon contemplated eating the attached bait.

A bobber disappeared. Something swallowed its tiny bag of horse files and carried it into the depths. No sooner had Chambo grabbed the fishing pole than his line snapped.

"What the heck?" he mouthed to himself. "I hope it's a good omen of things to come, hopefully."

His cell phone rang.

"Would you mind asking Rip and Rava to join me in the library?" Gar asked. "Include yourself in the group."

"We'll return to the river soon," Gar told them. "Now that there's a commando team in Elelim, the near-term potential for trouble is likely higher. I'd like to replace our injured native with another deckhand. That way, we'll still have three people in each canoe.

"I'd also like to carry weapons. We should be prepared."

Wu slept under a filthy bedsheet until the morning's oppressive heat became a sticky annoyance he could no longer ignore. Rather than turn on the corroded ceiling fan, he opened the refrigerator and grabbed a beer.

Thoughts of the Siraj girl exploring for plants along the Taritatu River tormented him. He considered her and her brother to be clever and also the biggest threat to his operation. If Siraj found a cure for his new viruses, it'd negate all his work. He'd get them this time and eliminate 'em for good. But first, he'd take their research.

He grabbed his phone and called AMA, an emerging aircraft operator based in the western portion of Papua. AMA occasionally flew pickup missions to remote strips along the Mamberamo and Taritatu rivers. Wu preferred using them because their manifests didn't seem as readily available to the government as those of commercial airlines.

"Hello, I want to fly from Jayapura to Dabra next week. There'll be a total of six of us. Yes, a few pieces of baggage, not much."

The female voice sounded on the other end of Wu's call.

"May I please have the names of those who will travel? We'll verify them when they board.

"We don't currently have a scheduled flight, but I'll confirm a flight for you by tomorrow morning. Normally, we take less than ten days to schedule the aircraft and pilots. Is that okay?"

"Yeah," Wu responded after a moment's hesitation. "A week from now, but not more or I'll go elsewhere."

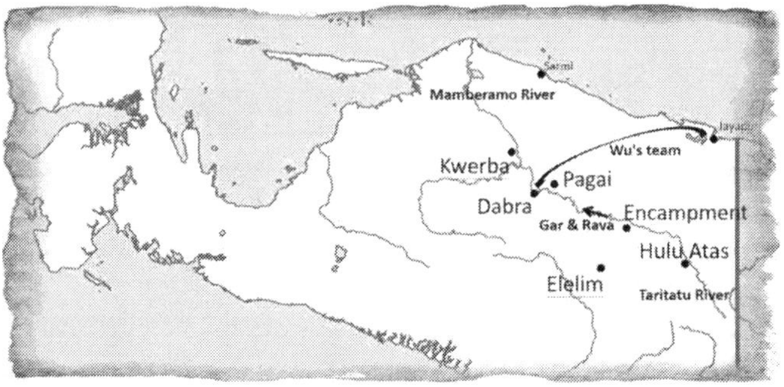

Key points along the Taritatu River

Wu returned to Chu's Bar later that night. A steady drizzle discouraged others from venturing into this backstreet section of Jayapura's run-down wharf area. As a result, Wu found himself alone in Chu's dimly lit back room. He rolled a cigarette and ordered a whisky.

Smoke hung in the air, obscuring his view of the accomplice as he entered Chu's.

"I don't like all this rain," the Oriental complained. "What's on your mind?"

"You're soft," Wu responded with a laugh. He shifted to a more somber tone, "Grab a bottle of that whisky and join me. Within the next couple of weeks, we're going to eliminate those two Siraj headaches."

"We already have the team at Hulu Atas to the east and another at Kwerba to the west. We've got them surrounded."

"You're an idiot!" hissed Wu. "Those two grass strips are over a hundred miles apart and that's as the crow flies. In reality, they're days apart on the river. Luckily, there's a closer strip at Pagai which is up a small tributary, and Dabra is another a bit farther downriver.

"We'll need someone at those airports to make sure they're not used as an escape route."

"Okay, if that's the case, all we need to do is send someone to each location. They can alert us and we'll move in for the kill."

"More whisky," called Wu. The rush of anticipation invigorated him when discussing his quarry's hunt. His focus sharpened. Feelings of conquest dominated. Wu wanted to formulate a plan that resulted in him personally pouncing upon his prey. "Here's what we're going to do . . ."

The phone at Luther Yawan Christian Church rang . . .

The AMA agent who'd taken Wu's call received her education at Luther Yawan. Its missionary pastor had infused her with confidence and loyalty, and a lasting friendship took root. She often shared this type of flight information with other flying organizations and welcomed the chance to talk with her old friend and mentor.

Everyone regarded these exchanges to be more of a safety precaution than a sharing of competitive information. Should an aircraft experience mechanical issues or worse and crash land in the jungle, it helped if everyone knew of the flight beforehand. The pastor's request for that type of information happened quite often.

"Is it you, pastor? she asked. "I have a message."

"Yes, what is it?"

"Remember a couple of weeks ago? You asked if any Asians booked flights, and you'd appreciate it if we passed the details to you. Well, I just booked such a flight."

TWENTY-THREE

"OF COURSE, I'M GOING," INSISTED RAVA. "He's one of my canoe-mates and I'm responsible for him. I'm concerned that his leg is healing properly. Plus, I miss Saturday."

"Whoa," laughed Gar with hands raised, palms toward Rava. "It's fine. You can come along. The only others will be the med-tech and Marlo. Poor Marlo stayed onboard during our stop at Rabaul and he's never experienced Icarus. I thought it about time he got that opportunity. Plus, he needs to stretch his legs on the planet's landmass before he forgets what that feels like."

Chambo approached Icarus with a forty-pound sack of rice over his shoulder.

"Here, let's put this in the back. It's for Grace as a token of gratitude for the special care she's given our injured warrior. Will you need help lugging it from the landing site to the village?"

"I think Rava just volunteered to carry it," Gar added with a laugh.

Devon walked from the aircraft to Gar with a series of routine updates.

"We've got a full charge but only need half of it for this out-and-back. We might want to run the LPs for thirty minutes and top off the Jet-A fuel tanks when we return. Other than that, we're good to go."

"Let's climb aboard and get started," Gar ordered.

He noticed Marlo fidgeting in the seat next to him and wondered if he'd become nervous. It seemed odd since he'd survived near-death experiences fighting to stay afloat in the middle of tropical typhoons and nearly capsized his trawler several times. Why would he wince at an afternoon flight in clear weather?

"Marlo, my friend, this is going to be a relaxed thirty-minute flight to a tropical island. I know there aren't any windows, but once Devon gets us moving, he'll activate an internal light show you won't soon forget. I swear, it'll feel like we're sitting behind Ali Baba on his flying carpet."

"Do my nerves show?" Marlo asked with an embarrassed smile.

Gar triggered his intercom. "Devon, is it possible to set the internal monitors before take-off? I'd like Marlo to see his beloved Tanigue as we depart."

The sides and top of Icarus virtually evaporated a moment later. Marlo subconsciously squeezed his fingers around the edges of his seat as Icarus levitated, dipped, and departed over the water.

"This is the greatest ride ever," he soon gushed. "It's … it's beautiful."

The approach to the old Wakde runway offered the same fascination. Gar showed Marlo the outline of the original runway and pointed to where the naval battle had taken place.

The group gathered outside Icarus.

"I hate to leave you here alone," Gar told Devon, "but someone needs to keep an eye on Icarus. We'll return in an hour or so."

Rava grabbed the rice bag with both hands, hesitated, and jokingly pleaded, "Won't any of you help me lift this sack of rocks onto my shoulder? Can't you see that I'm a woman in need of help?"

"I'll make a deal. with you," Gar interjected. "If you let me carry the rice, I'll let you lead the way to the village." He smiled and laughed.

"I suppose that'll be okay," Rava humphed, "but don't expect the same when it's your turn."

Now that Gar agreed to carry the heavy rice bag, lost energy returned to her body. She started toward the pathway and looked back over her shoulder.

"Come on, follow me to the best coffee on the island."

Rava felt the same warmth she'd experienced when first returning home from college. The village represented a safe place with interesting friends. She started down a sandy pathway leading into the gnarly brush

Wakde's sense of security and the sound of chirping birds released her lingering tensions. She felt carefree as she led the group through the village toward Momma's café. Each hut remained exactly as she remembered it. Two children halfway down the grassy trail added life to an otherwise tranquil setting.

More children appeared as Rava walked farther into the village, all smiling and shouting greetings. Most of them recognized Rava and Gar from their last visit.

Saturday poked his head out of a hut to their right, smiling as though he'd found a long-lost friend.

"Welcome back Ms. Rava, Mr. Gar. We've been hoping you'd return before long. Did you enjoy your trip to Rabaul?"

The procession stopped. Everyone smiled at the recognition.

"How's your son?" Rava asked, "Is he up and about?"

Saturday pointed toward the beach. "He's playing as he did before. When he comes here, I'll introduce you to him."

"Is our injured native making progress?" Gar asked.

Saturday laughed knowing the native had found a pleasant diversion to keep his mind off the healing leg.

"He's under the spell of Momma Grace and spends much of his time sampling her various coffees. She spoils him.

"Yesterday, he took a few first steps. Today he's walking more and I think he is recovering fine."

"We brought our med-tech to take a look at his cast," Gar said. "He'll examine his leg and give you instructions for him to follow. I think it'll be best if he remains here until our work is finished. We'll return to remove the cast and take him home once we're finished on the Taritau."

Grace's coffee shop lacked activity. Her lone table with its rickety wooden chairs sat empty in the shade of a large palm tree. It appeared isolated but ready for customers. Where's Momma Grace? Gar became curious before seeing her and the limping native along the beach. Momma noticed Gar's group and waved.

They returned to her coffee shop.

"Can you manage our injured native for a couple more weeks?" Gar asked. "I hope he hasn't been too much trouble?"

Momma Grace brought a joyful energy to the conversation. "Of course, I can manage this guy. I rather enjoy having him around. He needs someone to feed him and take care of him. Besides, it gives me something to do when I'm not busy cooking.

"Plus, he tells me about life in the jungle. He knows many fresh fruits and vegetables."

Gar found himself captivated by Momma's energy.

"We brought you this bag of rice as a way of saying thank you for helping him. But, it's yours on one condition. I'll need a cup of your coffee in return."

The med-tech took Saturday and the native inside Momma's café where he could examine the native's cast and explain how to best start walking again. Momma and Gar remained alone at the table, each with a cup of coffee.

"Mr. Gar," she started in a more serious tone, "a group visited our island and asked about Mr. Rip and Ms. Rava. They called them 'bad scientists' and wanted to track them down."

Gar listened intently. "Did you mention their whereabouts or our schedule?"

"Of course not. I don't share that information with foreigners, or Asians, and I don't think of them as good people. I told them that two backpackers had been here for a week, but they'd left without saying where they headed."

"How many foreigners?"

"Five, all young and angry. Saturday and the native slept in his hut at the time. I sent two children to tell them to stay out of sight."

Gar asked Devon. "After we get airborne, would you mind circling the island and making a low pass down the old runway? I may have plans for this place. The locals are supportive. It's isolated from curious eyes, yet close to the mainland. It holds potential should we ever find ourselves in the area again."

Preparations for tomorrow's return to the Taritatu River touched every corner of Tanigue. Chambo fussed with a canoe inspection. Quinn plotted a course and a landing site. One of the deckhands organized the food supply.

Devon approached Chambo.

"Did you actually have a fish on the line using a sack of horseflies?"

"Yep. Not only that, it measured almost three feet," he bragged. "Wanna keep the bet going?"

"Of course," answered Devon, "but I'm trying to attract those damned flies to Quinn rather than me. At the same time, I don't want him to enjoy the advantage of having so many to kill. Got any ideas?"

"Well, we could spray a little sugar water on his pants and enjoy the result," responded Chambo. "And maybe we could stay close and take advantage of having so many winged devils buzzing him. It'd be worth a try."

Rip and Rava joined Gar and Chambo in the dining room. Outside, afternoon clouds had given way to a golden sunset, and with pre-departure preparations complete, they relaxed with glasses of wine.

"After we harvest a few more plants from our last site, I'd love to venture farther downriver," Rava said. "There has to be more growth along the way and it only makes sense to find as many of those areas as possible."

"I have to agree," added Gar. "There's a riverside village called Dabra about seventy-five miles from our start point. I think it might be an excellent destination. We can restock our food if necessary and they have an asphalt runway.

"Chambo, if we're on the river for an extended period, you'll need to park Icarus somewhere along the way and remain on standby. Dabra will probably have a lot of curious eyes and possibly commercial flights, so that won't work. Also, you'll most likely get a call from Mac to move his team while we're doing other things, so you'll probably stay busy. See if you can find a staging area not too far away."

Rip absorbed the conversation and worried about the dangers Rava might face.

"Do you think it's safe to return to the river at the same time Mac and his team are busy stirring the pot?"

Gar had already given it some thought.

"It's up to Rava. We know there's a group of Asians a fair distance to the east and another enclave downriver where the Mamberamo joins the Taritatu. We're in the sweet spot between them and there shouldn't be any reason to cross paths if we work quickly."

"I'm committed to going back," Rava insisted. "Finding and collecting such a breakthrough plant far outweighs whatever risk might exist. I vote to proceed but with caution."

"That's why I'd like to take a few weapons along. The med-tech and I will carry Glocks. Chambo, I'd like you and the pilots to arm up as well.

"We'll have Saturday and the other native listen for any word of foreigners floating about. I think that should keep us safe and will allow us time to gather another, larger load of plants, and bark and water for Rip."

Quinn watched as deckhands attached the canoes to Icarus. His focus shifted to the open deck and the cargo yet to be loaded on the aircraft.

"Devon, this looks like a lot of cargo for a single flight. Did you compute the total weight?"

"I thought Chambo had done that. It looks like a lot to me too."

It soon became clear they'd exceed the safe limit for such a flight. Quinn felt hesitant about going to Gar with another planning issue but knew it had to be done.

"Sir, our weight is too much. I suggest taking all but the food and tents on the first flight. It'll give you time and the resources to gather plants before nightfall. I'll run the LPs this time and make a second shuttle for everything else.

"Chambo, Devon, and I should have camp pretty much established by the time the rest of you return from the river."

Gar had wondered about the weight earlier but said nothing.

"I understand. Good call. I'm sure we can make it work with two shuttles."

TWENTY-FOUR

PAPUA'S COOL MORNING AIR HELD LITTLE OF the excitement normally associated with a flight into the jungle. Gar stood on the open deck staring into the darkness, thinking it didn't feel routine. He felt the distant drums of danger and hoped for something else.

Quinn finished prepping for the first shuttle. Devon would remain on Icarus and take the second flight.

"Okay, let's get started," Quinn announced. "The sooner we arrive, the more time we'll have to gather plants before the rains come."

Backpacks and tents filled the space between Icarus' seats. They'd be heavy on departure, and as a result, Quinn would fly well below their maximum altitude. He'd illuminate the interior with a digitized night sky to conserve battery power. Projecting a simple display from a small batch file rather than directly from a hundred miniature cameras significantly reduced the power draw. It'd remain dark outside until after they landed and flying without stealth mode would save significantly more charge. He left it disengaged.

Gar heard the subtle sound of the LP engines after Quinn spoke into his microphone and started them. An imperceptible smile brightened his otherwise phlegmatic look.

The river appeared as a back-and-forth meandering ribbon along the jungle lowlands. Its light-brown color contrasted with the deep green hues splattered everywhere else. Quinn referenced his holographic visual display for the landing zone icon and looked outside to confirm its placement.

He talked to himself as he neared his destination. "This jungle changes so quickly … where is that opening? Wow, that's it? Okay, here we go".

The opening where he planned to land felt different, even though much of it matched his recollection. The undergrowth had begun its conquest of the open space over the past weeks. Quinn decided to commit to the approach. He didn't have time to reacquaint himself.

He commanded, "Fly approach." Icarus took control and descended in the morning twilight to a perfect touchdown.

Chambo exited ahead of the others and once they joined him, he organized the canoe detachment process. Saturday and the other native removed cargo from inside Icarus and temporarily stacked it in the grass. They moved away from the quadcopter and Gar gave Quinn a 'clear to depart' wave.

Icarus lifted into the air and flew away.

"I want to start searching right away," Rava told Gar. "We can nibble on snacks while gathering plants and we'll eat a bigger meal when we're done."

"Are you always so eager to get going in the morning?" Gar teased. "I thought you might prefer coffee with breakfast before traipsing into the jungle."

She glared at him with a hint of a smile. "I don't want to waste time."

"Well," Gar laughed, "it's going to rain this afternoon and I suppose I'd prefer getting back here early enough to set up our tents while they're still dry."

Chambo found himself alone and in charge of arranging the camp.

"Ouch!" He slapped the back of his neck at a pesky horsefly. "Damn, they know I'm here. Where's that hat with the mosquito mesh net?"

Sounds of birds and insects chatting amongst themselves began filling the air once the commotion of moving the canoes to the river subsided. It provided a calming backdrop as Chambo lugged equipment from the middle of the open area to a sandy stretch near the jungle. He unfolded a camp chair after he had everything organized and stacked, faced it toward the river pathway, and lowered himself into it.

"The world can wait a few minutes while I become one with the jungle."

He closed his eyes and breathed in the smell of the ferns, the soil, and the richness of the jungle floor. A hawk screeched as it flew across the opening. Insect chatter stopped for a noticeable pause before slowly returning. He'd start setting up in a few minutes.

Saturday pushed his canoe into Taritatu's slow current. The second canoe followed close behind. Rava almost immediately spotted a narrow tributary diverging west off the main channel and directed the team into it. They quickly found themselves in thick foliage.

The Taritatu River looped north and west from where they'd first launched. This passageway, along with two similar waterway tunnels, connected the east and west sides of the loop.

"There. There are more plants," exclaimed Rava. She and Saturday wedged their canoe between a couple of trees as close as possible to them before climbing into the water and pushing through the waist-deep swamp to within arm's reach.

Freeing roots from the tree bark, as they did two weeks earlier, took patience and meticulous undoing. They worked independently, with equal speed.

"Saturday. Let's gather bark from where we take the plants. Here's a saw for you to use."

He'd never used a hand saw before and fumbled with the one Rava had given him. She immediately realized the problem.

"Saturday, give me the saw. I'll show you how we unfold this thing and snap the blade into place."

She held the saw above where a plant had nested and wondered how on earth one could saw bark off a tree. It never crossed her mind that it'd be more difficult than pulling plants from the bark.

She eventually sawed back and forth across the tree trunk, cutting in a downward direction. They took turns cutting bark specimens. Each one approximated eight inches across by four inches down and an inch thick.

"I hope this satisfies Rip," she mumbled to herself.

Devon and Quinn quietly landed with the remaining tents and food coolers. When no one greeted them, they headed toward the already stacked supplies and found Chambo sound asleep in his chair.

"Don't wake him yet," Devon whispered to Quinn. "Let's tie his shoelaces together and go back to Icarus. We'll call him from there."

"Chambo . . . Chambo!" Quinn called with a touch of panic. "Run, there's a bear behind you!"

Chambo looked up, heard Quinn's call, and surged forward before falling unceremoniously on his face, he looked up to see the two pilots laughing.

"I'll get you two for this."

Quinn helped Chambo to his feet.

"Sorry, we couldn't resist. It looks good here. Let's get the rest of the cargo put away and set up the other tents.

"You can supervise. Devon and I will do the work. That should even up the scoresheet for now." Quinn said in a mea culpa moment.

Chambo couldn't help but smile and laugh.

"Not entirely, but it's a good start."

The two canoes slid out from the narrow passageway, back into the far side of Taritatu's loop. Gar scanned the river left and then right.

"Why don't we work our way upriver? That should eventually lead us back to the campsite."

Another passageway came into view to their right and led back into the jungle, parallel to the way they'd come.

"Go there," Rava called as she pointed. "It'll most likely take us back to the Taritatu again."

What seemed like a hundred plants clung to the tangled trees before them.

"Whoa! It's the motherload," Rava proclaimed. "Let's harvest as many as we can manage, and cut lots of bark too."

The native in Gar's canoe wandered off while Gar and the other deckhand harvested plants. He paddled close to Gar twenty minutes later, smiled, and held up a cloth sack.

"Here are snakes for our dinner. No need to fish today."

"Ssh!" Saturday called to the others in a hushed voice.

He pointed toward the Taritatu, which flowed parallel to their narrow passageway approximately fifty yards through the heavy growth.

Two canoes with several natives and foreigners passed from right to left. Gar noted their conversation sounded rough and undisciplined. It looked like four to six passengers in each canoe . . . maybe ten . . . and they looked Asian.

Gar signaled for the others to continue harvesting plants and bark once they'd passed.

"We'll continue for another hour before heading back to camp," he half-whispered.

Devon and Quinn donned hats with mosquito netting similar to the one Chambo wore. Horseflies remained in the air, but without easy targets, found alternative areas to occupy. Killing the little monsters became nearly impossible once they stopped attacking the three of them.

Their focus shifted and they voted on whether specific jungle sounds originated from birds or insects. They couldn't agree on an answer to everyone's satisfaction without an authoritative judge. Differences of opinion devolved into elaborate explanations of why a bird's vocal cords or an insect's leg rubbing generated a specific sound.

"Let's bet on the exact time someone feels today's first raindrop," Quinn suggested to Devon.

"Not just someone," Chambo added. I"t has to be a particular person. Someone not making the bet."

"Yeah, that makes sense," conceded Devon. "Let's ask Rava to tell us when she feels the first raindrop. The time will be when she tells us, not necessarily when she feels the raindrop."

"One more thing," added Chambo. "Let's say the winner gets credit for killing twenty flies. That way we can keep the fly bet alive."

The first canoe appeared from the grassy pathway. Two natives, the med-tech, and the deckhand carried it. Gar and Rava followed, toting ten-gallon plastic jugs filled with swamp water. After depositing the first canoe, the small group immediately disappeared down the path to retrieve the second one.

Gar headed toward Chambo, who sat under the tarp.

"We'll move to the next site tomorrow morning. Let's get these canoes attached to Icarus as soon as we remove all the plants and bark.

"The Asians paddled past us while we gathered plants. Maybe they're paddling downriver to Dabra for supplies or maybe they're exploring like us. But my gut feeling is that they're looking for us. Whatever they're doing, it's not a good sign. We'd be wise to remain out of sight."

Rava joined them, a look of satisfaction on her face.

"We did well today. I think we can move to our next location anytime."

"You must have read my mind," Gar added.

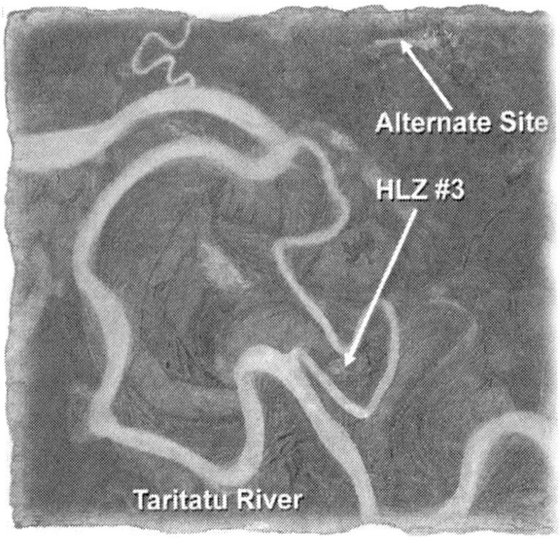

Taritatu encampment plan

Chambo as usual, wanted everything organized well in advance.

"Devon, Quinn, drag your butts over here so we can plan tomorrow's move."

He spread his area chart across a food cooler and pointed to a small open area with 'HLZ #3' penciled next to it.

"This is forty-two nautical miles from here and it's where we'll set up our next camp."

"It's exposed on both sides to that winding tributary," Quinn advised. "I suppose it's a suitable location for launching the canoes, but if the Asians come cruising along that shortcut, they'll definitely see Icarus and probably the tents."

"What's this clearing to the north?" Devon asked.

Chambo looked more closely and could see they had a problem.

"Hold on a few minutes … Gar! Can you come here for a minute?"

The section of the Taritatu under discussion flowed in the shape of a large 'C' with a smaller tributary winding from one end of the letter to the other. Travelers not familiar with the shortcut would naturally miss Gar's planned encampment. Experienced river travelers, however, would likely follow the tributary and notice them.

"We'll have to be flexible," Gar suggested. "Let's land along the tributary and take a look. We can at least detach the canoes and cover them with the ghillie nets. From there, we'll hop over to the alternate site in stealth mode. Let's evaluate it thoroughly before finalizing a course of action.

"Heck, maybe we can camp at one site and shuttle to the other for access to the canoes. We'll have to wait and see."

Gar's satellite phone beeped. A message from Mac. . .

Request pickup tomorrow morning at Elelim. Drop-off at Hulu Atas.
Regards, Mac

"Chambo, we should talk," Gar said. "We need to move Mac and his team tomorrow morning. I wonder if we could move most of our stuff on the first shuttle, get Mac moved, and after that return here to get the canoes.

"Scratch that. It's too complicated."

"Why don't we have Devon depart before dawn to get Mac," Chambo suggested. "Once he drops the team at Hulu Atas, he can come here and start the shuttles to our new site.

"If you like, I can go along to cover any maintenance issues."

"Yes," said Gar, "much better plan. Power management will be critical and we may need to plan for downtime along the way to recharge. I'd like you to go along. Not so much for maintenance issues, but to update Mac on our plans and to get any information that he's willing to share about his mission."

Rip paced about his floating lab, worried about Rava. She possessed a vastly more adventurous spirit while he flourished in the conservative world of academia. She'd always been feisty, full of life, and ready to tackle impossible challenges. She felt more at home in the jungles while he identified more closely with a well-equipped, and safe, laboratory. His thoughts shifted to her plants and the potion, and he started a one-sided conversation with himself.

"This potion definitely has positive curing powers. It strengthens the immune system with more flexible antigen antibodies and it seems to always create robust antibody-producing memory cells. This plant is really amazing.

"Wish I could say the same about my neurological cell development. Devon's and Quinn's last perception tests amounted to little more than an anomaly, and unfortunately, not a quantifiable progress."

Rip heated water in a glass beaker, poured it into his coffee mug, and added a green tea bag.

"First, I'll take a little break, and then start looking at the tannin levels."

TWENTY-FIVE

DEVON AND CHAMBO STOOD SIDE BY SIDE in the darkness, each with a coffee mug in hand. The cool, still air mass refreshed their campsite after having replaced the daytime heat and humidity. Rich jungle smells added an earthy flavor. Random insects chirped a chorus of wake-up greetings while others happily squeaked on moist grass reeds.

Chambo drank a last sip before emptying what coffee remained onto the ground.

"What do ya think? Shall we start toward Elelim?"

"It's time," Devon responded. "Besides, this should be an interesting little hop over the mountains. I'll bet you two-to-one there are clouds along that ridge heading into the airport."

Icarus came to life, idled at minimum power while the instruments stabilized, and lifted into the night before disappearing over the trees. Devon followed a narrow tributary heading south toward the mountains, and after five miles, started climbing to four thousand feet. The straight-line distance to Elelim stretched only twenty miles, so events came quickly.

The jungle remained dark and featureless beneath them. Mountains existed more like shadows than majestic karsts stretching to the skies.

"You got it right," Chambo commented as they leveled off. "Looks like we're gonna drive through a few 'puffies' over the ridge."

"Yep," answered Devon. "You might want to hold on to something for the next couple of miles. It could get bumpy."

No sooner had Devon suggested the possibility of turbulence than Icarus jolted up, then down. He started a bumpy descent that continued until the clouds spit them down into more stable air. The approach transitioned to a slow, steady descent to where they'd deposited Mac and his team a week earlier.

Mac had paid a small premium to the shop owner from whom he'd rented their motorcycles so that he and his team could return them to a parking lot closer to Elelim's runway. At 4 a.m. they hiked several hundred yards from the bikes to the airport pickup point.

At precisely 5 a.m. a large shadow settled onto the grass at the side of the runway. Its side door slid open.

"Come aboard," Chambo called out. "Next stop, Hulu Atas."

Devon added power, dipped the nose, and proceeded on a flight path to Hulu Atas that took them around the higher mountains he'd overflown earlier. With luck, they'd remain in clear skies.

Hulu Atas sat mostly east of Elelim. At the halfway point, Devon turned northeast across a series of two-thousand-foot-high ridges before descending toward the riverside grass strip.

Chambo leaned close to Mac. "We're moving to a new exploration site further down the Taritatu later today. Gar labeled it HLZ #3 on your map."

"That's good. It helps to know where you'll be, especially if we need help."

Mac pulled a small chart from his pocket and looked to confirm Icarus's projected location.

"We think those from the lab at Hulu Atas are in canoes close to our current location," Chambo added. "We saw them on the river yesterday morning."

"Interesting," whispered Mac. "That's good to know. It might change our timing if we don't have to contend with them at Hulu Atas. I'll update Gar should that be the case."

"Is there anything you can tell me about the Asians you left at Elelim?" Chambo asked.

"They won't bother anyone anymore," Mac answered. "That group, every last one of them, is pushing up daisies fifteen miles outside of Elelim. They won't be found, ever.

"Their laboratory, if you could call it that, has been completely emptied. I mean, we sandblasted paint off the walls. We leased a bulldozer, dug a large pit, and dumped the furniture, equipment, papers, and chemicals into it. The secure windows and doors also found their way to the pit. We burned everything and buried the remains."

"Do you think anyone will notice that they're gone?" Chambo asked.

"I'm sure someone will be curious," Mac answered. "That's why we made it look like a coconut warehouse inside. It now looks like the Asians processed coconut pulp into a deep hydration hair solution. We left a pile of paperwork to that effect, some basic tools, and so forth. They'll soon be forgotten.

"More interesting will be the reaction of their superiors. We've left a handwritten note in Mandarin that suggests they all contracted flu-like symptoms. That's the only clue, which should make their disappearance more of a mystery in the eyes of their superiors."

Morning fog hung above Taritatu's slow-moving current as Icarus approached Hulu Atas.

"Would you like me to overfly the area before landing?" Devon asked Mac. "If nothing else, it'll give you a look at where the main facilities are located."

Mac considered the idea for a moment. "Let's make a single pass along the runway. That should be enough."

Devon engaged stealth mode and hover-taxied a hundred feet above the runway's length. It appeared to be abandoned and quiet. He reversed course after crossing the Taritatu River and spoke into his mic. "Fly approach."

Mac and his team appeared out of nowhere once Icarus invisibly touched down and moved to the side of the runway where they once again disappeared into the jungle.

"See you guys later."

Devon added power and departed westward along the river.

He marveled at Papua's epic beauty as dawn brightened into morning and scattered raindrops gave way to sunshine. This section of the Taritatu transited rolling terrain with little sign of life. A single dirt road roughly shadowed the winding river. It alone held the secret of recent human activity.

Devon's mind flashed with questions like, "Who could have carved this roadway out of the jungle? Who maintains it after rain washes out sections along exposed ridges? I wonder if anything bigger than a motorcycle can use it?"

He looked left into the mountains and reminded himself of how different this country could be. Lowland swamps stretched for as far as he could see to his right. A canopy of ancient coniferous palms hid the jungle undergrowth and its multitude of distinct inhabitants.

"Can you believe all these trees?" he said to Chambo. "They go on forever."

Chambo recalled his earlier research and felt the need to share it with Devon.

"There are a thousand varieties of trees here, and tens of thousands of different vascular plants. It really is amazing. But I suppose that's why this is a place where explorers like us find previously unknown medicines.

"Rava once told me she spotted quite a few araucarias, which are the tallest tropical trees in the world. She also explained that because the topsoil is so thin here in the jungle, most of those tall trees have buttress roots to firmly anchor themselves to the ground. It makes me think twice every time I see them.

"Anyway, Papua's tropical jungle is as magnificent as it is primitive."

Gar greeted Devon and Chambo when Icarus touched down several miles east of Hulu Atas.

"Welcome back. We've got a little bit of organizing to do, but should be ready to go within the hour."

"That'll work perfectly," Devon replied. "I'd like to run the LPs while we're on the ground. The batteries could use a little more juice."

The flight to HLZ #3 crossed forty miles of flat swampy lowlands that stretched to the horizon. Clouds capped the rising mountains to their left. Chambo held the grandeur of Papua in his thoughts.

"This is a strange land," he confided to Gar. "Those mountains rise to almost six thousand feet before descending into the central highlands. The mountains abruptly climb to fifteen thousand feet beyond that high valley. I think there's a point near the Grasberg mine that's over sixteen thousand."

"We're lucky to be searching down here in the lowlands," Gar responded, "at least from a logistical perspective. Could you imagine fighting the weather every day? The higher altitudes would limit Icarus. Heck, the highland temperatures would dip below freezing and require us to carry cold-weather gear.

"Look at this river. It's the squiggliest mess I've ever seen, as though Mother Nature forbade straight lines. That road down there is equally amazing. How did surveyors determine in which direction to forge their way through the swamps?"

"That looks like our destination ahead," Chambo said while pointing to the 'C' shape in the river.

Devon commanded, "Fly Approach" through his mic and Icarus flew a perfect straight-in approach to the planned opening. The area consisted of dry ground under knee-high grass. The morning sky had heated everything more than expected. Fortunately, nearby trees temporarily blocked the sun's warming rays. Yet even with the shade, the air would likely become uncomfortably hot well before noon.

Gar and Saturday walked from one end of the opening to the other.

"Do you think it'll get too hot here?" Gar asked. "It's so open."

"Yes. Very hot, but close to the water."

"Let's leave the canoes here, for now, Gar replied. "I'd like to see the alternate site."

The advance team boarded Icarus for the ten-minute hop after having detached the two canoes. Devon engaged stealth mode and lifted Icarus into the air.

The jungle gave way to an open stretch of land not more than fifty feet across. It appeared isolated and lifeless, with no buildings or huts, and no signs of farming or mining.

Chambo leaned toward Gar. "I've seen areas like this in the Rockies where a lightning strike sparked a small fire. I think the chemistry of the soil changed, or something like that so that vegetation struggled to take root."

"Let's land and take a closer look," Gar suggested.

Devon flew his approach to the largest part of the open area. His intended landing zone consisted of hard-packed soil with more than enough room for Icarus to fit. It sat higher than the narrow portion closer to the river, and its flat surface suited their campsite better.

"Can we walk from here to the river?" Gar asked Saturday. "Maybe we could paddle the canoes close to this site and keep them hidden nearby."

"Good. I will lead us to the river. You decide." Saturday smiled.

Gar gathered Chambo, Devon, and Rava.

"I'm uncomfortable having the canoes so far away from us, especially in this swampy quagmire. Chambo, can you recharge batteries here while we find a path to the river? If we're successful with that, a couple of us can move the canoes.

"Devon, once you drop us at the canoe opening, fetch the rest of the team and bring them here.

"Questions?"

Rip puzzled over the condensed tannins he observed in the sample plants and wondered how they supported positive medicinal effects.

He knew that high levels of tannins usually became more detrimental than curative. It's why his mother added milk to his tea. It caused the tannins to bind with the milk rather than his stomach wall. He concluded that it's the binding nature that must promote neurological growth. He'd need more testing.

He didn't have enough tannin in solution to run meaningful tests.

"I'm just gonna have to wait for Rava to return with the bark," he muttered to himself.

It would soon be time for the hydroponic lighting system to automatically turn on. Rip's wristwatch alarm sounded and he headed down the passageway to verify that it worked properly. It felt crowded in the shared equipment room. Three twenty-foot sections of large-diameter PVC pipe filled the open space. They rested on a framework of welded angle iron and collected overflow water in plastic barrels placed at the end of each row. The barrels served as a mixing pot for added nutrients. Tiny submersible pumps pushed this enriched water to the upper end of the PVC feeding tubes, completing the feeding cycle.

LED light panels hung above each row of plants and brightened the room considerably when they illuminated. The two lone plants at the upper end of each row appeared healthy. Rip carefully examined their roots and noted key mineral levels for each independent row before returning to the lab.

Saturday gazed toward the river for several moments before looking over his shoulder toward Gar and Rava.

"This way."

The other native followed as they started toward the river. A fallen tree trunk provided the only dry footing along a pseudo-pathway that paralleled a narrow flow of water. Balanced footing came naturally to Saturday, but not so much to Gar or Rava. They stepped cautiously with barely enough confidence to maintain Saturday's pace.

The aroma of jungle flora permeated everything.

"This feels so invigorating," mused Gar to himself.

"You know, you're more than a little crazy for being so comfortable in such an inhospitable swamp," Rava jokingly chided him. "Look, an opening."

"Close now," Saturday announced. "We're almost there."

The far side of the opening descended slightly into knee-deep water. Twenty yards into the swamp, trees gave way to the Taritatu River. Gar found a long stick and hung it horizontally across several branches. It would mark the spot where they'd later paddle the canoes into the underbrush.

Devon flew Chambo and Saturday back to HLZ#3 so they could move the canoes forward. He then made a beeline back to those he'd left near Hulu Atas three hours earlier.

No sooner had Devon landed at the previous encampment than Quinn ran up to the quadcopter.

"I've got thirty-five more of those insanely aggressive horseflies."

"That's not fair," Devon protested. "I've been flying all day. So, how'd you do it?"

"You honestly don't deserve an explanation," Quinn countered. "Especially after laughing at me while getting reamed for the battery charging lecture that you watched."

"What if I tell you about Mac and his interesting exploits? I think you'd find them interesting. Consider it an information swap."

Quinn pretended to consider Devon's proposal.

"I felt bored, so I hiked to the river. This dead fish had a swarm of horseflies coming and going so I threw a fine-mesh net over all of them and started swatting.

"I collected what I showed you after only an hour. Not bad when you consider I didn't get attacked by any of them."

TWENTY-SIX

THE ONSET OF TWILIGHT BROUGHT WITH IT A natural inkling to sit around their small campfire and relax. It'd been a busy day of flying, relocating, hiking to and from the river, and setting up their tents. Rava appeared noticeably more energetic than the others, despite having worked as hard as any of them. She unfolded a camp chair and sat down.

"I think we've gathered almost enough plants and bark. The only job left to do is identify more potential harvesting locations."

"That's good news," Gar replied. "I suggest we explore Taritatu where it joins the Mamberamo River. There's an open area nearby that we can use to access Icarus. It'll also be a good spot from which we can return to the ship.

"Of course, we've still got a commitment to move Mac and his boys to at least one more site, but after that, we could very well conclude our mission here."

"I'd like to shuttle the plants and bark we've already gathered back to Tanigue," Quinn added. "That'll reduce our weight on the last flights."

"In that case," Rava interjected, "let's explore the nearby swampy areas tomorrow and include whatever we find on our flight to Tanigue. After that, we can relocate down the river."

Devon turned to Chambo with an on-the-spot suggestion.

"What do you think of this? The conclusion of the horsefly bet will be when we land on Tanigue with everyone else."

"Agreed," said Chambo. Quinn nodded in agreement.

Gar lay awake, regretting having to move on from the current site so quickly. The location turned out to be excellent, away from the river, on high ground, and dry. Best of all, they'd escaped those damned horseflies.

At midnight, the rains began. . .

An untrained observer might reliably predict daily weather patterns affecting Papua's lowlands. There is a wet season from December through April. Most often, the mornings arrive with clear skies and refreshingly cool temperatures. Clouds first appear in mid-morning and build as moisture rises from the jungle floor. Afternoon and early evening rains clear the skies before the cycle repeats itself.

But during this La Niña year, a low-pressure system pushed in from Papua New Guinea.

Rava awoke to the heavy patter of rain and crawled out from her sleeping bag. Rain would complicate things. Time for coffee.

She scooted across the open uncovered space between her tent and the large common-area tarp. The jungle canopy fortunately deflected most of the rain. As she heated water for coffee, she noted streams of accumulated rain cutting tiny channels in the soil as it drained into the jungle marsh. The lowlands would soon become really wet, possibly submerged

Chambo pulled up a folding chair and sat next to her.

"This will be a good day to stay under the tarp and play a long game of pinochle."

"I wonder if the river will flood or if the currents will get dangerous," she mused. "Maybe you're right, we'll have to see.

"Do you think Icarus can fly back to Tanigue today?"

"Well," he considered his answer for a moment, "I suppose we'll have to wait and see how windy and turbulent it gets."

Devon appeared from his tent and yawned as he listened to the others.

"I'm ready to give it a try."

"Why don't you and Quinn load everything that needs to go back to Tanigue?" Chambo suggested. "Take a break after that while Gar and the others complete their search for more plants."

He shifted his focus to Rava. "Do you think you'll explore today?"

"Of course, we'll go looking," huffed Rava. "At least we'll look until we decide the rains are too heavy."

The pathway to the canoes had become a sloshy calf-deep mess. They seemed dangerously close to floating away when Saturday eventually found them. The river had flooded along the shorelines.

"It's not good to move about the jungle now," Saturday advised. "Snakes and other animals have been displaced and are more angry."

Gar looked at Rava. "Let's relax today and try again tomorrow morning."

"Okay, this time I agree," she responded.

The rains and wind persisted. Most human activity along the river paused. Everyone sat under the main tarp, passing the time by telling stories. Gar asked Saturday if he remembered when the Japanese and the Americans fought on his island home of Wakde.

"I remember as a child, my father welcomed the Japanese when they first arrived on the island." Saturday laughed to himself. "He always told me they appeared too serious. He said they irritated our spirits by cutting so many trees.

"The spirits responded by feeding them disease from the mosquitos."

"I think the spirits probably fed them malaria," Gar interjected. "Soldiers throughout the South Pacific had problems with it."

"Yes," Saturday continued. "One night, my father sensed danger from the ocean. I don't think he saw the American and Australian ships but he could feel their presence.

"That night, he brought us to the shore, near Momma Grace's shop. We borrowed a canoe and paddled to the smaller island. He said it would be safer.

"The fighting started the next morning and lasted for almost a week. The Japanese eventually left and the Americans remained. They provided us with their extra food and seemed more relaxed.

"We all rejoiced when everyone left and life returned to normal."

Rava joined the conversation. "I remember being very young, growing up in India. My father told us stories about the war. He'd fought against the Japanese in Burma but never told us much about his personal experiences. India existed under British rule back then and we supported the Allied forces.

"I know that eighty-seven thousand Indian soldiers died during World War Two, more than a few of them in Papua. Over three million civilians met their maker. Those had been difficult times for the entire world. It seems little of it escaped the conflict."

Three days later the winds settled and the rain slackened to a drizzle.

Gar and Rava each directed one of the canoes. The river remained swollen but the current had again returned to normal. By noon they'd located another patch of plants. Cutting bark had become more difficult with the higher water levels, yet Saturday and Rava managed to fill two large bags.

"Let's finish up here and head back to camp," Gar called. "I'd like to add what we've harvested this morning to Icarus' load and get it headed toward Tanigue."

Gar sat next to Chambo under the tarp as the others finished preparing Icarus for its flight.

"I received a message from Mac. He somehow made his way to a riverside community called Pagai and wants us to retrieve his team from there tomorrow, if possible. It's located downriver from Hulu Atas but before our old horsefly-infested encampment.

"I think they wanted to catch up with the Asians we'd seen back there.

"Once you find them, take 'em to Kwerba and set up camp in the opening we identified near where the Taritatu merges with the Mamberamo River.

"We'll pack up our gear and start heading that way in the canoes. I'd like to stop at Dabra along the way and get an update on the river. It'll likely take us a week to complete the trip and if we need help, we'll call you on the satellite phone."

Chambo mentally tallied the logistics of the move.

"Let's be sure we've got everything that you're not taking loaded on Icarus. Devon, Quinn, and I will start toward Tanigue later today and spend the night onboard the ship. First thing tomorrow, we'll fetch Mac and his boys.

"Hopefully, we'll have this one wrapped up in another week."

Loading the canoes with their tents and other supplies proved to be more of a chore than first expected. Gar and Saturday stood in chest-high water beside the canoes.

"Saturday, the water here is too deep. Do you think we can safely pull them farther into the jungle before loading our gear into them?"

"Better," Saturday said with a nod.

They pushed through the brush until reaching the Taritatu. Rava realized that exploring would be increasingly difficult in high waters. The water flowing into the river generated strong crossing currents. She'd try to relax and enjoy the scenery for a change.

The river twisted much less than earlier and the channel widened. It provided an isolated thoroughfare that gently pulled them toward the southern mountains.

From Gar's perspective, the area appeared mostly flat, with open swamps giving way to the jungle canopy. They could easily have lost their way if the main channel hadn't been so wide. It now wandered into less obvious channels that had rerouted over time.

Another canoe filled with natives passed them heading in the opposite direction.

"Where are they going?" Rava asked Saturday. "It's so isolated behind us."

"I think maybe another small village. Maybe to a trail that leads into the jungle. Natives live deep inside the trees. Sometimes they come to the big village for shopping. Sometimes just to see."

Dabra filled an elevated clearing with steep-sloped mountain ridges on three sides, the tops of which remained shrouded in clouds. A variety of simple houses and small businesses surrounded an asphalt runway that accommodated several flights each week. Dabra sustained a meager economy and served as a launch point for palm oil farmers and struggling miners who operated farther into the surrounding jungles.

Gar, Rava, and Saturday walked from Dabra's shoreline into the village.

Devon and Chambo made one last sweep of the encampment area, looking for anything they might have overlooked. Quinn strapped himself into Icarus' pilot seat and started flipping switches.

Chambo took a last moment to scatter the firepit ashes before climbing aboard. Icarus lifted and slowly accelerated to the north.

The first significant point along their flight path, the village of Kwerba, came into view. Quinn looked for its runway to get a sense of how best to fly an approach to it. The sleepy village occupied a distinctive bend along the Mamberamo River and the runway started at its shoreline. Immediately north of Kwerba, rising terrain squeezed the river between sheer cliffs. White spray and frothing currents churned its flow for the next ten miles.

"There's Tanigue," Quinn announced an hour later. "We'll be on deck in ten minutes." He thought about sleeping in a bed once again and eating proper food.

Rip seemed anxious to find out what samples they'd delivered on Icarus. He met them at the landing pad.

"Did Rava send the bark? I'm convinced it's the key to improving your rock-bottom perception skills."

"Has anyone ever told you that you're a pain in the ass?" Quinn jokingly replied. "I mean, so self-absorbed. Aren't you interested in how Devon and I are doing? How our flight went? Just our perception training? And what about your sister? Remember her?"

"Okay, okay." Rip raised his hands in a sign of surrender. "I suppose you're right. How many plants did you bring back?"

Icarus lifted off Tanigue an hour before dawn and began the flight south toward Pagai.

Rip's phone sounded. His missionary friend, with whom he and Rava had spent a night after their escape from Jayapura, spoke from the other end.

"Rip, it took quite a while for me to find you. I've got an update on a group of Asians who leased a flight. Are you still interested?"

"Yes, absolutely," Rip replied. His hand began sweating as he talked. An empty feeling gripped his stomach.

"I'm sorry this is such short notice, but six Asians will fly to Dabra this morning. I don't have an exact arrival time, but my guess would be somewhere between 9 a.m. and 10 a.m. I'm afraid that's all I've got to pass along. Hopefully, it's of help."

"Yes," Rip half answered, "thank you. I've got to pass this information right away. Thanks."

He started toward the ship's bridge. Marlo needed to hear this and pass it to Gar. He hoped there'd be enough time.

At 9:30 a.m. Gar's phone beeped. Marlo passed the flight information.

"Let's go," Gar said with a sense of urgency. "We need to get the canoes headed downriver.

Saturday nodded and moved toward the canoe until Rava protested.

"Not so quick. I've got more to see and I'm sure Saturday could gather more information."

"Now," Gar shot back in a firm tone. "We've got an issue. A flight of Asians is about to land and we need to be gone when they do."

Saturday and the native pushed the canoes into the current. The others donned straw hats. Gar wrapped a patterned cloth around his shoulders.

A Cessna Grand Caravan flew low over the river and landed on Dabra's runway as they grabbed the oars.

"Did you hear of any Asians already staying in Dabra?" Gar asked Saturday.

"No boss. No one stays, but they have a house downriver in Kwerba." Saturday knew they would head toward potential trouble, but showed no emotion.

Gar subconsciously sensed himself being squeezed into a corner. It'll feel good to finish exploring this section of the river and get out of here.

TWENTY-SEVEN

PAGAI VILLAGE CONSISTED OF TWENTY-TWO rickety wooden houses that lined the sides of its grass airstrip. Villagers constructed them closer to the river rather than inland, providing easier access to the canoes and their associated commerce. It left the far end of the strip vastly more isolated. Two rusty warehouses that contained equipment for digging gemstones out of nearby mines stood in contrast to the much smaller structures surrounding it. Human movement along the airstrip occurred sparingly throughout the day and rarely during the early morning. Residents seldom ventured outside their homes before noon.

Most of the natives tilled the small gardens they'd cleared from the ever-encroaching jungle. Those involved with the mines spent much of their working hours keeping records of daily production, scheduling inbound supply shipments, and processing outbound movement of crude gemstones to Jayapura. Working hours routinely consisted of one hour in the morning and another later in the day. Local gossip and random storytelling filled the remainder of their time.

Mac's arrival would have been a heralded event had he not come ashore during an evening downpour. He and his team found refuge under the house nearest to where they'd beached their canoes. Mac had given up hope of catching the Asians who'd left Hulu Atas well ahead of them. He'd deal with them later.

The house owner provided them shelter in the space between the ground and the structure's raised floor. Like most other houses, this one perched four feet high on concrete posts. The design offered better airflow and kept the inside temperatures lower. It also allowed Mac and his team to quietly depart in the middle of the night without being noticed by others.

They left shortly after midnight. The grass remained wet but provided firm footing until they reached the section of the grass strip beyond the buildings. Mac noticed the grassy surface suddenly replaced by large sections of exposed soil. The rains had turned the area into a slick, muddy consistency that Mac considered excessively mushy for normal aircraft operations. He led the team to the side, closer to the jungle.

"This looks better. At least it's not muddy. Try not to think about the two inches of standing water."

A slight rise beyond the end of the runway provided dry ground for them to sit on while they waited. Mosquitos, rather than the dampness, became their primary irritation.

Devon entertained himself during the relatively boring night flight by quizzing Chambo and Quinn on Icarus' virtual reality system.

"How is the terrain database updated?" He asked. "How often? Where is it physically stored on the aircraft?"

Quinn followed Devon's questions with a series of his own.

"How does an icon . . . say, the landing zone icon, interface with the terrain data? Where does the associated math exist? What exactly activates the programming?"

They'd exhausted their mental question bank when Chambo caught them off guard with a question of broader scope.

"What improvements will make the system more functional?"

They overflew Pagai in the dark of night before Devon began a turning descent for landing. Moments later, Mac and his team climbed into the back. Icarus lifted back into the air, turned to the northwest, and started the one-hour flight to Kwerba. They remained on schedule to land well before sunrise.

"We didn't expect you to have traveled all the way to Pagai," Gar said to Mac. "Hope your visit to Hulu Atas met with success."

A hint of a smile appeared on Mac's face.

"The Hulu Atas operation felt a lot like the Elelim laboratory elimination. We relieved two guards of their earthly responsibilities and I honestly don't think they'll be missed.

"We located a dormitory-type building where everyone stayed. I think they've cleared out and are now moving elsewhere. We took the liberty of burning that place to the ground.

"The lab presented more of a challenge because we couldn't find a bulldozer to bury everything. We ended up moving all the furniture and other equipment to the dorm before we torched it. What a sight to behold. I mean, it burned hot."

"Do you think the locals will notice them being gone?" Chambo asked. "Do you think they knew what the Asians did?"

"Well, they'd already left so that sort of solved most of it. The locals already suspected them of infecting villagers with one of their diseases. They're more than a little happy having rid themselves of that human pestilence.

"We did another cleansing of the laboratory and seeded it with more coconut husks. Within a month someone else will occupy the building and put it to another use. Its past will fade into the present."

"What about the Asians?" Chambo asked.

"At first I thought we might find them on the river. That would've been a reach even under the best of circumstances. The rains changed everything and we found ourselves lucky to stay afloat long enough to reach Pagai. It's amazing how quickly the currents pick up and how dangerous they can feel. I thought we'd have to paddle into the mangroves and sit out the storm in the canoes, but our natives insisted we could make it to Pagai. Guess they had experience.

"I think the Asians are headed for Dabra. We'll come back for them after we address the Kwerba situation."

The darkness of night would keep Icarus hidden from curious eyes, but Devon felt it wise to engage the stealth mode for added invisibility. He verbally activated it as they flew low over the Mamberamo River approaching Kwerba. As a more routine matter, he'd activated the noise reduction system shortly after departing Tanigue and had never disabled it. Once he engaged quiet mode there would be no added electrical penalty to keep it engaged. He planned to land at the river's edge and quickly discharge Mac and his team.

Several local fishermen slept in their canoes when Icarus arrived. Something out of the ordinary stirred one of them. A sudden swirl of wind passed overhead and just as suddenly went calm. He sat up and looked out at the river. Nothing moved. He turned and looked back toward the airport. A series of shadows appeared out of nowhere before moving toward the trees and disappearing.

An icy chill gripped his heart. Something moved the air, but what? Another swirl of wind from above. He looked up. Again, nothing. An uneasy feeling filled his veins.

He pushed his canoe into the river later that morning and paddled against a slow-moving current toward the next village. A sense of relief soothed his mind once alone and around the first river bend.

HLZ Rivers awaited eleven miles to the south. Its entire clearing remained hidden from passing river traffic behind a strip of heavy jungle growth. Devon landed Icarus at the far side of the opening and hoped the added separation would provide even greater concealment.

Chambo joined the two pilots after Icarus had been secured under lightweight ghillie netting.

"Okay boys, let's get our tents set up and gather wood for tonight's fire. Do you think we can catch a stringer of fish?"

"I think we'll have more than enough time to try," answered Quinn. "We've finally got time to ourselves. Let's make sure it doesn't become boring."

"What are we gonna do on our next flight?" Devon asked.

"Well, if … if Mac completes his work at Kwerba quickly, we'll probably pick up his team and deliver them somewhere else.

"On the other hand, once Gar and Rava show up, we'll prioritize getting them back to Tanigue. We'll have to wait and see."

"In either case," Quinn added, "Icarus should be fully charged by tomorrow morning. Let's see if we can catch a fish or two for dinner."

The last forty to fifty miles of the Taritatu snaked back and forth so much that the canoes seemed to be in a constant turn. Around every river bend, another twist came into view.

A mountain tributary fed into the main channel several miles north of Dabra. Wide stretches of mangroves had taken root to either side. Rava noticed it immediately.

"Why don't we poke our noses in there and see what plants we can find."

Saturday turned their canoe and they glided into the brush. Gar followed twenty yards farther downriver. They'd pushed and pulled their way almost two hundred yards into the tangled trees when Rava excitedly pointed to an unusual plant near her canoe.

"Wow, look at that. I've never seen this species before. I have to harvest one or two of them. Who knows, it might be a swing and a miss, but it's a rare opportunity we shouldn't pass up."

Wu climbed down from the Cessna Grand Caravan ahead of the five others with him. Dabra seemed smaller and more remote than he'd imagined. He and the others grabbed their backpacks and started walking away from the aircraft.

"Which way to the river?" Wu asked one of the baggage handlers.

The native smiled to himself. Three sides of the airport hugged high mountains, leaving only one direction for the river. He pointed in that general direction and continued sorting the remaining baggage.

"This way," ordered Wu. He proceeded off the tiny tarmac onto a dirt road that headed in the direction the native had indicated. A block later the small group approached what appeared to be a coffee shop.

"Wait here," he said as he held out an open palm to reinforce his words. Wu continued alone into the shop.

"Coffee," he called in a mildly demanding tone. He took a seat at one of the two small tables.

"Have you recently seen any foreigners traveling downriver?" he asked when the coffee arrived.

"We often have foreigners pass through," the girl responded. "Most of them head to the jungle for work."

"No. Not them," Wu snapped. "I want to know about foreigners who are looking for plants. Not tourists, and not workers."

"I don't know of any," she finally said.

Wu paid for the coffee and left.

He asked the same questions of the canoe owners at the river's edge. Again, nothing.

"Wait," one of them said. "Not long ago, two canoes passed from upriver. They stopped here for only a few minutes before continuing."

"You, and you," Wu demanded. "I need you to take us to Kwerba. We'll leave immediately."

Neither fisherman cared for Wu's tone. Plus, they had families in Dabra to consider. Leaving on such a long journey would be fine, but not so quickly.

"We have family matters," The first fisherman responded. "They need food before we depart and I need to buy food for the trip."

"Okay, but hurry," Wu countered. I'll pay you when we arrive. Not before."

"Just a little," the fisherman begged. "I need something to buy the food."

The fishermen returned to their canoes late in the afternoon. Wu had become impatient.

"It's about time you returned," he snarled. "If you don't speed up, I'll take your canoes and we'll paddle them ourselves."

"We're so sorry, but the food store ran out of stock and we had to find another store almost in the mountains to get what we needed.

"The best time to travel is early in the day. Now, the rain comes. We won't get far before we have to find a place to spend the night. It's better to wait until morning."

"What do you mean!" he shouted. "We'll leave now."

They reluctantly moved their gear into the canoes and prepared to launch into the river when heavy rains began.

The second native turned to his passengers.

"It's dangerous along the river at night if we don't have a good site for sleeping."

"We won't get far tonight and won't have a safe place to sleep," one of the Asians called to Wu in the other canoe. "Do you think it would be to our advantage to remain here tonight, where we can get one last good meal and a night of restful sleep? If we start down the river at daybreak, we'll quickly make up whatever time we lose today."

Wu had always been impulsive, and with the taste of blood in his mouth, he hesitated to delay. He knew the river trek would drain their energy. He also understood that as much as he mentally resisted any delay, spending the night made more sense than rushing into the dangers of the river at night.

"We'll wait until dawn," he said with a hint of resignation.

Rip's laboratory smelled awful. Several small vats of alcohol boiled the bark's tannin into solution. He'd decant the concoction in another hour.

He examined the batch that had been processed yesterday under his microscope and found it to encourage a variety of tissue growths. The results remained very preliminary but looked promising. Unfortunately, he couldn't find enough time in the day to get everything done as fast as he'd like.

"If only I had a staff of ten helpers," he mumbled to himself, "I could get all those plants separated and into individual growing pots in the hydroponic garden . . . Rava will be proud of me when she sees it.

"What I need to do is set up a series of Rava's potions with varying amounts of tannin. I'm pretty sure we can optimize the potency of her anti-viral solutions."

TWENTY-EIGHT

RAVA KNEW HER OPPORTUNITY TO FIND MORE miracle plants neared its end. She'd in all likelihood have to make do with the specimens she'd already gathered and perhaps a few more.

"Let's push into that swampy area. It looks promising. Just this one more time." Progress slowed.

"I think we will sleep in the canoes tonight," Saturday called across to Gar from his canoe. No good landing areas along this section."

"In that case," Rava added, "we can look until the sun goes down."

Her request made good sense, but evening raindrops began splattering around them as if to announce that further exploration would come with a cost.

Gar wiped a drop from his forehead.

"I think it better to find an area free from the current and secure our canoes for the night. Besides, I'm interested in seeing Chambo's innovative setup for sleeping in them."

Chambo had explained his sketches to the Thai canoe fabricator, thinking at the time that he'd eventually suffer the consequences of whatever he designed.

Segmented mylar panels sat within the side walls and could be arched from one gunwale to the other. They shielded the occupants from rain, mosquitos, or any number of other annoyances when completely secured. The enclosure left Rava feeling slightly claustrophobic, like being inside a hotdog.

Foam pads lined one side of the canoe and could be pulled loose and repositioned along the centerline. This arrangement provided a firm, comfortable sleeping cushion.

Chambo's most interesting option, however, involved connecting the mylar panels from one canoe to a corresponding panel on a second canoe. Connected coverings provided a single arched top cover when Gar aligned the canoes side-by-side. Clamping the vessels together along the gunwales kept them from drifting apart during the night.

Gar and the med-tech configured the two canoes exactly as Chambo had envisioned. Rava sat across from Gar, impressed with her cozy accommodations.

"I hope you don't snore too loudly," she casually remarked. "I'm hoping to get an uninterrupted night's sleep."

"I've never awakened because of my snoring. Does that count? Better to think positive thoughts like drinking hot coffee over a crackling fire."

The rain intensified . . .

Everyone embraced the dry environment despite its closeness. Gar set up a compact camping burner and started heating water for coffee. The med-tech and the deck hand each set up identical burners. One pulled a small pot from his backpack and the other a frying pan. They waited patiently to ignite the burners once Saturday and the other native seasoned the fish they'd soon grill.

Several battery-powered lights that Gar had clipped onto the mylar framing illuminated the interior with a dim glow.

"Now, doesn't this feel cozy?" Rava mused. "Who'd have imagined we'd be camping in such luxury right here in the middle of nowhere?"

The river had turned angry at times during the past week. Its current quickly became treacherous when heavy rains increased Taritatu's volume. But its anger often faded as quickly as it flared. It defined the nature of the Taritatu. Today's slow current lulled everyone into a carefree state of mind. Each bend in the river led to another and another.

"That little inlet over there," Saturday pointed toward an opening along the riverbank, "has a path. We can walk along it to search farther into the jungle."

"Let's go," Rava enthusiastically responded.

Gar wondered how Saturday knew there'd be a path. He had an uncanny sense of his world.

"Let's pull the canoes out of sight."

He looked to the deckhand. "I'd like you to remain here and keep an eye on the river."

The path that Saturday followed consisted of little more than an opening through the brush and trees. Gar wondered if natives used this path, or if it remained the passageway of wild pigs headed to the river.

His answer came when the path dipped into a swampy low-lying area and he noticed bamboo sticks laid across it. It validated his suspicion that natives frequented the area.

"There," Saturday pointed. "An opening and hopefully more plants."

Rava smiled to herself for suggesting Saturday accompany them.

"Brilliant. Saturday, how do you know of such areas?"

"I know," responded Saturday. "Farmers use trails like this to find their sago trees which always grow in swampy areas."

"Look," exclaimed Rava. "Those are strange plants I've never seen before. Let's harvest a couple of them."

Saturday raised his hand after an hour of exploring the path.

"Stop. We've gone far enough."

"No, we can explore this area longer," Rava countered.

"Look there," Saturday pointed. "Crocodiles. I think better to go back."

Several prehistoric-looking creatures lay perfectly still, basking in the sun. The others quickly agreed and retreated toward the canoes.

"Seen anything unusual?" Gar asked the deckhand when they reached the river.

"Only two canoes paddling up the river toward Dabra," he responded. "They used the far side away from the current so I couldn't see them clearly. They looked like a mix of Papuan men and women transporting bundles of sago starch.

"Other than those two canoes and a group of monkeys playing in the nearby trees, it's been really quiet."

Gar's canoe approached a split in the channel along a section of the river lined more by swamp grass than trees.

"Which way?" he asked.

"We go to the right first," answered Saturday. "Maybe right way, maybe not. We'll know soon."

Gar led the team along a meandering waterway until its depth became too shallow.

"Wrong way. We go back," Saturday announced.

Twilight slowly yielded to night as they neared the main river channel.

"Let's secure the canoes here, off the river," Gar announced. "We'll get an early start in the morning when we can see more clearly which way we're going."

Rava helped Gar connect the canoes and secure the coverings in place.

"You know, you snored rather loudly last night. I worried that you might attract wild animals."

"Oh my," Gar laughed. "That's not good. Can you imagine having one of those giant monitor lizards snooping around?"

"Very funny," she responded. "Let's have a cup of fresh coffee and you can tell me more about how you started your business in Asia."

The heat of the day peaked hours earlier. It hung in the air as it gathered moisture and encouraged the ever-present flies to forage for human food. The Hulu Atas group of

Asians paddled their two heavy wooden canoes with weary arms. At long last, they approached Dabra.

Their journey had lasted nearly two weeks and although they'd paddled with the current, the effort exhausted them. The first two days started with a relaxed sense of adventure. Blisters inevitably formed on their hands and triggered a stinging pain each time they paddled deep through the water. Discomfort and speed formed an inverse relationship, and not surprisingly, their speed slowed considerably.

Most of them wrapped their hands in cloth strips torn from their shirts. They became slaves to the current and contributed little more than steering their canoes along the river. Scant enthusiasm remained for paddling. Most of them laid their paddles inside the canoe and resorted to staring aimlessly at the river banks.

Time passed with embellished tales of jungle experiences. One of the Asians recalled a particularly difficult trek into the jungle and shared his recollection of the natives and the wild animals that he'd encountered along the way.

"Have you ever seen one of those large jungle lizards?" one of them asked. "I walked deep into the jungles a month ago when I came upon an open area. There, on the path ahead of me, sat a three-foot-long lizard … ugly with beautiful colors, a tongue that nearly reached my face. He didn't flinch, but I knew he watched my every move from behind his slit-green eyes.

"I picked up a rock and threw it at him. That seemed to be a mistake. He rose on his legs and a circular shield expanded around his head. I saw teeth and waited for his attack.

"He somehow decided not to charge me. He held his ground."

"What did you do?" another Asian asked. "You know those ugly creatures are poisonous."

"I froze for almost five minutes," he answered. "Eventually, I stepped sideways into the jungle, never taking my eyes off that slimy devil. I could see his round shield retract. I kept going the other way and eventually found my way back to the path."

Another Asian added his experience.

"Remember last year when we headed into the lowlands on the far side of the Taritatu? We almost walked into a four-foot-long monitor lizard. I saw three of them.

"It felt chilling. No, terrifying. They have long red split tongues and if they'd been hungry, I think they'd have eaten us. We turned and ran."

The heavy rains caught them unprepared and pushed their canoes into the brush along the river's edge. They pulled further into the trees and secured themselves rather than push back into the current.

Rain-soaked them for two days. They bailed water from the canoes and tried to sleep. Backpacks and supply packages pulled over their heads blocked very little of the incessant rain. They found themselves without dry kindling to start a fire and resorted to eating cold rice and leftover fish. Storytelling faded to silence, replaced by a misery that chilled their bones.

Dabra existed in their minds like a place akin to heaven. When the village came into view along the Taritatu, it appeared much smaller than they'd imagined but it represented warm food and a decent bed. An anticipated return to normalcy filled their being.

They found refuge and slept under one of the local houses on their first night. The ground remained dry despite the rain and it felt much softer than the canoes. A small fire flickered for most of the night, the smoke a welcome mosquito repellent. One Asian brewed what tea remained while another cooked fresh fish he'd purchased along the river.

They'd find a building for their new laboratory in the morning.

Farther down the river, Wu and his small party pursued Rava and Gar much more slowly than Wu wanted.

"Paddle faster," he demanded.

The natives smiled to themselves while making an empty effort to paddle harder. They felt insulted and disrespected by Wu and his associates. If he wanted to go fast, they'd go slow. If he wanted to sightsee, they'd hurry up a bit.

The natives purposely paddled into false tributaries on several occasions. Each diversion humored them while offering an opportunity to venture along sections of the river they hadn't already investigated.

"There." The native pointed toward something in the brush. "It's a good-sized lizard we can kill and eat tonight. Be patient while we get it."

Wu's impatience with the natives resulted in noticeably slower progress than would have otherwise been possible. The natives stopped earlier than necessary each night, saying they needed to fashion a campsite before losing sunlight.

The natives cleaned the lizards they'd killed and wrapped them in banana leaves before burying them under the fire's coals. They heated flattened pancake-like slabs of sago and set aside hot water for tea. The Asians appeared angry and upset while the natives joked in their native tongue. One's yin balanced the other's yang.

The slow pace prevented Wu from closing the gap between his team and Rava.

That would change …

Saturday twisted his head back toward Rava.

"The other river joins us soon. Be careful of the current."

Gar thought he'd identified their destination.

"Let's turn toward the near shoreline and find a place to beach the canoes. Our encampment is close."

They coasted into the overhanging tree branches and found themselves against higher ground.

"Perfect. Let's see if we can find those darned pilots."

A short way into the jungle, trees gave way to a large opening. Gar immediately recognized Icarus under its ghillie nets.

"Chambo, are you over there?"

"Over here," came the response.

The three of them nestled around their fire with several large fish cooking on the grill.

"We've got several more fish we can cook," Chambo called back. "But I'm afraid you'll have to eat them with rehydrated vegetables."

Rava arrived at the fire pit and threw a large iguana toward Chambo. Saturday had caught and killed it earlier.

"Here, add this to your pot. You three look totally protein deficient."

"Are you ready to take us back to Tanigue in the morning?" Gar inquired. "After you drop us off, you can come back here and wait for Mac's call. His team should be ready to move again before much longer."

"She's fully charged and ready to go whenever you need a ride," said Quinn. "We'll be ready in the morning."

"Let's relax tonight," Gar concluded. "We can pack everything later."

TWENTY-NINE

GAR SHOOK CHAMBO'S SLEEPING BAG WHERE it covered his shoulder.

"There's been a change in plans. Mac messaged me a moment ago and requested a lift from Kwerba to Dabra as soon as possible. I don't know exactly how he gets updates on the whereabouts of his targets, but he thinks the Asians from Hulu Atas have finally arrived in Dabra."

Chambo nodded, still groggy from sleeping.

"I'll inform Devon and Quinn. It shouldn't take more than an hour to pick up and deliver Mac. We'll come back for you after that.

"We'll probably need to charge the batteries for an hour before heading to Tanigue. I hope that's okay."

Rava approached the two while they drank a 'wake up' coffee.

"Let's get started taking down the tents and packing the supplies. I'd like to get an early start."

"Rava," Gar said in a soft, almost apologetic tone, "we need to move Mac first. There'll be plenty of time to get everything packed. Why not enjoy a mug of coffee while Devon and Quinn get Icarus started?"

Quinn, Devon, and Chambo climbed into Icarus and started their checklist for the short flight to Kwerba. They'd cleared Icarus' interior after Chambo had directed them to remove the few containers already stacked inside. They never knew exactly how much cargo Mac and his team would bring, so they always planned for maximum space.

Quinn engaged the sound suppressor system and activated stealth mode before departing. Gar marveled at the technology whenever the cameras came on and ninety-five percent of Icarus instantly disappeared. It convinced Saturday and the other native that the pilots could perform magic, a gift they'd somehow received from the gods.

The one remaining clue suggesting Icarus existed disappeared when Chambo slid the cargo door closed.

A low whoosh accompanied by an invisible thump of air came and went as Icarus lifted from the clearing. Gar typed a brief message to Mac, letting him know Icarus would land, invisibly, at the runway's end in fifteen minutes.

Mac walked from the trees to the grassy area at the side of the runway. He noted that natives had pulled several of their canoes ashore but left them to sleep in their homes.

The air thumped . . . the side door slid open and Chambo's enormous smile appeared.

"Howdy boys. Welcome aboard. Next stop, Dabra."

He could see the team's fatigue.

"Rough night?"

"Not bad," Mac replied. "We've been up most of it. A couple of my guys traipsed quite a way into the jungle while tracking down two of their virologists. The terrain here gets mountainous less than a mile outside the village and it made trekking more strenuous than they expected."

Chambo couldn't contain his curiosity.

"Can you tell me about the operation here?"

Mac seemed open to sharing his experience with Chambo. With anyone else, he'd be tight-lipped. In fact, he'd say nothing unless the person had direct involvement in the mission. Chambo became the exception. He projected a Pied Piper of Hamelin personality that softened Mac's affinity for silence and Chambo also needed to understand the adversaries they both chased.

"It turned out to be another classic laboratory operation. Everyone lived in the same building as the lab, so it made dismantling their presence relatively quick. Yesterday's little fire interrupted Kwerba's usual calm, but I think the memory of that place will fade quickly. We piled all the critical samples and equipment in the middle of the room and covered them with a combination of thermite and iron oxide. The aluminum-rust combination is one of our specialties. That stuff burns at three thousand degrees."

"Did you have targets in Kwerba?"

"Ten in total," Mac replied. "Two of them had trekked into the mountains to infect another unsuspecting tribe with one of their new deadly viruses. The others remained in Kwerba.

"We disposed of those in town. They won't be found."

Chambo liked Mac but realized he and his team represented a lethal force. He wondered how such ruthless men could remain mentally balanced. They knew the harm their targets had done to the world and somehow rationalized doing what it took to stop further atrocities.

"What happened to those in the jungle?"

Mac looked as though he'd explained enough.

"It took two days to catch up to them. Our guys intercepted them on the trail as they headed back to Kwerba. If it hadn't been for that morsel of luck, it might have taken weeks to find them again.

"The experimentations they conducted on innocent natives must have been terrible. Eliminating those two came with a certain sense of pleasure, not in ending their lives, but in putting an end to the evil diseases they forced on others."

Chambo heard the pain in Mac's voice and could sense the mental burden he carried. He felt sorry for him.

"We'll arrive at Dabra in thirty minutes. Relax. I won't bother you until then."

Quinn turned to Chambo and briefed him on the landing.

"The best way to avoid detection when dropping off Mac will be to do it along the mountains. Houses border most of the runway, and the shoreline has all those canoes and fishermen. It might be tricky, but using the far end will be much better.

"Can you let Mac know the plan and then tell me if he has any concerns?"

Clouds formed low along the mountains surrounding Dabra. Rather than make the approach down the runway centerline and expose Icarus, Quinn hand-flew the aircraft along the mountain slopes west of Dabra and approached the runway at a ninety-degree offset.

"Hang on, everyone," Quinn announced. "This might get bumpy."

Icarus tossed moderately left and right as Quinn descended toward the vertical white stripes that marked the runway's end. His landing came with a soft impact and a noticeable 'whew'.

A swath of jagged-edged stones stretched from the runway to the mountain's edge. Along its midpoint, a babbling stream flowed left to right. Quinn's landing point wouldn't be ideal for departure because of the proximity of the stones. But, if he moved slightly forward before adding full power, he'd mitigate the danger of blowing them into the rotors.

Quinn watched as Mac's team disappeared into the tall grass. He shifted his focus down the runway and immediately noticed a commercial aircraft approaching from over the river. It would land heading toward him.

Just sit tight. Less movement meant less chance of discovery. The pilot would most likely go to the terminal and not to the end of the runway.

The de Havilland DHC-6 landed well down the runway but kept rolling toward Icarus until it reached the terminal ramp a thousand feet in front of them.

The pilot of the de Havilland watched the runway ahead with peripheral vision after his primary focus shifted inside the aircraft. He busied himself with turning off the landing lights and the navigational radios and eventually broadcasting the arrival message for his two passengers. Icarus' occasional blur at the end of the runway never caught his attention.

Quinn departed without taxiing forward. It seemed worth the risk of avoiding detection by those servicing the de Havilland. He took a deep breath, added power, and levitated in the same direction from which he'd arrived.

A single dull 'clack' caught the attention of one of the baggage handlers, who straightened and looked in Quinn's direction. The sound seemed unusual, but the handler couldn't see anything out of the ordinary. He grabbed another bag from the cargo pod, handed it to its owner, and reached for another.

Icarus' downwash dislodged a one-inch diameter stone and spit it forward until it ricocheted off a larger rock, shooting upward. An instant later, the number three rotor sucked it through its path.

The razor-like stone nicked the number three blade. Although damaged, it remained in one piece. Quinn felt a sharp tap when it contacted the rotor. Icarus' flight path remained normal and Quinn's mind shifted elsewhere. He turned north toward their encampment destination.

A thumbnail-sized piece of the number three rotor assembly tore loose from the blade fifteen minutes later. Quinn felt an immediate vibration and spoke into his mic, "Rotor monitor ON."

A schematic of the four rotors came into view across his visor. The sensors feeding data to Quinn's display primarily measured the rotor's mechanical integrity and since all the mechanical linkages remained intact the display appeared normal. Fortunately, another set of sensors measured blade balance and flashed an 'out of balance' warning. He reduced power.

The vibration subsided slightly but continued. Quinn feared that like most vibrations, it would intensify over time and that would exacerbate whatever damage already existed. He spoke again. "Shutdown number three engine." The electrical control module removed power from the engine but also did the same to the number one engine. This reduced overall lift significantly while keeping the lift aspect in balance. What lift remained would make it nearly impossible to take off from a remote location and would make it more difficult to perform a cushioned landing. But it would sustain cruise flight.

Directional control became sluggish, forcing Quinn to initiate turns sooner and more slowly. He decided to follow the general course of the Taritatu River to prepare for the eventual landing.

He briefed Devon and Chambo on the upcoming procedure.

"I'm going to make a long straight-in approach. Not sure if we'll have enough lift to fully cushion the landing, so expect a short rollout. Hold on tight and don't worry. I'm good at this kind of thing."

"If Chambo considers it to be a certifiably smooth landing," Devon added. "I'll give you an additional five horseflies."

The open field came into sight and Quinn initiated a slow descent to the middle of the opening. Chambo slid open the side door just in case they'd need to escape from a crash landing. Everything remained smooth and constant until ten feet above the ground. At that point, Quinn slid the throttle forward to its maximum position. Icarus shuttered as it continued to descend. Immediately before touching the ground, Icarus floated for an instant. Quinn pulled the power to idle and they came to rest.

"That'll be five horseflies," laughed Quinn.

Devon appeared relieved and upset at the same time. Chambo joined Quinn's laughter.

"What happened?" Gar asked as he approached Chambo.

"I think we chipped one of the rotor blades. We'll have to construct basic scaffolding and get up there to take a closer look."

Gar thought for a minute.

"Do you think the blade housings could be retracted so that you could climb on top of Icarus to do the inspection?"

"Well, we could very easily damage the stealth system by walking around up there and crushing cameras or the monitor wiring. I'd rather take more time and minimize the risk of creating further damage."

"Okay guys," Gar sighed, "explain to Saturday what you need and start constructing a work stand."

Rip nearly burst with excitement when he examined the nerve tissue under his microscope. The axons of his sample had been severed before being immersed in one of the curative concoctions he'd developed using Rava's plant extract and his tannins. The result shocked him. The axon appeared to have completely regenerated itself.

The gap between axon ends in one of his Petri dishes had been set to approximately a quarter-inch and even that sample had regenerated. Amazing.

Rip needed to experiment on an actual spinal column. Even with a severed spinal cord that wouldn't regenerate, the potion could very well create alternative pathways to return partial function. It seemed incredible. He couldn't wait to share his findings with Rava.

The four-legged scaffolding platform that Devon and Quinn had lashed together would suffice for their one-time inspection. They'd have to reinforce its flimsy bracing before they could use it for anything more technical, like replacing one or two of the rotor blades.

Chambo, Devon, and Quinn each weighed too much to safely climb the crude structure, leading Chambo to consider whether or not a non-flyer could adequately inspect the blade. He concluded that it would have to be one of them.

"We'll draw straws to see who climbs this toothpick contraption. Longest straw climbs. The other two will stand ready to catch him if our engineering wonder collapses."

Devon quickly plucked three strands of grass and cut two pieces shorter than the third. He held his hands behind his back and shuffled the strands before presenting them to Chambo and Quinn.

"Wait, this isn't fair," Quinn protested. "You know which one is longest."

"I don't get to pick," Devon responded. "Only you and Chambo. I get what's left."

Chambo drew a short straw. Quinn pulled one of equal length. Devon held out the long straw and reached for the scaffolding.

"Let's get started."

Devon looked down and gave his report after having pulled the rotor blades through several rotations.

"This blade assembly has a large chip. It'll need replacement."

"Once we get it swapped," Chambo added, "let's do a ground run to determine if everything is balanced. It won't take long to make adjustments, but first, I think this stand will need a fair amount of reinforcement."

"We're gonna be busy most of the afternoon getting this rotor blade replaced," he explained to Gar. "I recommend departing for Tanigue at first light tomorrow."

Rava joined the group with a fishing pole in hand.

"I think I'll try fishing while you grease monkeys repair my carriage. We can eat whatever I catch for dinner."

THIRTY

CHAMBO POINTED TO AN AIRCRAFT PANEL beneath Icarus' cargo door.

"If you'll remove that cover, there are two rotor blade assemblies inside." He then turned to Saturday.

"Can you fetch us about ten more bamboo poles? We'll need them to reinforce this rickety death trap of a stand."

Rava and Gar busied themselves with folding, packing, and stacking everyone's camp gear near the fire pit. They'd break down the tents in the morning, just before loading them on the aircraft.

Devon unscrewed several dzus fasteners, pulled the panel free, and smiled with a look of satisfaction at what he saw inside.

"They did this right. Quinn, this may be beyond your sense of appreciation, but look at how they secured the rotors to the frame. They coated the brackets with this non-degrading rubberized stuff. Everything is padded with foam. Pretty dope."

"Let me take a closer look." Quinn stooped and leaned toward the opening. "I didn't even know we had spares tucked away inside. I wonder what else we might have hidden in the side panels … hopefully a large bottle of Good Old No. 7 or an apple Chū-Hi."

Devon studied the upcoming work from a distance. He decided that unfastening the rotor assembly would take effort. The job itself seemed fairly uncomplicated, but squeezing and twisting his body into position to do it would be a challenge.

Chambo handed Devon several small wrenches and a wire cutter. Up to this point, Devon had subconsciously assumed that he'd simply reach in and begin work. But now, there didn't seem to be an obvious way to proceed.

He studied the situation again from atop the scaffolding and talked to himself while trying various options.

"Let's try reaching over the sound suppression housing. Ugh . . . nope, that's not going to work."

The housing encircled the rotor's rotational path its diameter extended almost eight feet, too far out for him to reach across to the hub.

"Maybe I can squeeze between the housing and the blades . . . why didn't I think of this first?"

He pushed his shoulders up through the opening, trying not to further damage the rotor blade that scraped his back.

Quinn stood to the side, and with nothing better to do, encouraged him.

"Now that you've become a permanent fixture on the rotor assembly, try not to strip any of the threads or muck up the nuts. Take your time."

They hoped that with luck they'd get the rotor changed by dark. They'd balance everything later in the night or early the next morning. It'd take time.

The rest of the team lounged around the equipment stacks. Rava eventually decided to head to the river. She'd bathe next to the canoes and later find the perfect spot to unfold her camp chair and relax while catching dinner.

The afternoon sun and its longtime companion, humidity, had drained her energy and left her feeling uncomfortably sticky. The few clouds in the sky foretold a rainless evening with little relief from the heat. She scanned the river and the wooded shoreline for any signs of life. Finding none, she undressed and slipped into the cool water. After rubbing the accumulated grit from her body, she grabbed her clothes one piece at a time and worked the waters between their threads while kneading them to her satisfaction. She then slipped them on and half-stood, half-crawled from the river.

The wetness felt good. The sun no longer clung to her body but felt more like a warm hug. She cast a fake frog into the river after having fidgeted with the lure and Quinn's fishing pole. A slow current floated the bobber out from under the overhanging trees.

Her camp chair wobbled when she sat in it. Its unsteady footing would normally have provided an acceptable diversion, but at the moment it detracted from her goal of total relaxation. She moved farther down the river and tried again. The new location provided a stable footing for her chair. Perfect..

Wu projected a frustration that his natives had come to tolerate. Another day passed without seeing anyone along the river.

"We'll paddle until dark," he rebuked them for their slow progress. "You two are slowing us down with your early stops. Do you think I'm stupid and don't notice your laziness?"

The natives nodded to express understanding and proceeded to paddle with less pull on their strokes. The currents would soon become tricky when the Tariku and the Taritatu merged to form the Mamberamo River. They continued slow and steady with the hope of avoiding the dangerous stretch until morning.

Wu spotted it first. . .

"There, up ahead under the trees. There's a canoe. Turn now. Paddle to the shore. Hurry!"

The two canoes pushed under the trees and came to a stop several hundred yards south of Rava. Wu drew up a plan in his head.

"The three of us in this canoe will sneak ahead on foot."

He called in a hushed tone to the other canoe.

"You'll remain here and chase anyone who tries to escape."

He'd taken several steps along the shore before turning back to the native in his otherwise empty canoe.

"You. Follow us from a short distance. Keep quiet or I'll feed you to the crocodiles."

Wu and the two others purposely remained in the wooded area, and as a result, never noticed Icarus or those at the campsite. They crept forward slowly, being cautious not to make unnecessary sounds. Wu again spotted the two canoes. Yes, it must be them. He spotted the woman and held out his hand as a signal for the others to remain quiet.

A twig snapped … quiet … another step …

Rava had fallen asleep watching the rhythmic rise and fall of the bobber. Out of nowhere, a hand covered her mouth. She tried to speak, to scream. Nothing.

"Stay quiet and you won't get hurt," Wu whispered in a harsh tone. "Where's your brother? Where are your plants?"

Rava tilted in a confused state. What? Why did this person want her plants? Her world suddenly didn't make sense. She shook her head to say no before pointing to the canoe.

Wu signaled for one other to search it. The two plants Rava had never seen before remained in her canoe in water-filled plastic bags. Wu's nearest accomplice spotted them, reached in, and grabbed the leafy plants.

A vile-looking kidnapper zip-tied Rava's hands behind her back and fashioned a gag for her mouth. Her mind began to clear and she realized they planned to kidnap her, the filthy cretins. She tried to think, to leave some sort of sign. She kicked Quinn's fishing pole toward the river. Wu pulled her in the opposite direction and forced her into his canoe.

The two canoes joined in the main channel where they slowly drifted into strengthening currents.

The rotor assembly change neared completion.

"Where's Rava?" Quinn asked. "It's time to start cooking whatever she's caught."

"I'll get her," Gar said as he started for the shoreline.

He found no sign of her when he arrived. The canoes remained as they'd been earlier. He spotted the empty camp chair.

"Rava," he called. "Are you here?"

Nothing.

Quinn's fishing pole lay on the ground. It didn't feel right. She'd have set the pole against the chair if she left. Where had she gone?

He looked out to the river. Darkness seemed only minutes away. He could barely make out two canoes in the distance. Queasiness gripped his stomach. He needed to take action, but how? Think. Think.

He ran to the campsite.

"We've got a big problem. Rava's missing and I think she's been kidnapped."

Chambo skipped a breath. "What? That's crazy."

Saturday and the young native, along with the med-tech and deckhand, gathered around Gar. The moment's commotion provided Gar with enough time to organize his thoughts.

"What's the status of Icarus?"

"I've finished attaching the new rotor assembly," Devon explained. "It's flyable, but we'll need time to reattach the loose panels. I think we'll be okay to fly it unless it's really out of balance."

"Okay," Gar answered. "They're probably headed for Kwerba. I suspect they'll try to fly out in the morning. Too bad Mac isn't still there.

"Here's what I want to do. Chambo, you take Devon and Quinn … and take Saturday and the kid. See if you can find them along the river. Slow them down, if possible. But, if necessary, fly ahead to Kwerba and keep them from leaving.

"I'll take the med-tech and deckhand in one of our canoes. We should at least get close to them if we run the motor at full speed.

"We'll see where the chase stands once we're all at Kwerba. Let's get started."

Gar and the others grabbed the weapons they'd thought to bring along. All three ran to the canoes. The deckhand pushed them free of the shore and they turned toward Kwerba while the med-tech started the motor.

The floor of the canoe where Gar sat had splashes of water. Then it hit him. The plants, Rava's rare plants had been moved. He knew the Asians had taken her.

Twilight would soon become darkness. Moving willy-nilly along the river's dangerous currents seemed suicidal. Nonetheless, catching Wu required just such a long and dangerous chase.

Chambo directed those remaining at the campsite.

"Saturday, can you and the kid move our maintenance stand out of the way? Once that's clear, get inside Icarus. We'll be there as soon as we tidy up everything else.

"Devon, climb up there one more time. Finish whatever needs to be done with the cowling and get our weapons before getting inside."

Quinn had moved the chipped rotor assembly to the area in front of the tents and began reattaching the access panel cover.

"I'll have this wrapped up in another minute."

Chambo feared they'd already missed too much.

"Devon, get the weapons."

The thought of a rotor vibration crossed his mind. He'd worry about that later.

"Quinn, I want you to fly this one. We'll keep Devon at the door, and I'll back him up."

Everyone crossed their fingers as Quinn flipped the start switches. All four rotors started spinning at low speed. Icarus remained stable.

"Okay, hang on," Quinn announced. "Here we go."

He pushed the throttle forward slowly, a small shutter. They lifted into the air and climbed toward the river.

Quinn switched on the noise suppression system and went into stealth mode.

Fifteen minutes remained before darkness would obscure all details of those on the Taritatu. Quinn spotted Gar's canoe as it neared the turbulent currents of the Mamberamo River.

Quinn knew they'd make it through the worst before the night got pitch black. It'd be a long night on the river for them.

Several miles ahead, Quinn picked out two canoes against the river's dark shadows.

"Okay," he announced primarily to Devon, who'd positioned himself at the open cargo door. "I'm going to fly over the canoes then turn around and come in for a closer look. Hopefully, that'll give them cause to slow their pace."

"I'm ready," he responded.

He pulled a short-barreled MK-18 rifle to his side.

Wu had relaxed since gaining distance from where he'd kidnapped Rava. He knew that darkness on the river would bring more safety than danger.

A sudden whoosh of air startled him.

The skies carried few clouds. The air had been calm all day. He looked up and saw nothing but could see that those in the other canoe felt it also. They confirmed Wu's senses when they grabbed their weapons and held them in a ready-to-fire position.

Quinn maneuvered around so he could approach from their rear. Devon updated the others.

"The canoe to the left has Rava in the middle. The other one has a native at the rear and three others in front of him."

Devon noticed the two with their weapons raised as if to shoot. They had unfortunately aimed in the general direction of Icarus. Devon fired two quick shots followed by two more. The kidnappers with weapons slumped forward.

The one at the bow rested his paddle across the gunwales before turning to reach for his weapon. His arm bumped the paddle, causing it to spin and fall into the river. He awkwardly reached for it as Quinn hovered low overhead. The strong downwash rolled the canoe left. The kidnapper disappeared into the river within an instant, only to surface moments later, well behind the canoe. The native continued to paddle, making no effort to go back for him.

Quinn looped around with the thought of rescuing the abandoned swimmer.

"There he is," Devon called, "to your right, swimming toward the shoreline along that calm stretch."

"Got him in sight," Quinn replied.

Neither of them could see the crocodiles along the shore who'd slid silently into the deeper waters. Their primary feeding time occurred after twilight, and the calm area where the unfortunate kidnapper headed had proved an effective venue for targeting larger fish.

"What happened?" Quinn asked in a surprised tone. "He just disappeared."

"Did you see that swish when he went under?" Devon added. "The crocs got him. I'm sure of it."

THIRTY-ONE

QUINN COULD BARELY SEE RAVA'S CANOE. Rather than switch to infrared operations or fly closer and risk capsizing it, Quinn turned toward Kwerba. He planned to land at the far end of the runway, closer to where he thought Wu might head. Hopefully, no one would be milling about.

Like most jungle villages, darkness brought children and adults to their homes for dinner. Fishermen occasionally returned from fishing after dark, but never more than an hour later.

Icarus flew an automated approach while Quinn looked for natives along the sides of Kwerba's short runway. Several fishermen appeared near the water's edge, but none farther inland.

"Let's turn off the rotors but keep stealth mode engaged with the LPs running," Chambo half-whispered to Quinn once they'd landed. "If we're here after an hour and a half, we can kill the LPs. I want Icarus quiet and invisible when Wu arrives."

Saturday approached Chambo with a sense of commitment.

"Sir, if it's okay with you, we'll visit the shoreline. We make the future easier for you."

Saturday and the kid didn't wait for an answer but turned and trotted along the runway into the darkness.

Chambo figured they'd blend in and if nothing else, they'd reduce interference that might originate from whatever fishermen remained with their canoes.

He looked to Quinn and Devon.

"If they come this way, I'd like to confront Wu myself and have you two provide cover from somewhere nearby, but out of sight. We'll plan to delay their movements until Gar and the others arrive."

"Why don't we get the ghillie net from Icarus and use it as cover?" Devon suggested. "If bullets start flying, we won't be such an obvious target."

Wu's canoe moved silently in the dark, apart from the second one. He hadn't quite figured out what had happened earlier along the river. His mind jumped from thought to thought, imagining that the others must have panicked in the current. Then he wondered if they shot at someone, or did someone else. It sounded close, but he couldn't see anyone else around. He couldn't understand why they lagged so far behind. He decided to regroup at Kwerba.

The darkness brought with it a feeling of unease. Chills shot up his spine when thinking of the dangerous amphibians, flesh-eating fish, and who knows what else, all swimming in the river beneath them. Noise from within the jungle might have sounded normal to the natives, but to Wu and the two other kidnappers, the sounds became increasingly ominous.

"Where's the other canoe?" he kept asking himself.

Rava knew that Gar and the others had taken to the offensive after the commotion with the second canoe. She convinced herself that they'd gotten Icarus in the air and probably chased in the canoes. She assumed the foul-mouthed dung heap who grabbed her to be their leader, the same one behind the death of Rip's laboratory friend in Jayapura. She wouldn't let him get any information from her. She told herself she'd die first.

The native unenthusiastically paddled while considering what to do with the dead kidnappers now slumped against the gunwales. He wanted to dump them into the river. They represented evil and he didn't want them in his canoe. He'd drag them onto shore at Kwerba and let that monster, Wu, deal with the consequences. The sooner he got away from Wu, the better. He'd join his friend at Kwerba and get a couple of hours of sleep before starting back toward Dabra. This felt like bad business.

Saturday and the kid selected two beached canoes from which they could get an unobstructed view of the river. Each lay down beside one, trying to relax. They'd deal with Wu when he arrived.

Two hours later, Saturday alerted to the sounds of someone paddling toward the shoreline. He glanced over the gunwale and saw Rava sitting between her three kidnappers. A native paddled from the rear.

Saturday signaled to the kid. They tensed and pulled knives from their waistbands.

One kidnapper climbed out and held the canoe steady for Rava and Wu. The last one delayed while looking for the strap to his rifle. He eventually took hold of it, slung the weapon over his shoulder, and grabbed the two plants.

Wu pushed Rava forward and forced her up the grassy slope toward the runway while the other two lingered. They'd all eventually find their way to the Kwerba laboratory and regroup in relative safety.

Not knowing that his local team had been eliminated, Wu felt confident that he held the upper hand should a confrontation occur.

"We are here. You pay me now," the paddler from Dabra demanded.

"Not so quick," the kidnapper with the plants snapped. "We may need you tomorrow. I'll discuss it with our leader and pay you after we decide what to do."

He turned away from the native and started up the slope in the direction Wu had headed. Saturday and the native moved quickly, silently, without so much as disturbing the air around them. Neither kidnapper sensed movement from behind. First Saturday cupped a hand over the kidnapper's mouth and pulled the knife across his throat. The kid reached for his target a moment later as the Asian turned toward the commotion. Too late. The kid grabbed and twisted his head until he felt it snap. Neither victim made a sound as they slumped to the ground.

"Good," Saturday said matter of factly, "let's drag them to the side. We wait for the next canoe."

It arrived moments later. Only the native paddling the canoe moved. Two others remained still. The first paddler approached the arriving canoe.

"They won't pay," he announced to his friend. "We should leave before they return."

Saturday appeared from the shadows and interrupted.

"Maybe I can pay if you'll help. Take those two in your canoe and pile them with the others," he pointed "over there. I'll talk to my boss. If he can't pay, you leave. Okay?"

"Okay."

Gar arrived in his canoe and approached Saturday.

"Where's Rava? Have you seen her?"

"That evil one pushed her up the hill. The pilots wait for him." Saturday pointed to the side. "All the evil ones are piled over there."

Chambo saw Wu pushing Rava in his direction.

"Stop where you are. Release the girl or I'll shoot."

Wu froze. There shouldn't have been anyone waiting for him. He raised his weapon and fired. Rava kicked the side of his knee, broke free of his grasp, and ran in the direction of Devon and Quinn. Wu turned toward her and fired again. She twisted and fell to the ground.

"No!" yelled Gar.

Wu stood directly between Gar and Chambo. Neither dared return fire for fear of shooting each other. They'd have to delay until their line of fire cleared.

Wu spun around and fired toward Gar, who dove to the ground for cover.

Before Devon or Quinn could shed the ghillie net and return fire, Wu bolted toward the jungle. Several additional shots rang out.

Devon and Quinn ran to Rava's side. She moaned while lying face down in the grass and holding her ankle.

"Are you okay?" Devon asked. "Are you shot?"

She looked up with a queasy feeling in her stomach.

"I twisted my ankle and fell. And no, I didn't get shot."

Chambo ran to Gar.

"Devon and Quinn are taking care of Rava. Let's find Wu before he causes more trouble."

Wu temporarily concealed himself behind a large boulder. His plan had gone all wrong. He needed to find his lab team and counter-attack. He noticed two shadows moving across the darkness in pursuit and fired again in that direction. It provided an opportunity to withdraw farther along the ridgeline. A narrow but relatively deep chasm complicated his escape. He bolted, and jumped, catching a limb on the opposite side. Before he could pull his way to firm footing, the limb snapped and he fell backward into the darkness.

Moments later, Gar and Chambo arrived and looked into the twenty-foot-deep crevasse. Darkness masked the bottom.

"We'll need to work our way to the bottom of this and pick up Wu's trail from there," Gar whispered to Chambo.

Saturday seemed to always appear when Gar most needed him, and he needed him now. Saturday trotted along the runway toward them. All three proceeded cautiously as tall grass obscured areas of sheer drop-off. Saturday found a narrow pathway leading down to the river. He turned to the others as they approached the spot where Wu had fallen.

"I think the chase is over. See there. The evil one is silent."

Wu lay face up, impaled on a hardened two-inch thick tree branch. It protruded from his chest.

Wu's reign of terror came to an end.

"Let's clean up this mess before a crowd gathers," Gar said as they returned to Icarus. He found Rava sitting in the grass and stooped beside her. "Thank goodness you're alright. I thought Wu shot you."

He put his arm around her shoulder and pulled her close to him.

"They won't threaten you and Rip any longer, I promise. I'm going to keep a much closer eye on you for the remainder of this excursion."

A tear ran down her cheek. "Thank you for chasing after me. I promise that I won't complain about your snoring ever again."

Saturday motioned for Gar to join him away from the others. "It's about the payment for those two natives who'd been forced to paddle Wu and his group from Dabra to Kwerba."

The fact that they provided the means for Wu to kidnap Rava complicated his thinking. Gar walked to the natives, looked at their canoes, and then addressed them.

"I suspect you two had no idea of Wu's motives. I'll pay you for your efforts but with one condition. I want you to forget about everything that happened tonight and to forget about the kidnappers completely. If you have stories to tell, make up a different client. Maybe talk about previous naïve tourists or something like that. Deal?"

The natives looked at each other, agreed, and smiled at Gar.

"Yes, thank you."

"Not a word," Gar added, "and I'll reward you in Dabra."

"Let's haul these bodies to Icarus and load them in the back," Gar told Chambo. "We'll make two trips to our encampment. Rava and I will remain here with two others until the second shuttle.

"And Quinn, when you land here again, do you think you could do it closer to the water? We'll need to attach the canoe before heading back."

"Sure thing," he answered. "We'll be back in thirty or forty minutes."

Chambo directed the team once Icarus landed at the encampment.

"Saturday, can you and the native dig a grave for the dead? I'd like to bury them before dinner.

"Devon, until they need us to help dig, we can set up the tarp and build a fire."

The two natives Gar had paid couldn't understand where the others had gone. Nor did they understand why they'd taken the dead kidnappers to the far end of the runway. They couldn't imagine how two men managed to carry their canoe with such little strain.

"These foreigners must have hidden strength," one of them said. "It'd take ten of us to carry a canoe up that slope."

Icarus silently departed the last time when one of the natives thought he saw the canoe that had been carried up the hill flying across the sky. It disappeared in the next moment, swallowed by the darkness.

Quiet returned to Kwerba.

"This is an unusual night, mostly evil," a Dabra native mumbled to the other. "But also, good. Let's see where the foreigners went."

Nothing remained to be seen once they crested the slope at the end of the runway. They walked the runway's length and explored along its periphery. Nothing.

"Where have they gone?" one asked. "It's like they're not here."

"Magic," the other added in a soft tone.

Icarus landed and the natives completed the burial. Everyone gathered around the fire pit where Gar stood to make an announcement.

"We have chased away the evil that has lurked along the Taritatu River," Saturday interrupted. "This is a good omen that we have no rain tonight. Tomorrow will be good."

"Chambo, if you could open that secret compartment on Icarus," Gar suggested. "I think we might all enjoy a shot of the Blue Label scotch I brought for an occasion such as this."

"I told you," Quinn whispered.

"Maybe someone could retrieve the fish that Rava caught for our dinner but left unattended near the canoes," Devon added.

Gar reached out to Rava.

"If you'll show me where you left them, I'll accompany you there."

"Bring your gun," she replied.

Rava's earlier excitement about returning to Tanigue had disappeared but now slowly returned. Her unsettling capture, the subsequent river chase, and her action-packed rescue had shifted everyone's focus elsewhere. Gar felt the weight of concern that had dramatically increased a few hours ago lifted from his shoulders. The threat he feared most no longer existed.

"Gar?" she asked softly. "I don't want you to get any ideas, but would you mind moving your sleeping bag into my tent? As much as it goes against my nature to say this, I'd prefer to have you next to me tonight."

"As a matter of principle," he kidded, "I feel somewhat obligated to … you know, your slightest wish is my command. I'll try to remain quiet."

Rava breathed out a lighthearted devilish laugh.

THIRTY-TWO

THEY AWOKE EARLY, RELAXED. GAR HEATED water while digging through the Pelican case for their coffee mugs. He found one, filled it, and handed it to Rava.

"Here. We'll remain along the river and relax for an extra day so we can fully decompress from yesterday's excitement. It'll be good to join Rip tomorrow. I'm eager to see what progress he's made while we've been out here swatting horse flies, fighting kidnappers, and avoiding crocodiles."

Rava chuckled.

"Yes, and I can't wait to show him those new plants I somehow kept with me.

"Gar, are those evil virologists gone for good?"

Gar sipped his coffee. A disappointed look revealed his inner frustration.

"Whoever directed their operations is still free to recreate this scenario all over again. I'd like to find that person, lock him in an isolated cell, and throw away the key.

"The immediate threat to you and your brother, on the other hand, has been eliminated … probably any future threat as well."

Sunrise on the second day greeted everyone with a feeling of closure. Spirits remained high. The time to depart had come before the morning's coolness dissipated. Everyone boarded Icarus. Devon finished the preflight inspection and the Before Take-off checklist, added power, and lifted above the Taritatu River one more time.

Icarus' internal optics displayed the outside view, all three hundred degrees from the floor's edge, across the top, and down the opposite side. Each passenger felt like a bird at five thousand feet looking down at the earth below, the immersion lessened only by the lack of wind in their faces.

Gar pointed to the Mamberamo River where it cut a narrow and frothy path through the Foja Mountains.

"Thank goodness we didn't have to paddle our canoes through that section. Look at those rapids."

"Oh, my goodness," Rava exclaimed. "I had no idea such turbulent waters existed so close to where we got off the river. Would you have followed us?"

"Possibly," he mused, and then in a more serious tone. "You're important to us, to me. I'd never forgive myself if I let you venture into that mess alone."

Marlo rushed to get the fake shipping container panels deployed before Icarus arrived and landed.

"Be careful and make certain the safety railings are in place."

He scanned the deck for the ship's cook.

"Yo! Is everything set in the dining room?"

"Yes sir. I've taken the liberty of placing a bottle of wine on each table."

"Very good. I think Gar will like that."

Gar turned to Chambo and Quinn once they'd landed and exited Icarus. Not everyone would party tonight.

"Guys, I received another message from Mac. He's eager to get extracted from Dabra and bring his team back onboard Tanigue.

"We won't need both pilots for this trip, so one of you can stay here and keep an eye on the wine. Chambo, I'd like you to go in case we have any sort of maintenance issues. And to keep you company, I'll ride along in place of the pilot who stays here."

"Devon is still busy getting Icarus post-flighted and recharged," Quinn quickly interjected. "It wouldn't be fair to make him fly all the way back to Dabra. I'll take this one if that's okay."

Chambo laughed and nodded.

"Alright, you win. But let's give the batteries a few minutes to charge before leaving. In fact, let's put more fuel in the tanks and run the LPs to Dabra."

Gar pulled Chambo to the side.

"Mac asked us to come quickly," he half-whispered. "He didn't care if we got there during daylight, so I suspect he may have issues he didn't want to talk about.

"Let's arrive in stealth mode and land in that cleared space between the river and the end of the runway."

Quinn turned Icarus toward Dabra's runway while descending through five hundred feet. He picked out the landing point from three miles away and through force of habit, double-checked the sound suppression system and that he'd selected stealth mode. A glance left and right along the Taritatu revealed a single canoe downriver of his intended flight path.

Gar anticipated a relatively brief stop but had one personal task to accomplish before they could depart.

"Quinn, I'm going to hike over to the canoes along the shoreline while we're on the ground. I won't be gone more than ten minutes."

They landed in a slightly uneven, grassy section of cleared jungle that fortunately supported Icarus' weight. Gar grabbed a sack of rice and disappeared along a narrow pathway.

Quinn didn't see Mac or his team. "Once Gar is clear," he called to Chambo, "pull the door shut until we see Mac. I'd like to remain as invisible as possible."

The two natives he'd paid at Kwerba sat together alongside their canoes, apart from the others. They appeared tired from paddling all night on their return voyage.

"Greetings," Gar said as he approached.

Both smiled but with a hint of caution and uncertainty. In their minds, Gar represented an unexplainable spirit. The last time they'd looked for him along Kwerba's runway, he'd simply disappeared from their midst. Thoughts of the flying canoe flashed in the mind of the second fisherman.

"I hope that the events of two nights ago have remained a secret," Gar said.

"We arrived from Kwerba an hour ago," the friendlier native responded. "We paddled hard because we wanted to see our families again, so we pushed day and night.

"How do you arrive so fast, and not exhausted?"

Gar chuckled.

"I have a canoe that can fly. I don't have to follow all the bends in the river.

"Here is a bag of rice for you to share between your families. Consider it a bonus payment for your unusual trip and a payment for your promise not to speak of the kidnappers, or me."

"Thank you," they responded with a look of disbelief on their faces. "Our families will be happy. No one cares about our trip. They only talk about the shootings here yesterday morning."

With that, Gar turned and started back toward Icarus. He wondered, what shooting? He needed to hurry back. It had to be Mac.

Mac led several limping team members from the brush. One had a cloth bandage wrapped around his arm. All moved slowly.

Chambo jumped from Icarus to help them climb on board.

"What happened?" he asked with concern.

Mac responded after helping one of the wounded to board.

"This stop turned out to be different. A little gunfire interrupted our usual sneakiness."

Gar joined them before Mac could continue.

"This isn't the best place to hide in the middle of the day," Quinn fidgeted.

A radio call from an approaching aircraft sounded in his ear.

"We gotta get moving," he blurted.

He added power and lifted Icarus into the sky. The invisible blur moved low toward the river and banked to the right, away from the approaching aircraft.

"How badly hurt is your team?" Gar asked Mac. "What happened?"

"Three of them have flesh wounds. Nothing life-threatening, but probably more than a bit painful."

Gar keyed his mic. "Quinn, call back to Tanigue and have the med-tech standing by to treat these guys. Superficial gunshot wounds … something for the pain."

He turned to Mac. "We'll get their wounds cleaned as soon as we land. How did you manage to get into a shootout?"

Mac didn't have a ready answer.

"Let's say that several Asians picked up on us. They sensed danger and without warning shot at two of us. We took cover and pressed our attack. Several of the boys caught a small portion of their lead before the shooting stopped.

"The bastards didn't last long and they didn't leave much for us to destroy once things settled down. They didn't have lab supplies yet. I think we destroyed all of that back at Hulu Atas. We buried the bunch of 'em in the jungle under cover of darkness before sneaking back to the edge of the runway.

"I think the regional authorities landed in that airplane. They'll conduct a small investigation, so it's good that we've left. Their daily routine will return to normal in a couple of days and I'll facilitate a little government-to-government chat that should clear up any misunderstandings."

Gar and Mac shared a carafe of Chianti Classico in the upper lounge while the wounded received treatment in the ship's infirmary. Marlo quietly monitored Tanigue's gauges, allowing the others as much privacy as they desired.

"Mac, I found these documents on a guy named Wu. He appears to have been the point man for all this riff-raff you've been cleaning up.

"He lived in a dump along the docks in Jayapura. I thought you might like to take a peek at his humble estate. There's a name of someone he worked with in Hong Kong. Hopefully, these will prove helpful."

Mac smiled.

"Interesting. I'd like to do more snooping. If I can tag one more of these dangerous actors, it'd be a gift to the world. Thanks."

After conducting a frustrating search of the lower decks, Rip found Quinn and Devon in the dining room. Quinn argued with Chambo about their 'world's greatest' fly-killing-contest results.

"What do you mean, it's a tie?"

"Well, you had thirty flies," Chambo explained. "Devon had thirty-four, and I had thirty-five. When I foolishly declared your emergency landing to be smooth, Devon gave you five of his flies. You ended up with thirty-five, the same as me."

"That's bad," Devon added. "And there definitely won't be room on that little plaque for both of your names."

Chambo didn't care if his name appeared on a brass plate that associated him with a fly-killing contest.

"We need a tie-breaker, something to kill the time between here and Thailand."

Rip tired of waiting to speak and simply interrupted.

"Look, you guys can figure this out later. I need to conduct a little evaluation using this new goop I created for each of you."

Quinn and Devon accepted the fact that they'd have to comply with Rip's memory test, even if they didn't like the interruption.

"So Rip, I heard you tossed your wallet into the ocean," Quinn noted.

Rip's face stiffened. "Ha ha, very funny. It actually fell out of my pocket when I reached for Rava's rare plants in the back of Icarus. You guys left in such a hurry that Icarus blew it overboard.

"Who told you about that? I'll get even with whoever spilled the beans."

"This is going to feel more or less like hot candle wax," Rip instructed. "I've heated the solution because I think it'll provide a more immediate effect. It won't burn you but it'll feel warm.

"Okay, blindfolds on. Quinn, what color is on the card?"

"Give me a minute to visualize it," Quinn demanded. "I see … wait, can you hold the card still? … okay, blue."

THIRTY-THREE

GAR WANTED TO BRING EVERYONE TOGETHER for a small celebration.

"I'm going to throw a little beach party on Wakde, combine a hero's return for Saturday with a medicinal rejuvenation for Mac's guys. We'll organize a barbeque, beach volleyball, and share a drink or two."

Smiles came to the faces of those within earshot. Even Marlo's normally mischievous expression brightened.

"Do you think the deckhands can come ashore? Bembol and I will keep an eye on Tanigue while the others join in."

"You need to schedule a rotation," Gar responded. "I don't want you to miss the fun. After all, it's an opportunity to walk among the ghosts residing on that historic ground."

Chambo naturally assumed duties as Party Director. His first task on Wakde would be to find a suitable section of beach for the festivities. Before flying to the island, he pulled out one of Marlo's area maps to get a sense of where to locate everything. The only place to land Icarus would be on the old runway. The closest beach existed along the north shore, but it seemed too far for the locals. Tanigue needed to dock on the opposite side of the island. He wondered how something so simple could become so complicated.

Quinn noticed the frustration on Chambo's face.

"Why don't we break down the festivities into two parts," he suggested. We can set up the barbeque and swim along the north shore. The beaches up there are sandy and there's a nice strip of coral offshore for snorkeling. Let's use the tender to get everyone to the village. That's where we'll welcome back Saturday, and where we can remove that cast from the leg of our native who fell from the tree.

"When the time is right, we'll organize a walk along the jungle path to the beach. It'll increase the excitement of finding the party and the beer."

A smile slowly formed on Chambo's face.

"We'll have to figure out what goes on Icarus and what goes in the tender. But, it could work."

The first group to arrive at Wakde's village included Saturday and the young native, Gar, Rava, Rip, Chambo, and the med-tech. The entire village would normally have been asleep so early in the morning, and that seemed to be the case as Saturday approached his house.

Before he could call to his wife and son, the young boy appeared at the door and ran to him. The sick little guy Rava remembered from several months ago hugged Saturday's leg with an abundance of life and gaiety. Rava beamed inside with happiness for the two of them. Saturday's wife emerged and walked to him more slowly with a smile that reflected inner joy. She took hold of his hand and squeezed it, which seemed a suitable substitute for a public embrace.

"We can go to Momma Grace," he suggested to Rava. "The native is with her, and my wife says he walks well on his leg."

Momma and the native walked along the beach looking for crabs. It had become their early morning routine and had motivated him to strengthen his healing leg.

"Rava!" Momma Grace called as she waved to the group. "I'll make coffee. Wait a minute."

The two hurried as best they could from the beach, set their catch of three crabs on the table, and greeted everyone again. Momma hugged each of them while the native simply smiled.

"Yes, coffee sounds perfect," Gar replied. "And it's time to remove that cast. Why don't we let the med-tech cut it free once you've heated the coffee?"

The young native explained to his fellow tribesman how the med-tech would make two long cuts from the top of his cast to the bottom, and pull it from his leg.

"When it's off, walk carefully. Careful for two days at least."

Momma excused herself from the coffee conversation so she could watch more closely while the med-tech cut the cast from her native's leg.

A battery-powered Dremel with a circular rotating blade pressed against the cast and began the slow cut from top to bottom. Gar noticed a growing excitement in the native's eyes as the tech peeled the two half-shells from his leg. Gar imagined him thinking the cast would be permanent and that he'd never have the freedom of movement that existed before his accident in the swamp. No wonder he looked so relieved.

Momma shared the same excitement. Once the cast broke loose and fell into the sand, she took the native's arm and helped him to stand. They sensed a miracle in the making.

Devon had flown several shuttles to Wakde's abandoned airstrip, delivering food and drinks. Besides supplies, each trip included several deckhands who experienced Icarus' magic carpet ride for the first time. Their job involved moving all the supplies to the beach.

Those who didn't ride on Icarus took Tanique's tender. When it arrived at the pier filled with Mac and his team, Momma looked to her native.

"Will you walk with me a short way toward the pier? I want to see you walk again."

The native smiled and slowly rose on his legs. He took a step, hesitated, and put weight on the unsupported leg.

He put his arm over Momma's shoulder. She wrapped her arm around his waist and together, they began taking one cautious step after another.

The sun warmed the beach while providing therapeutic energy to Mac's wounded team members. Beer flowed freely. Water and warm air mixed with pop music and conversation. Time became a lost dimension, something that flowed without thought or concern.

Mac sat in the sand next to Gar.

"Do you think I might borrow Saturday for another month? I could use his help getting me settled in Jayapura."

"Jayapura?" Gar questioned. "You surprise me at times. I suppose you should ask him. His attachment is to Rava, but if you explain whatever you need in a way that supports her, I think he might agree to join you."

"On another note," responded Mac. "I'd like to get my team airlifted out of Papua within the next few days. They won't be needed here any longer and the sooner they disappear, the better. I hope you can deposit them at Sarmi's airport sometime during the next night or two. As soon as I can arrange their airlift out of Papua, we can iron out the details. I'm gonna rent a car for Saturday and me, if he'll come, to drive to Jayapura. After that, I'll be out of your hair."

"Actually, I've got a convenient option for getting to Jayapura," Gar hinted. "Rip left a car in the jungle when we brought him and Rava aboard Tanigue. Let's talk to him about getting the keys."

Mac sauntered down the beach to where Saturday and the other natives cracked open several coconuts for the tasty juice inside.

"Saturday, would you be interested in coming with me to Jayapura for a short while?"

He wasted little time in responding. "No, Sir Mac. I will stay with my family now. Without me to fish and help gather food, it's difficult for them."

"If you could listen to exactly what I'm asking, I will accept your decision." Mac countered. "The work of Rip and Rava benefits all of Papua and more. They do good medical research but have been attacked by those with evil intent.

"We have eliminated all of them currently in Papua, but there is someone in Hong Kong who organized and paid those evil people. I want to find out more information about that person before I eliminate him. You could help me do that. I think Rava would approve."

Saturday's expression didn't change. He listened quietly but said nothing.

"If you will stay with me for one more month to help me settle along the docks in Jayapura," Mac continued. "I'll buy you a fishing boat with a motor and sails. It'll be the best boat between here and Jayapura."

Saturday turned to his wife. They exchanged a few words in their native language before he turned back to Mac.

"I will help you eliminate more evil. One month only."

Devon and Chambo flew Icarus from Tanique to Wakde two days later. They'd return the two natives they'd hired to their jungle village. Saturday and the two natives watched as Icarus landed near where they stood along the pathway from the village.

Chambo ushered them toward the aircraft when Saturday asked, "Can Momma Grace ride along with the native? She'd like to see her friend's home." Saturday leaned closer. "Maybe stay," he whispered.

"Oh," replied a surprised Chambo. "I think it'll be okay."

Wheel marks from their earlier landing on the tiny island sandbar had washed away with the persistent rains. Everything else remained exactly as Chambo remembered. He couldn't help but think that it all began here.

Several canoes filled with natives appeared in mid-river and diverted to their sandy beach. The two natives Gar had selected several months earlier to protect Rava smiled at the sight of their fellow tribesmen. Lighthearted discussion ensued, followed by the formal introduction of Momma Grace to the others.

Saturday nudged Chambo.

"I think Momma Grace and her native will return with me to Wakde. They don't want to separate and she prefers to stay on our island. He won't leave her."

"I love it," Chambo confessed with a smile. "Let's get all that rice we brought into their canoes."

The conversations lessened and the time to depart drew near. Momma and her native boarded Icarus last before Chambo pulled the cargo door closed.

"Contract complete," Devon announced. "Let's find our way back to Wakde, and let's do it in style."

He engaged the sound suppression system, causing the already whispery sound of turning rotors to all but disappear. He added power and levitated above the sand before accelerating out over the water. That's when he engaged stealth mode and Icarus disappeared as though flying into another world.

Quinn deposited Mac's team along Sarmi's sleepy runway the following night. Thirty minutes later, the muffled sound of reversing propellers broke the silence. The pilot feathered the props and noise levels dropped to near quiet. A dark-colored King Air 350i rolled to the end of the runway and turned around, props feathered and engines running in low-speed ground idle. The side access door lowered, team members scurried aboard, engines went to full power, and they departed.

Quiet returned before anyone in Sarmi realized what had caused the noise. No one gave it another thought.

Quinn landed at Sarmi again an hour before dawn, this time to deplane Gar, Mac, and Saturday. As quietly as he'd come, Quinn disappeared back into the night.

Saturday would remain at the airport until Gar and Mac fetched him later in the morning. The two waited with him until nearly 9 a.m. before walking off to rent a scooter. Gar remembered a small rental shop near the airport and that's where he and Mac headed.

Their tandem ride into the jungle appeared only slightly less comical than when Gar had ridden the reverse route with Rip. An aura of knowing where they headed somehow made them less obvious to those they passed along the way.

Rip's old car remained exactly where he'd parked it a month earlier. Its filthy veneer consisted of dirt and grime that rains had streaked and partially removed. Mac tried opening the door and found it locked. Gar felt a sense of relief for having thought to lock it. Otherwise, someone would have stolen it long ago.

He reached under the front wheel well on the passenger side and felt around until finding the magnetized keyholder. He inserted and turned the key. Click. He tried again, another click.

Mac rolled down the window.

"You don't suppose we have jumper cables in the trunk?"

"As a Boy Scout many years ago, I learned to always be prepared."

He removed his backpack and pulled out a small zippered pouch.

"Hang on just a minute, let me unlatch the hood."

He opened the hood and pushed aside the protective covers over the battery terminals, unzipped the pouch, and removed a portable battery charger.

"Okay, try it."

The engine sputtered for several seconds before starting.

Gar winked at Mac.

"I'll follow you. Let's meet at the bike rental shop."

They rode together in the car from the bike shop to Sarmi's operations building. Saturday had gone inside to drink coffee with the same kid behind the counter who'd told Rava about Wakde.

"Have you ever been to Wakde Island?" the kid asked.

"Maybe once or twice," Gar replied. "I'm looking forward to going back. I've heard it's quite historical."

Mac drove. Saturday occupied the passenger seat and Gar relaxed in the back as they started down the coast toward Jayapura. They neared an inconsequential village abeam Wakde Island and pulled to the side of the road.

"This should be good. You can leave me here."

Mac pulled to the side of the road. Gar climbed out and walked around to Mac's window.

"Take care, my friend. And Saturday, one of these days I'll return to visit."

Tanigue's tender found Gar along the shoreline thirty minutes later.

Mac and Saturday surveilled from half a block away the hovel of an apartment that Wu had listed as his address. The location appeared on one of the documents Gar took from him at Kwerba. They returned later to take a look inside. Mac tried the door. Locked. He stooped and removed a pic from the top of his shoe and, after briefly fiddling with the lock, pushed open the door.

Very little existed inside. Saturday watched for others while Mac gathered everything he could find and stuffed it into his backpack. He pulled Wu's phone from his pocket before leaving, connected it to a battery charger, and left it unattended on the only table in the room.

They broke into Wu's second apartment minutes later. The two hammocks inside would become their beds for the next month. . .

THIRTY-FOUR

RAVA AND GAR LOOKED OUT FROM THEIR favorite forward observation deck. The Papuan coastline off to their left had become a familiar sight, but would soon disappear when Tanigue began churning toward Thailand. Their conversation remained subdued. Leaving behind Saturday and his natives, and Papua in general, tempered their excitement with sadness. The night brought calm. Rava relaxed and felt more contented than she'd been in a long time.

Gar quietly listened as she explained the unique properties found in the plants she'd analyzed.

"In a nutshell, there are a million variations in the molecular growth and healing qualities of jungle plants. It's like searching for a needle in the haystack, except when we find it, we can sometimes enhance its positive qualities."

"Do you think you've found something special in the plants we've gathered?"

"Oh, I'm sure we've done that. It'll take time to figure out exactly why this new plant potion fights off viruses so effectively. But, with time, we'll improve it and make it available to millions of others."

Gar listened with a curious mind. He sensed Tanigue's motion.

"Can you feel it? We're starting the journey back to Thailand. Marlo tells me it'll take eight days if the weather holds. It should be a smooth trip with plenty of time for you and Rip to focus on the plants."

"Well," she replied, "I'll give you an update on my progress one of these beautiful nights, maybe with a glass of wine."

Rip grabbed a wooden pointer and tapped it on the whiteboard in front of the conference table.

"I've taken the liberty of comparing your mental imaging to that of a much broader sampling. No primates this time.

"Look here. You two are presumably smart guys, but your mental perception is . . . well, atrocious."

Devon raised his hand before speaking. "Wait, that's only raw data. It doesn't account for the fact that we're at sea. The motion must impact perception. Plus, we're more like conscripts than volunteers."

"Ha!," Rip laughed. "I don't buy it. But, don't feel bad. Your abysmal scores have at least established an easy-to-improve-upon baseline. There's not much room for regression."

Quinn felt confused. He'd always met or exceeded standards. This didn't feel quite right.

"Okay, let's work at this in the morning when my brain is generally pretty clear, and again each evening when it's more relaxed. I bet you'll see consistent improvement."

"It's interesting you mention improvement," Rip interjected. "I've already noticed a slight improvement ever since I added the goop to your headsets."

Chambo spent the first day at sea going over Icarus' system readouts and maintenance data. He'd brief Gar on the quadcopter's overall performance and hope the findings would be satisfactory. He found Gar in the library.

"I've got preliminary analytical data on Icarus and I think you might find it interesting. Got a minute?

"The LPs haven't run long enough to establish meaningful wear trends. But, from what I can tell, they should remain within our wear tolerances and compression targets. It helps to run them at a constant speed in diesel mode.

"Next, I took a cursory look at the electric motors …"

Gar wandered into Rip's onboard lab and smiled when he noticed Rava assisting him.

"I've got an update on your future lab work and hydroponic project. Care to hear where you'll be living for the next year or two?"

Rip flashed a curious look that transformed into a smile.

"I've grown accustomed to the steady feel of waves along the hull. It'll be impossible to replicate, and I'll miss it.

"Can we keep the lab on Tanique?"

"I think you might like this more," Gar hinted. "When I talked to General Smithberger last night, he emphasized his desire to continue pursuing medicinal and neurological research. When I told him the importance of keeping the plants in a warm environment, he suggested building a large state-of-the-art hydroponic facility with an attached laboratory in the industrial park near our hangar."

"You mean in Thailand?" Rava blurted.

"Yep," he answered with a smile. "You can work on Tanigue until the new facility is completed. Once everything is set, we'll move the plants and equipment to U-Tapao.

"Of course, you'd have to put up with me and my gaggle of misfits on a more-or-less daily basis."

"When can we see the land?"

Rip summoned Quinn and Devon to the training room for their last afternoon session aboard Tanigue. Gar had settled in a chair toward the rear. He wanted to hear what Rip had to say about their progress.

"You're not going to believe this," Rip started, "but you guys are actually starting to see images without using your eyes."

"I'm not surprised," Devon said. "Yesterday, I picked up partial mental images. It felt like I could see one or two pieces of a jigsaw puzzle."

"Yeah, me too," added Quinn. "A couple of images remained incomplete, but stuff like colors and basic shapes became easier to see. I didn't think much of it. Maybe my time had come for guessing right."

Rip smiled like a proud parent who'd just potty-trained his impossible son.

"What I'm seeing under the microscope is truly encouraging. And now, you guys are validating the neural linkage.

"I'd like to set up an MRI for each of you within the month. Imaging your temple area should provide tangible evidence of any neural growth. I think we'll be pleasantly surprised."

Gar couldn't wait to start testing the inputs during the flight.

"We're on the verge of something evolutionary," he mused.

"The ability to regenerate neural pathways in targeted areas of the body is going to open up a whole new realm of medical research. This is a big deal."

Gar and Rava leaned against the railing of their private viewing deck at Tanique's bow. They dreamed of exploring Thailand together once her hydroponic garden got going.

"Don't get any ideas," she warned. "I'm only interested in exploring Thailand's history."

Gar put his arm around her waist and gently pulled her to him.

"Yes, of course." He kissed her and she relaxed in his arms.

"This idea of yours will be an exception," she whispered. "Maybe I'll make a list of approved exceptions."

"Make sure you can see the mooring line when it hits the pier," Chambo called to Rip. "What time is it?"

"It's two-two past the hour. Get ready . . . there! It hit the pier at precisely two-four."

"I got it." Devon welled up with excitement. "I won the horse fly contest."

THIRTY-FIVE

GAR ARRIVED EARLY TO REVIEW THE FINANCIAL records from the past month when his phone beeped twice. A message. That seemed odd. Who'd send a message this early in the morning?

> Gar,
> It's your old friend Mac. I'm watching waves curl and tumble along an isolated Kauai beach with a morning brew in hand. Thought you might find our experience interesting. Perhaps it'll provide a bit of closure on Papua.
>
> Saturday and I slipped into a beggar's existence after you and your gang left us. We broke into Wu's dump of an apartment and the two of us set up casual surveillance of the neighborhood. I met with the local authorities and explained our connection with the government and our purpose in Jayapura. They confirmed my identity with Jakarta, after which I suddenly noticed quite an increase in respect. At least they offered me coffee after hanging up the phone.

I'd left Wu's cell phone in his apartment. We could hear if anyone called from our digs in the adjoining shack. It started ringing six days later.

A stranger appeared at Wu's place late one afternoon. He called a number and Wu's phone rang. Wu's contact became our target for the next day. Saturday shadowed him the first night while I collected ancillary information. It didn't take long to establish that he'd come from Hong Kong to look for Wu.

He came to Wu's apartment again the next day and a police swat team arrested him. Ka-ching.

The Papuans held him in shackles until Indonesian authorities could fly in to transport him back to Jakarta's Cipinang Penitentiary Institution. They've confined him in one of their deep underground single-occupancy cells.

Prisoners down there rarely see sunlight again. The Chief of Police in Jayapura assured me that because of the inhumane nature of his crimes, he would be persona non grata. No one will know his identity and any inquiry as to his whereabouts will be met with shoulder shrugs . . . as though he never existed.

On a brighter note, Saturday is the proud owner of a small and efficient fishing trawler. I slipped him enough cash to keep it fueled for a year and paid slightly more to get him lessons on how to operate it. Our last virologist could have easily slipped from our grasp without good old Saturday's help.

Take care of that girl, Rava, and give my best to Chambo, Quinn, and Devon.
Mac

Terms & Locations

140,000 Indonesian rupiahs Equals approx. $9.75
Alternate Site An encampment approximately one mile from the Taritatu River. An opening caused by a lightning strike and subsequent fire.
Bajaj An Indian car manufacturer, however, its brand name has become synonymous with three-wheeled taxis in Papua. It's called an auto rickshaw in India, a CNG in Bangladesh, a three-wheeler in Sri Lanka, and a tuk-tuk in Thailand.
Chu-Hi A Japanese canned alcoholic drink. Traditional chūhai is made with barley shōchū and carbonated water flavored with lemon. There are various other flavors, such as apple.
Dabra Small village with an asphalt runway along the Taritatu River. Used by palm oil farmers and miners as an access point. Nestled against the central mountain range.
Decoction involves first mashing the plant roots and stems to allow for maximum dissolution, and then boiling in water to extract oils, volatile organic compounds, and other various chemical substances.
Dzus fastener also known as a turn-lock fastener or quick-action panel fastener is a type of proprietary quarter-turn spiral cam lock fastener often used to secure skin panels on aircraft and other high-performance vehicles. It is named after its inventor William Dzus.
Elelim Administrative center of Yalimo Regency. Located in the central mountains and has an asphalt runway. Used by Asians as a virology staging point. They also ran a crude laboratory.
Foja Mountains Considered by many as a lost world, it is ecologically isolated, rugged, and remote. These highlands

have seen the evolution of scores of endemic species. Mountains rise to over 6,000 feet.

HLZ #2 An open area along the Taritatu River that is infested by horse flies.

HLZ #3 An open area filling a loop in one of Taritatu River's tributaries. Used to offload Gar's canoes.

HLZ Rivers An open area near the confluence of the Taritatu and Mamberamo rivers.

Hulu Atas Small village with a grass strip along the Taritatu River. Used by Asians as a virology staging point. They also ran a crude laboratory.

Icarus Highly modified quadcopter with revolutionary radioisotope generators, advanced Wankel-like engines, and new-technology batteries. Incorporates artificial intelligence and virtual reality. Features low visibility and low noise operations.

Infusion An extract prepared by soaking plant leaves in liquid, like making tea.

Konbini Japanese convenience stores, including 7-11, Lawsons, and many others.

Kwerba Small village with an asphalt runway along the Mamberamo River. Used by Asians as a virology staging point. They also ran a crude laboratory.

LP engine LiquidPiston X4 High-Efficiency Hybrid Cycle engine resolves the issues associated with Wankel engines, including high oil burn, compression blowby, and low power. Icarus uses two relatively small and lightweight engines to charge batteries. The canoes each have an LP for propulsion.

Mamberamo River The second longest and widest river in Indonesia. The river, formed by the confluence of the Tariku and Taritatu rivers, has an interior basin with extensive freshwater, swampy forests, and grasslands. It cuts through the Van Rees Range and Foja Mountains in a series of rapids and gorges. Known for tremendous biodiversity.

Night-Vision Goggles (NVGs) Require some ambient light (moonlight) for the best results. Provide a green monochromatic view.

Pagai Small village with an asphalt runway along a tributary of the Taritatu River.

Radioisotope Thermoelectric Generators An improved version of the power generators currently powering the Perseverance Rover on Mars.

Raptor Experimental aircraft purchased by Gar. They appeared stealthy and carried a variety of airborne sensors.

RHIB Rigid Hull Inflatable Boat. This is the type of tender used by Tanigue to transport crew and passengers to and from the ship to shore.

Sarmi A coastal town and administrative center of Sarmi Regency. Has an asphalt runway. Escape destination of Rip and Rava.

Tanigue 210-foot fast support vessel originally bought by the U.S. Navy and later acquired by Gen (Ret) Smithberger of the Department of Homeland Security. Gar operates Icarus off its landing pad.

Taritatu River Also known as the Baliem River. The headwaters of this extensive waterway originate in the mountainous central region of Papua. Gar and his team explored the easternmost north-south branch of the river before moving to the east-west main branch.

Tincture A process where the plant is placed in a mason jar and covered with boiling water. The resulting pulp is soaked in alcohol to separate the extract.

U-Tapao Airport Located two hours south of Bangkok near the town of Rayong. Previously a U.S. Air Force Base; now a Thai Royal Thai Navy Base with a long, wide runway.
Wakde Island Group Consists of two islands: Insoemoar and Insoemanai. Of these, Insoemoar is the largest, although it is only 1.5 miles long and 3,000 feet wide. The islands lay 2 miles offshore NE Papua. The Japanese and Americans fought between 17 and 21 May 1944, for control of the Wakde airstrip.

Fact or Fiction?

The state of advanced technology is often difficult to determine and often blurs the line between fact and fiction. Much of what I've written in this book already exists in one form or another, but some elements venture a step or two into fiction. This pinch of clarity will hopefully bring value.

For example, the storyline is fictitious. I don't know of any viral experimentations taking place in Papua nor do I know of a large quadcopter such as the one described in the story. On the other hand, many of the technical aspects are accurate or exist in another form or application. Here is a short list of fact or fiction.

Geography and history. All locations exist and the names are accurate. While the existence of Grey Hawk International at U-Tapao Royal Thailand Naval Base is fictitious, everything else about that location is accurate, including Delta Golf Operations and the abutting town of Ban Chan. Zamboanga City's history and port facilities are depicted accurately. The Japanese occupation of Wakde Island occurred during WWII. They cleared the interior jungles for a short runway and stationed several fighters there. U.S. and Australian forces fought for and seized control of the Island as described. Rabaul's historical recollections are accurate in every detail.

Icarus represents my version of a state-of-the-art government-operated quadcopter. Most of its capabilities already exist in one form or another while some are exaggerated to fit the story. Here's a breakdown.

Sound deadening. The preponderance of sound generated by a propeller-driven aircraft originates from the propellers, specifically the tips of the propellers. That's where their speed through the air can become supersonic and can get noisy. While I don't know of a system to capture propeller sound waves to noise-cancel them, I do know noise-canceling headsets adjust sound wave amplitude similar to what I've explained. Theoretically, Icarus' system should work, but it does represent a stretch from similar effects using a headset.

Current helicopter blade technology includes rotor blade tip modifications coupled with localized and super-fast surface modifications to reduce sound.

Artificial intelligence and augmented reality currently exist in other applications. For example, Siri software on a computer, or even in stand-alone systems, interprets voice commands and then responds. Other software applications such as Microsoft Flight Simulator 2020 and X-Plane 11 integrate geographic position, weather, and terrain elevations into a real-time display of the world. This largely accurate representation is used during the story to provide internal wall-to-wall displays within Icarus.

The external displays for Icarus require technology that to my knowledge, does not yet exist. A single camera can capture images in infrared, visual, or low light and can then display the image elsewhere. Projecting those images onto multiple conformal and integrated screens may happen in the future, but not yet.

The rotary LP engine depiction is accurate. There are issues with the durability of these engines, but for a constant-speed application, they do represent a significant reduction in weight and size. As written, the LPs represent significantly more fact than fiction.

The radioisotope thermoelectric generators exist on many current satellites and space probes. Their output power is much less than the systems described in the book, however.

Utilizing brain impulses to control a computer mouse, or to activate a prosthetic device currently exists. Moving the nerve impulses in the opposite direction to form mental images is possible, but as written is, unfortunately, a work-in-progress.

Building or filling in neural network gaps remains a work in progress. For example, a severed spine cannot yet be reconnected. Great strides have been made in achieving that goal, but to my knowledge has not been fully attained.

I hope this helps to separate fact from imagination.

Author Notes

Thank you for reading this adventurous tale and experiencing a bit of my wandering imagination. As an author who writes and self-publishes, I very much value your readership. Even more deeply appreciated is your reaction to the book.

Whether you found my words to be gold-encrusted nuggets of brilliance or belabored wanderings fit for the dung heap, I'll never know without your feedback. Potential readers will find your unbiased comments helpful in their purchase decisions. Please leave an Amazon rating, or better yet, a written reaction to what you've read. Feedback is the lifeblood of a good author and the best insight for potential readers.

Please consider reading one of my other novels, or if you want to know about me, take a look at Walk Run Fly, a most interesting autobiography. Thanks again!